I0584072

GRAVITY STORM

SHADOW VANGUARD, BOOK ONE

TOM DUBLIN
MICHAEL ANDERLE

LMBPN

DISRUPTIVE IMAGINATION

JIT Beta Readers -
From all of us, our deepest gratitude!

Kelly O'Donnell
Kimberly Boyer
Larry Omans
Peter Manis
Joshua Ahles
Sarah Weir
Paul Westman
Tim Bischoff
John Findlay
James Caplan
Larry Omans
Kelly Bowerman
Micky Cocker
John Ashmore
Erick Cushman
Daniel Weigert

*If we missed anyone, **please** let us know!*

To Kirsty, the brightest star in my universe.
— Tom

To Family, Friends and
Those Who Love
To Read.
May We All Enjoy Grace
To Live The Life We Are
Called.
— Michael

ICS Fortitude, **Bridge - Yoll Space**

Captain Jack Marber's chair screeched as he spun to face his two colleagues.

"Fucking chair," he grumbled. "Remind me to-"

An alarm sounded, cutting him off mid-sentence.

The bridge crew turned toward the view screen. Jack reached across to activate the feed, his chair crying out again. He'd tried repairing the battered old seat on many occasions yet, no matter how much oil he slathered over the mechanism, it continued to object noisily to any movement.

At the moment, however, he had more than mere comfort on his mind.

"This is it," he said grimly, gesturing to the radar display. "Those Skaine bastards are pulling alongside."

In the co-pilot's seat, Tc'aarlat rubbed his mandibles together in anger. "I thought the Etheric Empire was supposed to be ridding Yoll space of pirates," he growled.

"At least, that's what their precious Empress promised

when she took control of my planet. All this time and we're still fighting off the thieving scum."

The blood red feathered bird of prey perched on the hard exoskeleton of his shoulder shrieked angrily.

"See, even Mist hates pirates."

"I don't think they'll ever eliminate the Skaine," said Dollen Stonebrand from the navigation console, banging one of his claws against the desk in a vain attempt to stop the radar screens from flickering. "The Empire is too nice about it. They refuse to conduct a proper universal cleansing of the bastards."

"They're like fleas. Once they get through a gate and infect your system, they're almost impossible to eradicate."

"Well, one of those fleas is hailing us," said Jack, gesturing to a flashing light on the console. "Opening the channel." He flicked the necessary switches.

The view screen before them hissed with static for a moment, then a leathery blue face emerged into view.

"*Interstellar Cargo Ship Fortitude*, this is Captain Bamston of the Skaine Patrol Vessel, *Narvalt*. Whom do I have the pleasure of addressing?"

Jack's upper lip curled into a snarl. "My name is Captain Jack Marber," he growled, his British accent causing him to hit the 't' sound in 'Captain' hard. "And you can cut the crap about being a patrol vessel. You're pirates, plain and simple."

Bamston pulled a face Jack supposed was attempting to approximate the human expression of offense. "Pirates?" the alien spat. "And what brings you to that uncharitable conclusion, Captain?"

"It's obvious," Jack replied. "You're Skaine, and that's all your kind ever does."

The face on the screen glowered. "My kind, Captain? I shall ignore the vile speciesist slur, if you would be good enough to please tell us the type of freight you are currently transporting..."

"No chance," barked Tc'aarlat. "Go stick your head up a dead Bistok's ass!"

Captain Bamston's image turned to glare down at the co-pilot, giving the impression that he was able to look around the entire bridge instead of just where the *Fortitude*'s fixed, low resolution camera was pointing.

"You really should keep a tighter rein on your staff, Captain Marber," he hissed. "Such a foul mouth could easily hamper diplomatic relations between my kind and the Etheric Empire."

"We don't work for anyone, least of all the Etheric Empire," Tc'aarlat responded, "so I can say what I damn well want, especially to the likes of you."

"And I'm not staff," he added, gesturing towards the figure in the Captain's chair. "We're partners."

"It's true," Dollen put in from behind them. "I'm the staff."

Bamston laughed unpleasantly. "Well, well... A human, a Yollin and a Baroleon putting aside their many cultural differences in the pursuit of capitalism. It does a soul good to see such harmony at work. Now, back to the subject of your cargo..."

Suddenly, the elongated ears on top of Dollen's bald head angled themselves to the left, and his tail began to twitch at the back of his seat. He hit the button that would cut the line of communication. The view screen flashed with static again for a moment, then fell dark.

"I hear something," the Baroleon hissed.

Jack turned in his chair, causing it to squeak again. He strained his own ears but couldn't pick up any abnormal sounds. However, despite only having known the Baroleon for a few months, he'd already come to trust his keen hearing. "What kind of something?"

Dollen raised a claw to hush his colleagues for a few seconds, allowing him to concentrate. "Tools," he said, his expression darkening. "Someone's forcing open one of the port side hatches.

Tc'aarlat sneered up at the view screen. "That Skaine bastard kept us talking so we wouldn't spot his boarding party. Can we get a look at them, see how many of the shit-suckers are out there?"

Jack's fingers darted across the controls for the ship's external cameras but was rewarded with little more than screen after screen of white noise and dancing pixels. "Gott Verdammt!" he cursed. "The CCTV system's on the fritz again."

"Can we run?" inquired Dollen. "Their ship is a lot smaller than ours. The engines won't be as powerful."

"Not while we're fully loaded," said Jack. "They'd be crawling all over us before we could pick up enough speed. Our only hope is to dump the cargo..." He reached out towards the control panel that would allow him to open the freighter's loading doors and eject their consignment.

Tc'aarlat shot out an arm and grabbed his partner's wrist. "No way!" he barked. "Do you know how much that would cost us?"

"We can't collect payment if we're dead!" Jack retorted.

"So, your solution is to just give them what they want and run away like a frightened schoolchild?"

Mist cried out again, ruffling her feathers.

"They're going to get the cargo one way or another," said Jack, flicking a disgusted glance up at the Raal hawk. "This way, we get to keep our lives. All we lose is our money."

"Wrong!" snarled the Yollin, his mandibles wide and angry. "All we lose is my money. You still owe me your half for the cost of this ship, remember?"

Jack fixed his partner with a hard stare. "You're bringing this up? Now?"

"If you're about to ditch any chance of me recouping my investment into deep space, then yes. I'm bringing this up now."

"Investment my arse!" Jack said with a cold laugh. "You paid for this freighter with stolen cash."

Tc'aarlat didn't look away from Jack's furious stare. "Which I stole fair and square," he spewed. "We are not handing this consignment over to pirates and bolting with our tails between our legs."

"Too late for that, anyway," said Dollen. He slid open a drawer beneath his console, retrieved an old-style kinetic pistol and tossed it over to Jack, who checked that the ammunition magazine was fully loaded. "The Skaine are already on board."

ICS Fortitude, **Upper Deck, Port Side Access Hatch**

Fonk heaved open the metal door, the broken locking

mechanism clattering to the floor of the dimly lit corridor. The pirate pulled his breather from between his mottled lips and ushered the small boarding party inside.

This was the first time he had been charged with leading an attack on another ship, and he was determined to get it right.

Not to earn Captain Bamston's approval in any way - he despised his superior more than any other officer he'd had the displeasure to serve under - but more because of the extremely violent way his predecessor had been executed for failing to secure the crew's last target vessel.

He could still taste the seared Skaine flesh Bamston had ordered the rest of the defeated boarding party to dissect, cook, and devour.

It was delicious.

And, as much as he'd love to give Captain Bamston crippling indigestion, he wasn't prepared to give his life to do so.

"Artok, Tuss - head to the cargo hold and find out what these dregs are hauling. Shizz, you're coming to the bridge with me."

Shizz scowled. "Just the two of us?" he grunted. "There are three of them up there. And..." he paused, his pock-marked face crumpling with the obvious pain of thinking, "three is more than two."

"What's wrong?" glowered Fonk. "Afraid of a little brawl?"

"No!" Shizz insisted, his pride stinging. "It's just that Orkov used to take more of us to seize command before plundering the rest of the ship."

"Orkov's dead," spat Fonk. "I'm in charge now, and we do things my way."

Artok looked from Fonk to Shizz and back again, half hoping the argument between the two would escalate and prove entertaining. Then a hand clamped down on his shoulder.

"Come on," snarled Tuss. "We've got a job to do."

Reluctantly, Artok unholstered his weapon, and followed his older brother in search of the cargo bay.

Signaling for Shizz to remain silent, Fonk led the way towards the freighter's deck, following the faded signage fixed to the corridor walls. The two pirates paused outside the door to the command area, readying themselves for attack.

And that's when Fonk's right shoulder was torn apart by a bullet.

The Skaine twisted in agony, quickly switching his weapon to his left hand and firing at the tall figure emerging from the shadows beside the door. His blaster was set to project a wide beam for maximum destruction but the combination of his left hand being less accurate than his right, and the sickening pain in his shoulder caused his aim to go wide.

The deadly beam missed its target, instead hitting and destroying the pilot's chair in the bridge beyond.

Jack glanced over at what remained of his smoldering seat. "I know I need a new one," he snarled, "but don't expect me to take that sitting down."

Spinning on the spot, he struck out a leg and kicked the Skaine's blaster from his hand, then darted forward to head-butt the pirate, shattering the bones inside the creature's nose with a sickening crunch.

"Glark!" yelled Fonk, clutching at his face with his now free left hand, blood pouring between his fingers.

The sudden counter-attack finally registered with Shizz, and he reached for his own weapon, ready to spring to Fonk's defense. But, before he could pull the gun from its holster, a second figure appeared from the darkness.

This one was brandishing a long, black rod with a pair of razor sharp prongs protruding from one end. Sparks of blue electricity spat and danced from one metal point to the other.

"The great thing about only having one gun on board this ship, is that the rest of us are forced to improvise," rumbled Dollen as he thrust the electrified end of the rod towards Shizz's terrified face.

"Say hello to Mr Sparky!"

The pointed prongs sank deep into the Skaine's eyes, causing his eyeballs to burst, trails of off-white viscous liquid dribbling down Shizz's cheeks. Dollen hit the button at his end of the weapon and held it down, sending 50,000 volts of sheer hell coursing through Shizz's brain.

"Amazing what you can do with a modified Bistok prod that doesn't like pirates!" Dollen yelled over the convulsing Skaine's screams. Pungent, black smoke streamed from every orifice as the inside of the pirate's skull was instantly brought to the boil, and his thick, grimy hair burst into flames.

Tugging the prod free, Dollen allowed his victim's still jerking body to crumple to the floor, where he proceeded to stamp out the fire engulfing Shizz's head with his heavy-soled army surplus boots.

"Safety first," he quipped, spinning the still-spitting prod.

Across the corridor, Jack advanced on Fonk who began to back away in horror as he realized that, even if he were to somehow get out of this fuck-up alive, he was almost certainly destined to be the main course at Bamston's dinner table that evening.

His eyes widened as Jack raised his pistol and took aim.

"Wait!" Fonk cried, holding up his bloodied hand. "I- I surrender. I'll join your crew, work for you. Do whatever you tell me to. For nothing. Less than that. You can have everything I own. Just let me live, and get me out of here. Please!"

Jack paused to consider the offer for a brief moment, then he closed one eye and squeezed the trigger.

"No deal, wank-stain!"

ICS Fortitude, Cargo Bay 4, Level 3

Tc'aarlat pressed his body into a shallow alcove in the wall and watched as the two remaining Skaine invaders wandered among the cargo bay's loaded pallets. Mist gripped his shoulder pad tightly, the bird's piercing yellow eyes fixed on the unsuspecting raiders.

The larger of the pirate pair paused beside a tall stack of wooden crates and sliced through the thick plastic wrapping with his fingernails, tearing it away to examine the delivery label pasted to the side of the box beneath.

"Com-poo-ter sar... sarv...," said Tuss, attempting to translate the unfamiliar words as he spoke.

The second pirate glanced over at the label. "Server," he said, correcting his brother. "Well, well... These mugs are carrying computer servers."

The taller Skaine blinked, his expression blank. "Great!" he announced in as confident a voice as he could muster. "They're really good, those computer servers, aren't they?"

Artok sighed. "A computer is like the screen thing we use for navigation on the ship. A server is a really powerful version."

Tuss grinned, revealing two rows of blackened and broken teeth as he stepped back to view the hundreds of identical pallets filling the hold. "And they've got loads of them," he announced. "We're gonna be rich!"

Not if I've got anything to do with it, thought Tc'aarlat twitching his shoulder to signal Mist to take flight. The hawk's powerful wings lifted her silently into the air, the deep red feathers fading to black as her natural camouflage ability took hold.

Once Mist was airborne, Tc'aarlat took a small step forward, his foot nudging against something. He looked down to discover a large, rusted metal toolbox on the floor beside him, and he smiled.

Tuss rubbed his hands together greedily. "The Captain will be able to flog this lot for a tasty profi-aaarrrgghhh!"

The final word became a scream of pain as a huge, dark bird swooped over the stacks of servers and shot down towards him, her sharp claws digging deep into the pirate's cheeks. The hawk gripped tightly to the rapidly bloodying skin as Tuss swung his arms about wildly in an attempt to dislodge this feathered foe.

"Get it off me!" he bellowed, not suspecting this would be the last sentence he would ever speak clearly.

For as soon as she spotted the pirate's moist, wagging tongue, Mist gripped the lump of flesh in her pointed beak, and tore it free of its terrified owner's mouth.

Artok raced to his brother's aid, only to feel a painful *thud* as Tc'aarlat hit him over the head with a heavy, metal wrench. As the stunned pirate reached for his weapon, the Yollin tossed the bulky tool aside, grabbed a pair of screw-drivers from his belt, and plunged them hard into the furious Skaine's ears.

There was a muffled clink as the tips of the two tools met deep inside the pirate's skull.

Artok's eyes rolled back in their sockets, then he slumped to the ground, dead.

"Ar'ok!" yelled the tongueless Tuss, finally tearing Mist away from his face, thick flaps of skin ripping away in the process. "Oo kiy mah ovvah! Ow oo unna ie!"

Tc'aarlat spun to face the blood-soaked Skaine. "Sorry pal," he said with a mock frown. "Could you run that by me one more time?"

The pirate whipped out his gun and aimed it directly at the Yollin's face. "I ed, ow oo unna ie!" Tuss pulled back the old-style weapon's hammer with his thumb.

Suddenly, a long whip-like tail lashed out from between two of the packed pallets and coiled itself tightly around Tuss's throat.

"Not today, you cockwomble!" spat Dollen, backing out of his hiding spot. His tail squeezed tighter and tighter, cutting off Tuss's supply of air and causing the Skaine to cough up a fine cloud of blood as he choked.

"Cockwomble?" queried Tc'aarlat as Mist soared in to land on his shoulder, her sleek feathers gradually returning to their usual burgundy hue.

Dollen grinned. "Heard it on one of those old British radio recordings Jack listens to at full volume in his quarters," he said. "I quite like it."

The pair watched as the Baloreon unwound his tail from Tuss's throat, allowing the deceased pirate to crumple to the floor beside his equally dead sibling.

"How did it go on the bridge?" Tc'aarlat asked.

Dollen wiped the blood from his tail with the flap of his shirt. "Good guys two, pirate pigs nil," he replied. "Positive result, if you ask me."

"Until their captain sends over another batch of these pox-ridden sac-suckers to find out what happened to their boarding party, that is."

"In which case, we'd better-"

Both Tc'aarlat and Dollen grabbed hold of the torn plastic hanging from the pallets of servers as the engines roared and the ship suddenly lurched.

"What the fuck is Jack doing up there?" spat Dollen, glaring in the direction of the bridge.

"He'd better not be getting ready to dump any of this cargo!" cried Tc'aarlat, setting off at a run.

Dollen followed at his heels, the two aliens staggering from side to side as the ship's erratic movement caused the corridor to tip and buck beneath their feet.

By the time they crashed onto the command deck, Jack had the *ICS Fortitude* running at top speed - in reverse.

"What are you doing?" demanded Tc'aarlat, leaping into the co-pilot's seat and strapping himself in.

"Getting rid of these Skaine bastards once and for all," exclaimed Jack, perched on the smoldering remains of the captain's chair.

He slammed his forearm onto the nearest console, dragging it down to flick an entire bank of switches at the same time, diverting every last drop of extra power to the engines.

"By flying towards them?" cried Dollen, securing himself into his own seat.

"Not towards them," said Jack with a wink. "Right into them! Hold tight..."

There was a crunch and the freighter rocked violently from side to side. Tc'aarlat activated the external cameras once more, pounding his fist on the control panel repeatedly until the system finally flickered to life.

All three crew members stared up at the view screen in time to see the severely damaged Skaine vessel, *Narvalt*, tumble away into space before exploding in sheets of white-hot flame.

Jack pushed hard against the main control levers, forcing the screaming engines into forward gear in an effort to escape the rapidly expanding fireballs.

He flashed a wide grin to his two astounded colleagues, then gestured to an image fading into view on the navigation screen. It showed a colossal space station

"Next stop, *Etheric Federation Base Station 11!*"

2

Federation Base Station 11, Jean Dukes R&D Labs, Vacant Office

Her hand trembling slightly, Adina Choudhury raised her particle beam gun and aimed it squarely at Ecaterina Romanov's heart.

"I've been waiting to do this for a long time," she said.

Ecaterina steeled herself. "Then, what are you waiting for?"

Needing no further encouragement, Adina concentrated and pulled the trigger.

Deep within the gun, a well-guarded, top secret mechanism dipped into a reservoir of neutral atoms, stripping a single electron from each one as they were pulled almost instantaneously into the firing chamber.

Less than thirty picoseconds later, the collection of now fully charged atoms were accelerated close to the speed of light and fired as a beam from the weapon's hardened barrel.

The beam, normally invisible to the naked eye, had been colorized to glow a bright cobalt blue, allowing its path to be tracked as it streaked towards its quickly-beating target.

Ecaterina screwed her eyes shut as it approached - only to be deflected just centimeters in front of her at the last moment, zipping past her left arm and blasting a coin-sized hole in the reinforced wall of the room.

"You can open your eyes now," said Adina as the blast point sizzled and burned. "It worked."

Ecaterina turned to look at where the particle beam had struck, working hard to slow her exaggerated breathing and heart rate.

"I can't tell you how delighted I am that it did," she said with a smile. "Although I still don't completely understand how."

Adina flicked the gun's safety into position and laid the still-cooling weapon on a nearby table. "Try to think of yourself like a planet," she said, tapping a command onto the screen of her tablet.

"A planet?" commented Ecaterina, her eyebrows rising. "Are you trying to say this new armor makes me look fat?"

Adina giggled. "Anything but!" she said, looking her colleague up and down appreciatively. "I wish I could rock a protective suit like that."

"No reason why you couldn't..."

"No need for body armor in a sensible job like mine," replied Adina with a shrug. She tapped on the tablet screen again. "Here we go; this will show you what I mean by a planet..."

Ecaterina joined her to peer at the display. It showed slow-motion footage taken by a camera mounted high up on one of the room's walls which had tracked the path of the particle beam as it left the gun.

"I added a color to the beam so we could follow its trajectory," Adina explained. "OK... I pulled the trigger, and there goes the beam, straight towards your heart."

Ecaterina nodded, her pulse once again beginning to race, even though she knew that she had survived the experiment.

"Now, watch as it approaches the breastplate of your updated armor..."

The two women concentrated on the screen as the searing line of atoms sped closer and closer to its target. Then, at the last second, it appeared to glance off a barrier, an invisible force field which deflected the beam harmlessly to one side.

"Brilliant!" breathed Ecaterina.

"Thanks!" said Adina, blushing slightly. "But all I've done is upgrade your armor so that it generates a force field. It acts as a shield, diverting the beam away from your body..."

"...like the magnetic field of a planet deflects harmful radiation from its parent star," finished Ecaterina. "So, you really weren't calling me fat, after all!"

"I know enough about your reputation to understand that wouldn't be a good idea," grinned Adina, grabbing the gun and heading for the door.

Ecaterina followed. "So, when does this armor update go live?"

TOM DUBLIN & MICHAEL ANDERLE

"Not for a while yet," explained Adina, stepping out into the main weapon testing area of Jean Duke's R&D labs. "We've got more tests to run, and we have to find a way to keep the field charged throughout an extended battle."

"Sounds like you've got a long day ahead of you."

"Not me," beamed Adina, sliding the gun through a hatch in a reinforced glass window where a uniformed guard returned it to its storage slot. "I've got the afternoon off."

Ecaterina began to remove the prototype armor. "Doing anything fun?"

Adina signed to say that she had returned the borrowed weapon on a clipboard and sighed. "I don't know yet," she said quietly. "Not until I get there at least."

Alma Nine, Taron City, New Hospital Building

The camera operator perched on top of the Channel Three News van, wiped the sweat from the teal-colored skin of his brow and trained his lens on the slowly approaching limousine.

Like all male Malatians, he was the proud owner of a shock of thick silver hair, which he styled in order to attract a female partner. If this ancient mating ritual went as planned, the men would then leave their hair to grow long and wild, the unkempt look announcing to the world that a match had been made, and the person in question was living in a long-term relationship.

The cameraman had yet to attract a mate, however, and so he had styled his hair into a series of long, spike-like spirals. As a result, he was happily receiving admiring glances from several of the unattached females in the vast crowd of onlookers.

The limo drew to a stop and, after a moment to check for any obvious dangers, several burly security men climbed out and took up their well-choreographed positions around the vehicle.

All wore their hair in an extravagant style, except for one. Hip Win, the President's head of security, kept his head shaved completely bald. He deemed his species' constant preening and displays of courtship to be a distraction from the serious task of ensuring the President remained free from harm. So, he did away with his silver plumage altogether.

A decision which only made him more desirable to a large portion of the population - both female and male. Social media based fan clubs swelled with photographs of 'The Smooth Operator', as he was known among fans.

But, Hip Win wanted nothing to do with all that attention. He stood rock still, scanning the exterior of the new hospital building and the crowds gathered behind barriers on the opposite side of the road from behind mirrored sunglasses.

This may only have been a ribbon-cutting ceremony on a new hospital, but the safety of the colony's President was paramount.

As promised, it was another beautiful day in the capital city of the planet Alma Nine. Rain had been forecast, but that had been arranged to fall only over farmland outside the perimeter of the city. Here, the sky was a cloudless blue; the color causing the silver spikes rising from the camera operator's head to glimmer slightly.

Eventually, Hip Win was satisfied that no direct threats were posed to his employer, and he spoke this particular day's code word into a microphone stitched into the end of his coat sleeve to give the all clear.

Upon hearing the signal, the guard nearest to the left side of the limousine opened the door, allowing the single passenger to climb out into the sunshine. Alma Nine's twice-re-elected President, Tor Val.

The crowd went wild with applause. They cheered, whistled and jostled for a better view of the beloved woman. This moment made standing in such cramped conditions for hours on end worthwhile.

Tor Val turned to face her well-wishers, a beaming smile etched across her features. Dressed in her political colors of navy blue and lemon, she looked just as stunningly beautiful as in her official Presidential picture, now being waved by many of her supporters.

That photograph had been taken on the day of her inauguration and, despite now being almost a decade older, her looks showed no signs of fading.

Her dark blue hair was extremely short, allowing the shining teal skin of her scalp to show through. But this was no chosen style. All Malatian women were born with a fine covering of extremely short hair, which barely grew throughout the course of their lives.

They left the extravagant coiffured preening to the menfolk.

The Channel Three camera zoomed in to catch her piercing eyes as they caught sight of a baby clutched to its mother's chest at the front of the crowd, and she hurried over causing her security detail to fan out into yet another pre-planned configuration.

The young parent turned her daughter as the President approached, and the gathered well-wishers let out a collective 'AWWW!' As the baby stretched her chubby teal arms out towards the approaching figure, giggling.

One swift cuddle and press photo opportunity later, Tor Val once again made her way towards the microphone festooned podium standing outside the new hospital's main doorway.

Waiting there, his long silver hair swept into a tall, rigid mohawk studded with blinking white LED lights, was her Vice President, Saf Tah.

He watched closely as Tor Val slowly made her way along the barriers, pausing every few steps to shake hands with, kiss the cheek of, or provide a selfie and autograph for some star-struck member of the public or another.

Dear God, all this 'press the flesh' nonsense made him sick.

Politics should be executed across heavy desks in rooms deep within the capital's parliament building, not out on the streets with the great unwashed.

He shuddered.

Tor Val could catch any number of diseases the way she willingly touches these people. Not that she ever would.

He wasn't quite that lucky.

And today's obvious support for Tor Val showed no signs of waning. Despite being the President for ten years, her approval ratings were as high as ever.

If only there was a way to force her to relinquish her grip on power.

The President briefly paused her meet and greet session

as a pair of young twins - one girl and one boy, who had already taken to styling his hair in a perky quiff - stepped up to hand her a bouquet of flowers.

The amassed cameras of the press corps exploded with bright white flashes when the girl curtseyed, and the boy bowed, then cheekily kissed the back of Tor Val's hand.

Tomorrow's front pages were in the bag.

Around twenty minutes later, Tor Val reached the podium and shared a handshake with her deputy. As soon as she turned back towards her eager audience, a staffer surreptitiously passed him a wipe and a pocket-sized bottle of hand sanitizer.

Pausing just long enough for anticipatory energy to crackle through the air, Tor Val began to recite her memorized and rehearsed speech. A speech she had written especially for this occasion, the content of which only a handful of her closest aides were aware of.

"Vice President Saf Tah, esteemed political colleagues, assembled medical professionals, ladies and gentlemen, and everyone gathered here today and all across Alma Nine..."

The speech continued with the usual positive political rhetoric about the colony's impressive healthcare system, and how this new hospital and its staff would continue the government's excellent record of care for the elderly and infirm.

The crowds were lapping it up, but Saf Tah found it all to be exceedingly boring. He forced himself to imagine in detail how he would have Tor Val's office re-fitted and re-decorated once his name was on the door in order to keep himself from yawning.

Tor Val's speech continued to please her fans.

"Eleven years ago, when we brave settlers were climbing aboard the *interplanatary Vessel Dessia*, and preparing to leave Malatia behind, we received a lot of unwarranted criticism..."

The gathered citizens began to mutter softly among themselves as they recalled how their journey to this new world had come about.

"They claimed Alma Nine was too distant a world to be successfully colonized, but we proved them wrong!"

Now, the crowd cheered.

"They told us our terraforming technology was too primitive to successfully transform 'that barren lump of rock' into the opulent, benevolent world it is today - and we proved them wrong!"

The crowd's cheering grew louder.

Saf Tah's eyes began to close as sleep crept over to wrap its warm arms around him.

"They assured us our plans for a comprehensive weather control system that would guarantee us bountiful crops and safeguard us from the kind of natural disasters that were tearing apart our home world were all just a pipe-dream..."

The audience held their collective breath.

"And. We. Proved. Them. Wrong!"

The loudest cheers of all forced the sound technician inside the Channel Three News van to quickly pull off his headphones.

"Which is why, today, I have a special announcement to make. A special announcement that will guide our incredible colony into the next millennium, and ensure its future as a citizen of this galaxy and beyond."

Saf Tah's eyes shot wide open as his attention was suddenly fibrillated back to life.

"For the past few weeks, I have been communicating with a representative of the Etheric Federation..."

Cheers turned to uncertain chatter as wave after wave of rumors concerning this new galactic superpower and their rumored methods of expansion and control washed over the crowd.

Tor Val raised a hand to calm them.

The assembled audience grew quieter.

Saf Tah's eyes grew narrower.

"I ask you to believe that I will never place our world into the hands of anyone who would treat it with anything but the utmost care, love and protection," the President insisted.

Her words echoed off the fresh white paint of the hospital exterior, and all around the now utterly silent plaza.

"And so, after considerable thought and lengthy negotiations, I have arranged for Alma Nine first to align itself with, and soon become a full member of the Etheric Empire."

"We are going interstellar!"

Tor Val's hands shot into the air, her fingers spread wide in the Malatian gesture for unending peace. All around her, the crowd went crazy with wild applause and exhilarated cheering.

The President had done it. She had won the trust and support of her planet's colonists once again.

Behind her, Saf Tah clapped politely, his eyes flicking over to meet the mirrored sunglasses stare of Hip Win. The bald security guard's face betrayed no emotion whatsoever but his hands, hanging down at his sides, were balled into two tight fists.

3

ICS Fortitude, **Crew Quarters**

Tc'aarlat stepped into his tiny cabin, closed the door behind him and let loose a long, exhausted sigh.

Turning on the spot, he sat on the edge of his bed without the need - or indeed, the room - to take a single step, no matter how small. The sagging metal springs complained loudly as he leaned back to kick off his boots, then turned to lie down on the bunk's thin mattress and well-worn blankets.

The Yollin tucked his hands behind his head, fingers interlaced, and a hazy image of a much larger room materializing from somewhere deep in his mind. The memory wasn't powerful enough for him to recall many of the room's individual features, or to remember doing anything interesting while in there.

Instead, it was like looking at a faded photograph of a forgotten location found tucked between the pages of an ancient, dusty book.

The comparison stung, so Tc'aarlat banished it from his

thoughts. There were many reasons why he should be able to remember more about the vast, well-appointed room, the primary one being it had been his childhood bedroom.

If he concentrated, he could picture himself in the room sitting beside an older, female Yollin on an exquisite yet tasteful couch. He suspected this figure might have been his mother as she held herself with poise and grace. And, of course, she was blessed with a clear indicator as to her status as one of the planet's elite upper caste...

She had four legs.

In this blurry memory, Tc'aarlat was perched beside her while she read to him, his own legs swinging back and forth several inches above the surface of the expensive carpet covering the floor.

Both of them.

As a child, he had never understood the scandal of being a two-legged child born to a family of wealthy, four-legged Yollins. Of course, he had sometimes wondered why he looked more like the family's servants than either his parents or his older sister.

And he was never privy to any of the hushed conversations where the fidelity of the lady of the house was both questioned and served up as juicy fodder among the under-the-stairs gossips.

An obvious embarrassment to the family, Tc'aarlat had been banished to boarding school shortly before his sixth birthday. If anything, the dorm where he slept was even bigger than his room at home - although here he had to share the space with a dozen or more similar aged boys, each of whom enjoyed the same number of lower limbs as he did.

It was at this school that Tc'aarlat learned how to look after himself, in every way possible. After all, it wasn't as if his fellow pupils were doing anything to aid his protection from the ignorant bullies, self-centered prefects and downright evil members of the teaching staff.

He may have been slight of build, but his mind was as sharp as a wild cat's teeth. Before long, he was selling sheets of answers to forthcoming examinations, and bartering appropriated bottles of staffroom booze for second helpings from the kitchen porters.

By the time he started his second year at the school, Tc'aarlat was the person you contacted whether you needed a saucy magazine or the keys to the safe in the headmaster's office.

Tc'aarlat was the go-to guy.

Stretching his legs to ward off the cramp he was likely to endure as a result of the morning's exertions against the pirates, he accidentally kicked Mist's tall, home-made perch at the foot of his bed.

He leapt up to grab the indoor birdhouse before it could clatter to the floor, spilling the contents of the Raal hawk's food and water dishes.

Mist was already displeased with him for leaving her on the bridge while he took his break. If she came back to discover her home broken as well, Tc'aarlat was likely to face the following day sporting a number of fresh scratch marks on either his arms, his face, or both.

Sliding a wooden chair - his only piece of furniture - aside, the Yollin struggled to slot the base of Mist's birdhouse into the only spot it would fit. Not for the first time he wished his personal quarters on board the ship were even a fraction the size of his old bedroom, and not some cramped converted broom closet with an old, broken cot wedged inside.

He frequently told himself this was the only place he'd ever lived where he could switch off the light and be in bed before the room got dark.

The tablet lying on the floor beside the bunk bleeped, causing Tc'aarlat to sigh once more. His break was over. It was time to return to the bridge and hammer at the antiquated controls while listening to Jack's endless anecdotes about his time in the Corps, and Dollen's questionable solutions for the problem of interplanetary immigration.

Sliding his feet back into his boots, he prayed there would be a decent bar on board this damned *Etheric Federation* Base Station.

Federation Base Station 11, Residential Zone 9, Rosemere Care Home

Wendy Lintern collected a clean set of bedding and made her way across the day room towards the south corridor. The light from the base stations' internal sun shone brightly through the windows, bathing the home's immaculately maintained grounds in a spring-like glow. Shadows from the trees danced across the walls of the comfortable communal lounge.

"Morning Mr Hutchison," she smiled to a tall, grey-haired gentleman sitting alone at a chess set. "Who's your opponent today?"

"My son, Kyle," replied the pensioner, waving his tablet

in the air. The screen was covered with strings of letters and numbers indicating the game's previous moves.

There was a faint ding from the gadget, and Mr Hutchison chuckled as he read the latest message, then moved his son's bishop towards the center of the board. "He thinks he's leading me towards checkmate, but I have a little trap of my own he'll have to get out of first."

"Sounds like he's getting better each time you play," said Wendy. "Say hi from me, and remind him to bring you a few bottles of that All Guns Blazing dark ale you like so much."

She winked as the old man's eyes widened in surprise. "I won't tell Head Nurse if you don't," she said conspiratorially as she headed down the corridor.

Wendy had worked at Rosemere for almost six years now, ever since her own father had died peacefully in his sleep at the home. She had been so impressed at the standard of care the home's staff had provided for her dad in his final years that she had resigned from her job as a financial advisor and retrained as a nurse so that she could help provide that same level of welfare to future residents.

One incident in particular had convinced her that she was making the right decision in changing her career. A few weeks after she lost her father, the home had held a memorial service for the families of everyone who had passed away there during the previous year. It was an unforgettable day, and one which had prompted her to write in the book of remembrance that she 'had met angels at Rosemere. Angels who were disguised as doctors and nurses.'

Wendy Lintern decided she wanted to be someone's

angel and, although she wasn't supposed to have favorite residents in her care, Yousuf Choudhury was someone she looked forward to seeing each day.

"Good afternoon, Yousuf," she said as she tapped on the white-painted door and let herself into the room beyond. "What would you say to some fresh bedding?"

The elderly man sitting in a chair by the window didn't respond. Instead, he just gazed at the patients, staff and visitors enjoying the sunshine out in the grounds, not really seeing any of them at all.

Wendy smiled sadly. Yousuf was becoming more and more distant by the day. Lost inside a labyrinth of his own memories, and only occasionally finding his way back to the real world.

So different from the chatty retired security guard who had moved into the home just over a year ago.

She turned to close the door when an unexpected visitor appeared carrying a large bouquet of flowers.

"Adina!" cried Wendy. "Here to see your uncle? You don't normally find time to visit on weekdays."

"Got the afternoon off," explained Adina, laying the flowers on the sideboard. "Thought I'd make the most of it."

"Well, I'm sure Mr Choudhury will be delighted to see you," said Wendy as she began to strip the resident's single bed.

Adina crossed to where her uncle was sitting and crouched beside his chair. "Hi, Uncle Yousuf," she said gently. "How are you feeling?"

Yousuf Choudhury didn't respond at first. Then, just as Adina was about to repeat her greeting, the old man's eyes faded back into focus, and he smiled down at his niece.

"Fatima!" he exclaimed. "How lovely to see you!"

Adina tried not to let the dismay show in her expression. "No, I'm not Fatima, uncle," she said kindly. "I'm Adina. Fatima was my mom."

Yousuf's brow furrowed. "Not Fatima?" he said uncertainly. "Well, I'm sure she'll be along soon. It's not like my sister to stay away for long."

"Fatima isn't coming, uncle," said Adina, her voice catching at the back of her throat. "She's... She's busy."

The elderly man cupped his niece's chin with a wrinkled hand. "Oh, she's always busy, that one," he beamed. "Got a little one to look after now, you know. A beautiful baby girl. Her name is Adina."

Adina closed her eyes, falling silent.

Wendy, having finished changing the bedsheets, grabbed the bouquet of flowers and came to stand behind the young woman. "Look at these beautiful flowers, Yousuf," she said. "Would you like me to find a vase for them?"

Yousuf Choudhury's expression turned blank for a second, then he looked down at Adina as though seeing her for the first time. "Fatima!" he cried again. "I knew you'd come to see me today. Did you bring the little one?"

Wendy gave Adina's shoulder a gentle squeeze, then made for the door with the flowers. "I'll go put these in some water."

Adina waited until Wendy had left the room, then she angled herself so that she was looking deep into her uncles eyes. "Uncle Yousuf," she said. "I need to know the name of the guy you get my meds from. The ones that stop me from... being me. I've almost run out and I need more."

But the old man was no longer present. He stared, unseeing, out over the sun-drenched gardens.

Adina clutched at the old man's thin wrists. "Please," she urged. "Give me a name, a number, anything. Where can I get them?"

Once again, she didn't receive any response.

"Must be here somewhere," hissed Adina to herself as she jumped to her feet. She took a moment to check that no-one was approaching along the corridor, then she slid open the drawer in her uncle's bedside cabinet and began to root through the mishmash of items inside.

There were paperclips, still wrapped pieces of ancient hard candy, a couple of pens and a stack of old letters tied up with a length of red ribbon.

But not the item she was looking for.

The cupboards in the sideboard were next to be searched. Adina found porcelain figures that had belonged to Yousuf's wife, Isir, which her uncle had kept after his wife passed away. After years on display at their home, they were now wrapped in newspaper and packed away out of sight.

Aside from a few boxes of old photographs and a stack of cloth napkins, that was about it.

Her frustration beginning to grow, Adina stood in the center of the room flicking her gaze from object to object, looking for anything that might contain an address book, or a scrap of paper with the details she wanted scribbled on.

She was considering whether she should rummage through the pockets of her uncle's robe when her eyes fell on a small tobacco tin sitting on the windowsill.

"I wonder..." said Adina to herself as she hurried over.

Glancing back to the door to check she was still alone, she grabbed the tin and removed the lid. The sudden smell of her uncle's pipe - something he hadn't used in years - threatened to drag her back to her childhood, but she forced herself to swim against the current and remain in the present day.

Inside the tin was a small collection of old buttons, a few yellowing stamps torn from the corners of ancient letters, and a couple of dead batteries; items which must have enough meaning to the old man in order for him to keep them so long. Adina quickly rifled through them all.

And then, she saw it.

Nestled at the bottom of the tin, beneath the pull tab of a zipper that had once fastened Adina's jacket through much of elementary school, was an old, off-white business card.

She recognized it immediately. This was the card her uncle always referred to when it was time to call... him. The man who sold Yousuf Adina's black-market medication. The pills he had last ordered for his niece six months ago, before his condition had deteriorated to such a point.

A few moments later, Wendy re-entered Mr Choudhury's room carrying a crystal vase, inside which she had arranged the flowers Adina had brought with her.

"I had to borrow a vase from Mrs Shelly's room, but I'm sure she won't mind-" she said, then stopped when she realized Mr Choudhury was asleep in his chair, and Adina was gone.

4

Federation Base Station 11, Dock 17, Freight Bay C

Nathan Lowell leaned against a railing and watched as two men - one human and one Yollin - exited from the hulking cargo hauler, *ICS Fortitude*, and headed his way.

"Eight hundred and forty-two computer servers ordered by..." Jack glanced at the name on the shipping docket attached to his clipboard before he passed it over, "...a Marcus Cambridge."

"Thanks," said Nathan, signing for the consignment before returning the clipboard and holding out his hand. Both Jack and Tc'aarlat shook it. "I'll get the dock crew to unload them. While they're doing that, can I treat you gentlemen to a drink?"

"Sure," said Jack with a smile. "I never say no to a cold one."

"Sounds good to me," added Tc'aarlat, his mandibles tapping together. "Don't look a gift whore in the mouth, huh?!"

"Horse!" Jack corrected quickly. "Don't look a gift *horse* in the mouth."

He turned to Nathan: "Tc'aarlat's working on including human proverbs and phrases in his day to day conversation."

"He's, er... doing well," said Nathan, looking beyond the newcomers. "So, is it just the two of you?"

Mist ruffled her feathers and shrieked from her perch on Tc'aarlat's shoulder.

"Sorry," Nathan corrected. "Three of you."

The Yollin reached up to scratch the top of the hawk's beak, causing her to caw softly. "She doesn't like to be left out," he grinned.

"Tell me about it," Jack muttered under his breath.

Tc'aarlat shot him a brief look of irritation, but decided against bringing up Jack's intense dislike of his pet in front of their client. "There is another member of our crew somewhere," he said. "Where's Dollen?"

Jack shrugged. "He disappeared as we finished docking. Said he wanted to get changed as he had blood on his shirt." He noticed Nathan's raised eyebrows and added: "We had a little trouble on our way here..."

"Sorry!" called a voice from behind the group. Dollen jogged over to join them, a jacket with the haulage company's logo branded on the breast pocket fastened all the way up to his throat. "Couldn't decide what to wear."

Nathan shook the Baloreon's hand, then led the small party through the customs and security zones to a large, well-appointed shopping mall filled with tourists of several different species.

They passed jewelers, perfumers and stores selling all

manner of souvenirs. Tc'aarlat spotted a window display featuring ornamental models of Federation Base Station 11 itself and fought the urge to make a sarcastic comment.

After a few minutes, the group approached a bar with a large illuminated sign proclaiming it to be called *All Guns Blazing*.

"Nice place," remarked Jack as they entered. "Do you treat all your delivery guys this way?"

"Not bad, is it?" Nathan beamed. "It's a new franchise of the most popular bar at the *Etheric Empire's* home base. And, you've seen right through me. You are getting the special treatment. I've got something I'd like to talk to you guys about, if you can spare the time."

Dollen was quick to nod his agreement. "We don't have another delivery slated for a few days. We can hang out for a while."

Tc'aarlat shrugged, jostling Mist and receiving a gentle peck to the side of his head as a reward. He was slowly getting used to mimicking Jack's human gestures, which he was growing to realize were useful in avoiding confrontational situations sometimes caused by his more Yollin-friendly movements of his mandibles.

"Don't see why not."

The establishment was around half-full. Waiters in white shirts buzzed from table to table, taking orders and delivering drinks and food.

Nathan led the freighter crew up to a second level where they settled at a table near to a huge, floor to ceiling window looking out into the enormity of space.

A waitress with curly, shoulder length hair hovered a few feet away while they settled into their seats, then stepped up sporting both a well-used notepad and a welcoming smile.

"What can I get for you?" she inquired.

"I can highly recommend the Crofian Cream Ale," said Nathan, producing a tablet and turning it to show his visitors a slow-motion clip of the frothy brew being poured into a tall, frosted glass. "The guys who run the original bar have it imported from the Su-Sallok System, and it sells out fast. You should try it while they still have a couple of barrels left."

"Sounds good to me," said Jack, his throat suddenly dry at the sight of the dark amber beverage. "I'll go for that."

"Me, too," agreed Tc'aarlat. "And some chilled water for Mist, if that's OK?"

The waitress nodded, turning to Dollen. "Sir?"

"I'll stick with something non-alcoholic," Dollen replied. "Do you have anything like that?"

"I'll get you a Coke," smiled the waitress. "Is that everything?"

"Yes thanks, Kirsty," said Nathan.

The group exchanged pleasantries, and chatted about the view of space from the bar's outer window until the waitress returned with the requested drinks, and a range of snacks. She placed a bowl of pistachio nuts in front of Jack, handed Tc'aarlat a platter of drungen chips and dip, Dollen was given cubes of soft, white cheese, and there was even a plate of diced meat for Mist.

"Wait, is that muri flesh?" Tc'aarlat asked as Mist hopped onto the table and began to tear at the chunks of food.

Nathan nodded. "Isn't that what Raal hawks eat in the wild?"

"Yes, but those vile little rodents are a bitch to catch. Most hawk owners have to buy synthetic muri meat and..." Tc'aarlat's voice trailed off as a realization dawned. "You're trying to impress us. I'm guessing Jack has a particular liking for whatever snack he's already digging into."

Jack discarded another pistachio shell onto an already growing pile and popped the nut into his mouth with a nod. Lifting his glass, he took a long drink of his ale, his gaze firmly fixed on Nathan.

Dollen pushed his cheese cubes away from him and sipped at his Coke. "What do you want from us?"

"Can't a man treat the guys who delivered his long-awaited computer servers?" asked Nathan as innocently as he could. "Which reminds me..."

He turned his head and spoke aloud: "Turing, has the cargo been unloaded from the *ICS Fortitude* yet?"

A voice with a clipped English accent seemed to come from every direction at once, causing Tc'aarlat to peer around the otherwise deserted upper level for hidden speakers.

"Allow me to find that out for you, Nathan."

"Thank you, Turing."

Tc'aarlat's eyes narrowed. "You guys heard that weird disembodied voice as well, right?"

Nathan smiled. "That is the base station's Entity Intelligence, Turing," he explained. "He's in charge of everything from regulating the oxygen supply to arming our weapon defense systems."

"Wise to stay in his good books, then?" quipped Jack.

Turing's voice sounded from the speakers once again. "In answer to your question, yes Nathan. The dock workers finished disembarking Marcus's order a little over 15 minutes ago."

"Good," said Nathan. "Could you please send the entire consignment to be burned in the central furnaces?"

"Of course."

Jack spat out a half-chewed pistachio. "You're *burning* the computer servers?"

"That's insane!" growled Tc'aarlat.

Dollen took another drink, but remained silent.

"Not really," replied Nathan. "They're not genuine servers. Just shoddy casings filled with used pinball machine parts."

"What?!"

"You'll still get paid," Nathan added.

Jack snarled. "I'm not concerned about the money!"

"I am!" Tc'aarlat interjected.

Jack threw his colleague an angry look, then returned his furious glare back to Nathan. "Do you know what we had to go through to get those things here? We were boarded by Skaine pirates."

"Of course I know," said Nathan, matter of factly. "I was the one who tipped them off as to your location."

Jack sprang to his feet. "You did fucking what?!"

Nathan's expression didn't waver. "I needed to see how you would cope against a dangerous adversary," he explained. "And you will be pleased to hear you passed with flying colors."

Jack almost threw himself across the table, grabbed the front of Nathan's shirt and dragged him to his feet. "First you incinerate our entire consignment, and now you're admitting that you sent a ship full of inbred piss-gargling bistok-fuckers after us," he hissed. "You've got some serious explaining to do, pal!"

Tc'aarlat looked from Nathan to Jack and back again. Even Mist paused, a strip of sinewy muri meat dangling from her beak.

Nathan glanced down at where Jack had hold of his shirt, and back up at his attacker's furious expression. Nathan's eyes flashed yellow, suggesting Jack was treading on dangerous ground.

"I promise you, it was all for a good cause, and now, if you would be so kind, let go of me."

With a final furious sneer at Nathan, Jack released his shirt, and turned to his shipmates. "Come on," he growled. "We're leaving."

Nodding, Tc'aarlat stood and whistled for Mist to flap back up to his shoulder, which she did without hesitation.

The two men looked towards Dollen as he stood and pushed his right hand deep into the pocket of his jacket.

It was then that Jack noticed the Baloreon's brow was coated with sweat.

"Dollen, what's wrong?"

But Dollen didn't reply. Instead, he unzipped the front of his jacket.

Both Jack and Tc'aarlat stared at their colleague in horror. Strapped to the Baloreon's chest was a home-made bomb.

. . .

Federation Base Station 11, Residential Zone 4, Geldings Strip Mall

The exterior of Geldings Strip Mall was in need of a lick of paint.

Adina wandered past a pet store, an engravers and a health food outlet, actively trying to look as though she belonged in the area. She hoped the effort of doing so wasn't making her stand out even more.

Finally, she reached Happy Garden, the all-you-can-eat Chinese buffet near the end of the mall, and turned into the narrow alleyway that ran alongside it.

This is where the voice on the phone had told her to meet him.

"H- Hello?"

A figure stepped out from behind a dumpster. The man was much smaller than Adina had expected; short and skinny to the point of appearing malnourished. He was informally dressed in dark trousers and scuffed boots, and the hood of his jacket was pulled up, causing it to cast a dark shadow across his face. Still, Adina could make out the moist, yellow teeth of her contact's leering smile.

"You the one who called?" he sneered.

Adina nodded, suddenly not as confident as she had been when she had first set off from the nursing home, and she hadn't felt very certain of herself back then.

"Yes," she croaked. "Are you Mosco?"

Mosco Asdale pulled back his hood, revealing a face peppered with acne scars and short greasy hair that looked as though it had been cut towards the end of an all-night drinking session.

With cutlery.

He nodded, his watery eyes lapping up and down her figure. Adina shivered involuntarily and wrapped her arms around herself, making a mental note to take a lengthy shower just as soon as she got back home.

"Where's the old guy?" questioned Mosco. "The one I usually deal with."

"H- He's ill," replied Adina, not wanting to give away too much information. "My uncle won't be able to meet with you any longer."

Mosco's mouth twisted into a wicked smile. "Your uncle?" he cooed, taking a step closer. "So, you're the girl, huh? The girl who doesn't want to be a-"

"Yes," said Adina, interrupting before he could finish his sentence. "That's me. I'm the girl."

She pulled a roll of banknotes from the pocket of her jeans. "Three hundred you said, right?"

The scrawny man shifted his weight onto his left foot and gave an exaggerated sigh. "I wish it was, girly," he said, pulling a mock disappointed face. "I really do. But the price has just gone up."

"Gone up?" exclaimed Adina. "Since when?"

"Since I just decided," Mosco sneered. He reached into the pocket of his hooded jacket and produced a crumpled plastic bag. Inside were scores of tiny black pills, each with a single yellow dot stamped onto one side.

"Six hundred."

Adina felt her eyes sting with tears. "But... But I don't have six hundred," she explained. "I can go to three fifty, maybe three eighty, but that's all I've got."

"Then you don't get the merchandise, do you?" said Mosco, turning away.

"Wait!" cried Adina, scurrying after him. "Give me half for three hundred, and I'll get the rest of the money to you next week."

Mosco slowly turned back to face her. "I've got a better idea," he grinned. "You give me everything you've got now, and then you and I can find another way for you to make up the rest of what you owe me..."

He began to advance on her, pulling a knife from his pocket and unfolding the blade from its slot inside the handle. It glinted in the only shaft of sunlight brave enough to extend this far down the alleyway.

"So, what do you say, little girl?" Mosco hissed, a stained tongue flicking back and forth over the chapped skin of his lips. "Do we have a deal?"

Adina backed away, preparing herself to turn and run as soon as she was near to the main street. There hadn't been many shoppers around when she had arrived but, if she could get into one of the nearby stores-

She backed into something solid and stopped dead.

There was someone standing right behind her. Someone large, who clamped a hand down on her shoulder.

"'Ello," grunted a deep voice.

Shit!

Adina closed her eyes and worked to keep her breathing under control

She'd walked straight into a trap.

Shit! Shit! Shit! Shit! Shit!

Stupid girl!

Of course, Mosco wouldn't be alone. Of course, he'd have an accomplice ready to bar her escape route. And now the two of them were going to drag her into the shadows and she'd never be heard of again.

She turned her head slightly and glanced over her shoulder. The figure behind her was huge; at least six feet tall, and almost as wide. It felt like she was backed up against an immense, immovable boulder.

The newcomer had cropped hair, an expansive sloping brow, and small dark eyes sunk into sockets so deep they appeared to be nothing more than empty holes leading directly into the depths of the accomplice's skull.

At just under five feet tall, Adina has been teased for her height - or, rather, lack of it - all through her childhood. She'd always been the smallest in her class and, whenever she'd hurried home from school in tears due to a bully's cruel taunts, her uncle had held her close and promised that she would have a sudden growth spurt one day soon.

Now in her late 20s, she was still waiting for that to happen.

The figure behind Adina wrapped its arms around her slender frame, the cheap nylon of its zipped-up jacket rubbing against the back of her head. However, beneath that, she didn't feel the hard chest muscle she was expecting. Instead the flesh was softer, and concentrated in two vast areas of swelling.

Adina's breath caught in her throat.

The assailant holding her from behind was a woman!

Mosco's face was just inches from hers now. She could feel his hot, rancid breath sting her eyes as he flicked open the top button of her blouse with his blade.

"So," he slathered wetly. "Do we have a deal?"

Adina's thoughts flicked back to her Uncle Yousuf,

struggling to retain his remaining memories in his single room at the rest home. He'd been dealing with this criminal - and others like him - for years in order to provide her with the medication she required.

Not that any of that mattered now. His illness meant that her only living relative would soon completely forget that he'd ever had a niece.

If Adina was going to walk out of here alive, she was going to have to do something she had promised herself would never happen again.

And it was really going to hurt.

Federation Base Station 11, All Guns Blazing, Lower Level

Aliporta squealed with excitement as her three friends led her, blindfolded, towards a table near the bar.

With just a week to go until her wedding to Graylaw, she had tried to turn down her bridesmaids' offer of a three-day hen party, but their detailed schedule of spa treatments, shopping and long nights drinking had persuaded her to reconsider.

Now, after a morning of manicures, pedicures and all-round pampering, her best friends clearly had some sort of surprise up their collected sleeves. Her fellow Snowbirals had stopped her among the crowds in the busy shopping court and produced a patterned headscarf, which they proceeded to tie over her eyes before moving on.

"You sit here," said Clercarp, guiding her into the chair at the head of the table, "and put this on..."

"Put what on?" asked Aliporta, reaching up to touch

whatever had just been placed on her head. Whatever it was, it was made of ornately twisting strips of metal and sat snugly around her horns.

"It's a tiara!" exclaimed another of the girls, clamping a hand over her mouth.

"Dycroft!" cried Loosamul. "It was supposed to be a secret!"

"Oops!" giggled Dycroft. "I couldn't help myself; she just looks so beautiful."

"Let me see then!" said Aliporta, excitedly, reaching up to remove the scarf.

Clercarp grabbed her hands and pushed them back down. "In a moment," she promised. "We just need to get the waiter's attention and order some of that bubbly drink you're always talking about."

"Champagne?" asked Aliporta with a gasp. "It's amazing! Graylaw's family had it imported for his sister's wedding last year."

"That's the stuff," agreed Loosamul.

Aliporta heard footsteps approaching, and then a gruff male voice spoke up. "Welcome to All Guns Blazing. Can I get you ladies something special?"

At that, Clercarp whisked off Aliporta's blindfold. She blinked with both sets of eyelids as her pupils adjusted to the bright lights of the room, her gaze finally focusing on the well-built Shrillexian waiter standing in front of her. For some reason, there was already a bottle of champagne chilling in an ice bucket beside four glasses on the table.

"I thought you still had to order-" she began, before a raucous song began to play from hidden speakers all around the bar. It was an old Earth recording in which the human singer was enticing his 'baby' to slowly remove her coat, dress and shoes - although he was still allowing her to 'keep her hat on' for some unknown reason.

Then the waiter began to dance seductively and unbutton his crisp white shirt!

Aliporta's normally cerise pink skin flushed a deep fuchsia color, and she covered her eyes with her hands as her friends cheered and clapped.

"I said no strippers!" she shrieked, peeking at the Shrillexian through her fingers as he tore open the rest of his shirt, sending the few remaining buttons pinging off the champagne flutes.

"Since when did we ever listen to you?" laughed Clercarp, whistling loudly as the stripping waiter grabbed the bride's wrists, pulled her hands from her face and pressed them against the thick, leathery skin of his chest.

The Shrillexian pumped his pecs beneath Aliporta's perspiring palms, then dropped his own hands and began to unbutton his pants.

Aliporta squealed as he pushed the trousers down. She screwed her eyes closed, and stomped her feet repeatedly.

She screamed with excitement, but her shrieks of joy were quickly drowned out by the screams of terrified patrons running for their lives.

5

Federation Base Station 11, Residential Zone 7, Sycamore Block

Adina entered her apartment, ensured the door was locked behind her, then tossed her keys into a metal bowl on the table in the hallway.

The flat was silent, just as it had been ever since her roommate had left to move in with her new boyfriend. Adina sighed at the memory of Tracey's excited voice as she announced news of her sudden engagement to Rocky.

Rocky! Who the hell calls their kid Rocky?

Even worse, the name totally suited him. Rocky looked - and acted - like a troll trying to pass himself off as a human. A former member of a high school gang, the guy considered himself a genuine 'bad boy', and hadn't let his poor education stop him from decorating his body with a range of self-administered tattoos.

Tracey had sulked for almost a week when Adina had pointed out that, according to the home-inked letters adorning Rocky's knuckles, the big goon was admitting to L-O-V-E H-A-T-S.

Now Tracey was gone and the soul had been drained from the apartment, which was probably just as well. Adina knew her friend would demand to know why she was returning home with blood splashed across her face and clothes.

She'd only been allowed on the tram after convincing the driver that she had been tending to a work colleague who suffered from severe nose bleeds.

She pulled the bag of black and yellow pills from her pocket and held them up to the light.

Selecting one, she popped it into her mouth. Then she opened the refrigerator, grabbed a bottle of water and twisted off the top. One big gulp later, and the medicine was gone.

Dumping the rest of the pills on the kitchen counter, she discarded her jacket and peeled off her shirt as she made her way towards the bathroom and her shower.

On the way, she grabbed a trash bag from the closet where she kept her cleaning supplies and stuffed the items of soiled clothing inside, making a mental note to keep them separate from the rest of her weekly laundry.

And, if the blood stains didn't come out in the wash, to destroy the evidence in a way that couldn't be traced back to her. The jacket, shirt, pants...

"Don't forget the soles of your shoes," said a voice as if someone was reading her thoughts.

Adina spun around as a lamp flicked on to reveal a woman with long blonde hair sitting on the sofa.

"Ecaterina?!"

"Your shoes," Ecaterina repeated. "Even if you manage to get all of the blood out of your clothing, you're likely to have traces lodged in the tread patterns of the soles. Especially as you walked through a pool of it on your way out of the alley."

Adina stared, seemingly unconcerned that, aside from her bra, she was naked from the waist up. "What are you talking about?"

Ecaterina pulled a small tablet from inside her coat, tapped on the screen and held it out. Adina's heart pounded as she watched video footage of herself leaving the alleyway she had visited earlier that afternoon.

"But, there... There weren't any..."

"Security cameras," finished Ecaterina. "Yeah, I know. This was taken by a drone a hundred feet or so above you. We have a team recovering the bodies you dragged behind the dumpster before you fled the scene."

Adina's brow furrowed. "Wait - you were following me?"

"No," said Ecaterina. "Not you. The Federation has had Mosco Asdale under surveillance for a few months now, gathering evidence we could use to put him away. Then, a new face shows up. A customer the camera operator hadn't seen before. So, he called me to take a look. Imagine my surprise to see you there..."

"Then you saw what he, and his... friend tried to do to me."

Ecaterina nodded. "And how you dealt with them. Very efficient, although some might consider your response as somewhat extreme."

"They were going to kill me!"

"So, you killed them?"

"I had no choice."

"You did have a choice," Ecaterina countered. "You could have chosen not to buy illegal drugs from a known criminal."

Adina opened her mouth to reply, then closed it again. Backing up, she slowly sat in a chair facing the couch and covered her face with trembling hands. When she pulled them away again, her eyes were wet with tears.

"I had to go there," she said softly. "I had to get my medication."

Ecaterina stood and retrieved the bag of pills from the kitchen. "This stuff is extremely dangerous, Adina," she warned. "DNA suppressants are banned for a reason, especially where nanocytes are involved."

Adina blinked back her tears. "You know what they are?"

"I do," said Ecaterina. "And, aside from being amazed by your behavior today, I'm more than a little offended. Why didn't you come to me?"

"Because you wouldn't understand," croaked Adina.

"Of course, I would," said Ecaterina. "I'm one of the few people who can understand."

Adina dropped her head, avoiding Ecaterina's accusing stare. Her shoulders shaking as she sobbed quietly.

Ecaterina took advantage of the lull in the conversation to return her attention to her tablet. She tapped an icon and swiped through a collection of video files until she found the one she was looking for.

She hit play, and turned the screen around so that both she and Adina could see it.

Adina wiped her eyes and stared at the crisp, color footage in horror. The drone had shot the footage so that she and her attackers filled the frame. Two violent thugs threatening an innocent young girl.

It looked like a scene from a movie.

A movie in which she had a starring role.

"Please..." she begged as she looked away, her throat dry. But Ecaterina held the tablet steady.

"I need you to watch this," Ecaterina urged.

Adina reluctantly returned her attention to the video.

She watched as Mosco Asdale ran the blade of his knife across her chest, playing with her while the oversized woman pressed down on her shoulders, ensuring she couldn't break free and try to escape.

Mosco turned the knife in his hand, aiming the point at Adina's throat. Then he leaned in and whispered in her ear.

The camera hadn't picked up his words, but Adina couldn't forget what he had said to her.

"I'm going to enjoy this," he had hissed. "I'm going to enjoy you!"

That's when the Adina on screen raised her hands, turning them over to stare at her palms. She screamed in agony - a sound the drone's microphone had recorded.

Her cry was so sudden, it caused Mosco to take a step back. His eyes flicked nervously from left to right, looking past his vast accomplice to check that no passing Good Samaritan had heard the shout and come looking to see who it was that required assistance.

Adina cried out again as she stared down at her now trembling hands. Her palms were moving unnaturally, the skin rippling and stretching as though something was squirming around underneath.

Whoever was operating the drone must also have spotted this, as the camera zoomed in to get a closer look.

Adina turned her hands over just as her fingers began to stretch and swell, growing before her eyes. Her neatly manicured nails bulged outwards, splitting and lengthening as they became long, yellowing talons.

Her wrists grew wider, thicker, stronger; quickly followed by her hands themselves. It now looked as though she was wearing a pair of oversized gloves made of thick, cracked leather.

And then came the fur.

Just a few strands at first, sprouting from the pores over her knuckles. The hairs grew quickly, reminding Adina of the clips of time-lapse footage of pea shoots sprouting she had watched in science class at school.

Then the fur spread, like an ocean wave washing over the backs of her hands. The terrified woman flipped her palms upwards again, only to discover they were now also thickly covered with the dense, grey-brown pelt.

Finally, the transformation ended. Adina stared down at two fully-formed wolf paws, her chest heaving.

The camera pulled back out to show all three participants of this bizarre spectacle once more.

Adina looked up, straight into the panicked eyes of Mosco. He dropped his knife to the ground as he backed away, his own hands raised in a gesture of surrender.

Even the bulky, big-breasted beast behind Adina had released her gargantuan grip on her shoulders.

The drone swept through the air above the alley, stopping to hover above and behind Mosco, earning a clear view of Adina's face as it split into a wide smile. This time, its microphone caught her trenchant words.

"I'm going to enjoy this," she intoned. "I'm going to enjoy you!"

Ecaterina paused the video just as Adina's razor sharp claws carved out the majority of Mosco's fleshy throat. The scarlet shower of blood freezing in mid-air.

"How did you do it?" she asked.

Adina couldn't meet her friend's gaze. "Do what?"

"How did you only change one part of your body into your werewolf form?"

"Don't say that word!" Adina said, turning away. "I hate it!"

"Werewolf is not a bad word," Ecaterina assured her. "And being a werewolf is nothing to be ashamed of. I should know."

"It is!" Adina countered. "I have to stop myself from completely changing into that... thing ever again. I need to!"

"Why?"

Adina didn't reply.

"Why, Adina?" Ecaterina demanded. "I can't help you if you don't tell me what's going on!"

Adina turned back to fix her red, swollen eyes on her friend.

"Because the first time I transformed into that thing, I killed my mother!"

. . .

Alma Nine, Aaron City, Department of Justice, Parole Offices

Vix Mil was in the midst of typing up an urgent report when the tap came on her office door.

She paused, closing her eyes for a moment as she wondered whether to remain silent and pretend she wasn't at her desk. The report she was working on was due to be delivered an hour ago, and an entire court case had been paused while she wrote it.

The knock came again, causing Vix Mil to sigh. She didn't have any appointments down in her diary, so she could just hide away. If she refused to answer, whoever was out there *might* go away, leaving her to type the final page of this extremely urgent document. Or, they might try the door - which, as always, she'd left unlocked.

If she was caught hiding away - no matter how honorable the reason - she would almost certainly get into trouble with her superiors, and that was something she didn't want to happen.

Sighing softly, she saved the document and switched off the screen of her computer. Not yet knowing the identity of her visitor, she didn't want anyone catching a glimpse of something they shouldn't see.

Vix Mil replied on the third knock. "Come in!"

She continued as the handle lowered and the door swung open. "I'm so sorry - I was lost in concentration and didn't hear anyone-"

Her voice trailed away as she realized exactly who her unexpected caller was. He stood on the other side of the desk, smartly dressed in an expensive suit, and wore his silver hair streaked with flashes of gold.

"Hen Wic," she said, gesturing to the visitor's chair. "I didn't expect you so soon. I take it you got the message I left for you yesterday."

"I did. No doubt you invited me here to congratulate me on my early release," smiled the guest as he sat. Crossing his legs, he picked at an invisible piece of fluff from his trouser leg. "Good behavior, if you can believe it."

"So I've heard," replied Vix Mil, opening a drawer in her desk and sliding out a thin folder. She flipped open the cover to examine the single-page document inside. "Consistently polite to guards and fellow inmates, a job in the prison library, and even teaching the Governor's daughter to ride her bicycle."

"What can I say?" said Hen Wic with a shrug. "I'm a people person."

Vix Mil closed the folder and sat back in her chair. "Not when you were busy intimidating members of the jury in the Loz May case," she commented.

Hen Wic's easy smile didn't so much as flicker. "I've changed," he said. "Serving time showed me the error of my ways. And, now I presume you calling means you've been assigned as my parole officer. Everybody wins."

"Actually, one of us doesn't win," said Vix Mil, retrieving the only other item inside Hen Wic's file. A color photograph. She flipped it around for her guest to examine. "You were spotted outside the home of the judge who convicted Loz May and his accomplices.

"As you'll be aware, that's a clear breach of the terms of your parole."

Hen Wic snatched the photograph and studied it.

"That's not me!" he protested, stabbing at it with a finger. "It could be anyone!"

"We have several independent witnesses," said Vix Mil with a sigh. "We know you were watching the judge's house, and I cannot imagine you wanted to help either of his children with their bike riding skills."

She reached over to press a button beside her communicator on the desk. "I don't want to do this, Hen Wic, but I'm duty bound."

Before Hen Wic could respond, the office door opened and a pair of burly security guards stepped into the room.

"These gentlemen will escort you to a holding cell downstairs while I contact the necessary authorities for your return to jail."

"You can't!" spat Hen Wic as the guards took him by the arm and forced him to stand. "I've served my time. I'm an innocent man!"

"Please could you close the door?" Vix Mil asked one of the guards as they turned to lead their prisoner away. The larger of the two men nodded and did as he was asked.

Hen Wic continued to rant and shout as he was escorted away through the outer offices.

Vix Mil calmly returned the file to her desk drawer, then she switched her computer screen back on, and continued work on her report.

6

Federation Base Station 11, Residential Zone 7, Sycamore Block

It was Ecaterina's turn to be silent. When she finally spoke, her voice was little more than a whisper.

"You killed your mother?!"

"It was my 13th birthday," Adina explained. "Until then, I had no idea I was... you know..."

"Wechselbalg," Ecaterina put in.

Adina nodded. "Right. That. No-one knew. There hadn't been a changeling in my family for generations, and the few people who had been told that our ancestors had once possessed those abilities had put the story down to rumor and superstition."

"So, what happened?"

"My mom had made some party food to celebrate my becoming a teenager," Adina continued. "Nothing fancy, just some snacks for a few friends and relatives. Then, when it came time to blow out the candles on my birthday cake, I leaned too far over it and the ends of my hair caught fire."

She paused, her eyes slipping out of focus momentarily as she relived the traumatic event.

"My Uncle Yousuf batted the flames out with his hands. I wasn't hurt in any way, but I panicked, and that must have been what kick-started the changes."

Ecaterina reached out to take Adina's hands in hers. "You began to transform?"

"I don't remember much after that - just flashes and images and sounds. I heard everyone scream, I saw them run. All except my mom. She stayed with me. She tried to help, but..."

Adina pulled her hands free and pressed her palms over her eyes, her body wracking with sobs.

Ecaterina could only wait until Adina had control of her tears and was ready to continue her story.

"When I came 'round, there was blood everywhere," she blubbed. "My mom was lying beside me, and she was... she was..."

Ecaterina climbed off the couch and knelt before her friend, wrapping her arms around the girl and holding her tight. "It's OK," she soothed, stroking Adina's hair. "It's OK."

"At her funeral, my dad told me he wanted nothing more to do with me," Adina wailed into Ecaterina's shoulder. "He said I'd destroyed his life, and he never wanted to see me ever again.

Uncle Yousuf took me in. He was so kind, so caring. He tried to get me help, to teach me how to deal with what I was. But I wanted none of it, so he tracked down somewhere to buy those pills for me. The ones that stop me from changing.

I've been taking them ever since."

Adina pulled away, grabbing her discarded blood-drenched shirt and using one of the few clean spots to dry her tears.

"I tore my family apart," she said dispassionately. "All because of that thing.

"And, today, that thing stopped you from being violently raped and murdered," Ecaterina reminded her. "I can't imagine how painful it must have been forcing yourself to change form while under the effect of DNA suppressants."

Adina shrugged. "So, what now?"

Ecaterina brushed Adina's bangs out of her eyes. "Station security will report exactly what happened," she explained. "The drugs, the attack, and how you resolved the situation."

"Will I go to jail?" asked Adina, gazing at the older woman through tousled locks of hair, looking for all the world like a lost little schoolgirl.

"I expect not," Ecaterina admitted, pulling Adina in for another hug. "I'll be fighting for you, insisting you had no choice but to fight back in the only way you knew how, along with managing who sees the report, but..."

She sighed heavily.

"You were in danger because you were engaged in criminal activity and, at the very least, it could be decided that you aren't capable of looking after yourself."

"So, they'll lock me in some hospital instead of a jail

cell," groaned Adina, pulling back and staring at the floor. "I'm shafted, aren't I?"

Ecaterina gently took hold of Adina's chin and lifted her face up to meet hers. She was smiling.

"Not if it turns out you were there working undercover for me..."

Federation Base Station 11, All Guns Blazing, Upper Level

People screamed and ran, overturning chairs and tables, coating the polished wooden floor with a mix of broken glass and spilled alcohol.

Near to the bar, a group of pink-skinned girls raced for the nearest exit. Immediately behind them, a shirtless Shrillexian waddled as quickly as the pants pulled down around his knees would let him.

Jack stared at the contraption strapped to Dollen's chest.

It was a vest made from some off-white material, onto which were sewn pockets stuffed with bricks of what appeared to be harmless grey clay. However, the colored wires connecting the clay blocks together and the blinking LED light suggested they were something far more sinister.

The wires continued down the inside of Dollen's right coat sleeve, where they ended at a black plastic box, about the size of an old-fashioned cellphone. A red button protruded from the top of the gadget, above which the Baloreon's thumb now hovered.

The pounding music stopped, and a thundering silence flooded the bar.

Jack felt his throat go dry. "That's..."

Nathan nodded. "Enough explosive to take out this entire bar..."

"...and a good portion of the docks, as well," finished Dollen. "Unless you agree to my demands."

The Baloreon was visibly shaking now, and Jack kept a close eye on his nervously twitching thumb. One false move, and this would be the last conversation any of them would ever have.

Nathan flicked a glance towards the windows in the main doors and was relieved to see figures in black armor already on the scene outside. Some of them helped to evacuate terrified shoppers from the mall while others took up positions around the bar, weapons drawn and ready.

Jack tried to work out how he'd come to bring a suicide bomber right into the heart of the Etheric Federation.

He and Tc'aarlat had met Dollen while delivering a shipment of medical supplies to a recently occupied moon in the Taserra Quadrant. He claimed to have been working as a navigator on board a passenger shuttle, but said he had overslept after a night of heavy drinking with a handful of locals.

He'd woken on a stranger's couch, then raced to the docks in an effort to get to his ship before it left. He missed the departure by minutes and was now stranded.

Jack spotted him wandering the loading bays, asking the captains of various ships if they could give him a lift to the nearest transport hub in return for working with their crew.

Despite the *ICS Fortitude* having three more deliveries to make before they would be close enough to anywhere where Dollen could arrange passage back to his home world, Jack was happy to take on an extra pair of hands.

It transpired that, not only was Dollen a hard worker when it came to loading and unloading cargo, he was also an experienced navigator. And so, Jack and Tc'aarlat had offered their new friend a full-time job.

But, the whole thing appeared to have been a clever ruse. A cold-hearted ploy, devised purely to get inside one of the Etheric Federation's bases.

Jack had been tricked by a terrorist, but he wasn't going to allow himself to be used by this bastard any longer.

"Take it easy," he said to the jittery bomber, glancing quickly at both Tc'aarlat and Nathan to check they were willing to back him up. "Tell us what you want, and we'll do our best to help you."

Yeah, thought Jack, *we'll do our best to send you straight to the fires of Hell you shit-sucking piece of trash!*

With a trembling hand, the Baloreon pulled a crumpled sheet of paper from his left jacket pocket, unfolded it with his fingers, and began to read.

"We demand that all political prisoners are released immediately, and safe transport is arranged to return them to their homes and families."

Nathan frowned as his face turned cold, his look murderous. "Understood," Nathan told Dollen. "What else?"

Jack was furious and his face betrayed his emotions.

"We demand the Etheric Federation withdraw from every world they have illegally invaded and retreat back to whichever corner of the galaxy they came from."

"O... K..." said Tc'aarlat, drawing out his response. "Is that it?"

Dollen shook his head, his left eye twitching as he focused on the sheet of paper once more.

"Finally, we demand that the so-called Empress of the evil Etheric Empire hand herself over to be tried and executed for her many war crimes."

A heavy silence hung in the air for a moment while everyone considered what Dollen had just said. The Baloreon attempted to fold up his list of demands with his free hand, eventually resorting to simply scrunching up the piece of paper and stuffing it back into his pocket.

"Can I ask a question?" said Jack after a moment.

Dollen turned to look at him, the movement causing more of his brow sweat to run down into his eyes.

"You say 'we demand'," Jack pointed out. "Who's 'we'?"

Dollen blinked, his eyes growing wide as he realized that he had missed out a key part of his speech.

Jack pictured him practicing his big moment in the mirror of his cabin. The traitorous piece of puke.

"We," croaked Dollen, "are *Dark Tomorrow*."

Jack's eyes flashed with rage. "You're one of those dick-less fuckers?" he spat.

"Tomorrow, the blood of our enemies shall rain down from the heavens!"

"Not this tired old shit," groaned Jack, rubbing the bridge of his nose.

Dollen's face twisted into an expression of rage. "Dark Tomorrow is a non-partisan organization dedicated to the freedom of-"

"No!" Snapped Jack, shaking his head. "You're a truckload of terrorist twats!" Snatching up his empty beer glass, he hurled it at Dollen's head.

The glass slammed into his temple, shattering into a dozen razor sharp pieces, several of which embedded themselves into the side of the Baloreon's face, with one particularly pointed sliver slicing into the corner of his eye.

As Dollen screamed, Tc'aarlat grabbed hold of the bomber's tail, pressed his boot into the small of his back and tugged as hard as he could.

There was a sickening ripping sound as the muscle beneath the hairless blue skin tore away from the tendons fixing it to the bone.

Furious, Dollen raised his hand and tried to focus his one working eye on the small button on the top of the detonator.

Nathan's fist made contact with his jaw, and it was only the extremely strong bone structure possessed by the Baloreon that stopped the punch from being a fatal blow. Instead, the bone splintered, sending a lightning bolt of pain through Dollen's face and causing his brain to initiate an immediate shutdown in the cause of self-preservation. The Baloreon's eyes rolled back in his head and his legs buckled as he crumpled towards the floor.

All eyes fixed on the detonator as - almost in slow motion - it slipped from his hand, spun in the air and fell towards the floor, the button now facing down towards the solid, varnished planks.

Before anyone could react, Mist launched herself from Tc'aarlat's shoulder, swooping down and snatching the device from the air just inches above the ground.

Pumping her wings, she flew back to her usual perch,

the wires connecting the detonator to the explosives in Dollen's vest street pulling taut as she landed.

Seeing their chance to help neutralize the situation, the armed guards burst in through the bar's main doors and spread out to take up positions around the establishment.

"It's OK, Keith" said Nathan to their sergeant as he hurried over. "It's just this guy. No other threats present."

"Thank you, sir," said Keith nodding. "If you and your guests could vacate the premises, I'll get the bomb techs in here to make the device safe."

"What about Dollen?" asked Jack. "What will happen to him?"

"I'll take care of him," said a voice from behind the group. Jack and Tc'aarlat turned to see a large man in gleaming black armor striding towards them.

"Gentlemen," said Nathan. "This is Ricky Milton Smith."

"The reputation of the New Rangers precedes you," Jack announced, shaking the newcomer's hand warmly.

"Yeah," agreed Tc'aarlat. "I hear you're the toughest sons of a bitches around here!"

Ricky shook his hand. "I'm sure you're a brave guy, as well."

"Too right!" crowed the Yollin. "Birds of a feather fuck together!"

"*Flock* together!" Jack put in.

"Same difference," said Tc'aarlat, stooping slightly so that one of the armed guards could retrieve the detonator from Mist's beak. "What will you do with this dick-splash?"

Ricky looked at the unconscious terrorist at his feet. "I'll interrogate him once he wakes up, and ensure he receives the appropriate punishment."

"Good," said Jack. He gestured to both Tc'aarlat and himself. "I just hope you understand that neither of us had anything to do with this. He used us to get in here and act like a grade A ferret-fister."

Ricky flashed a grim smile. "We have your arrival on board, and your entire conversation recorded," he assured them. "We appreciate the mechanics of the situation."

"And we'd better not have our payment docked for this, either!" insisted Tc'aarlat.

"I assure you that won't be the case," smiled Nathan. "In fact, there may even be a small reward for the safe capture of Mr Stonebrand here..."

The Yollin's face split into a wide grin. "The moment I met you, I knew you were one of the good guys," he proffered. "Now, when you say small reward, exactly how small are we talking here?"

Ricky turned, partly to hide his grin, and partly to wave the newly arrived bomb techs over to get to work.

"What say we continue our conversation in my office," suggested Nathan. He led Jack and Tc'aarlat down to the lower area of the bar and the main doors. As Nathan pushed them open, the men heard a fresh chorus of screams.

"What now?" sighed Jack.

On the far side of the mall, just outside the yellow exclusion tape, the group of Snowbiral girls were chasing a terrified Shrillexian, now wearing only his underwear and socks. He skidded on the polished floor as he tried to stop at the door to the male restroom.

With a haunted glance back at the girls, he slammed open the door and dove inside. Giggling with excitement, the bride led her three bridesmaids straight inside after him.

This time, it was the Shrillexian's turn to scream.

Nathan extended an arm towards another door positioned next to the beer cooler cabinets behind the bar.

"We'll take the long way around."

7

Alma Nine, Taron City, Government Building, Vice President's Office

"That devious fucking bitch!" spat Saf Tah, slamming his fist down onto the dark wood top of his desk, and sending a container of brushes, combs and tubes of hair gel crashing onto the floor.

Mol Gat, one of the Vice President's longest standing aides, hurried over to pick them up and return them to their spot beside a small but well-used mirror.

"I, um... don't understand, sir," he admitted as he refilled the pot. "Why would the, um... President enter into negotiations with the Etheric Federation without, um... informing you?"

Saf Tah glowered down at his assistant. "Because, you moron, she knew I would have put a stop to her plans."

Mol Gat cast a nervous glance over at his fellow staffer, Jus Clo, before standing to replace the collection of hair products.

"Oh yes, of course, sir" he cooed, hoping the faint

tremble in his voice wouldn't betray the intense feeling of dread Saf Tah's rages always filled him with. "And, um... you would put a stop to it because...?"

"Because, you pathetic gutter slime, aligning ourselves with those Etheric bastards will put us on the path to utter destruction!"

He pounded on his desk again, toppling the pot of combs and gels once more.

"We'll be nothing more than a puppet planet, expected to come running whenever their pathetic excuse for an Empress clicks her fingers."

Snatching up the mirror, he peered at his reflection, carefully repositioning one of the tiny white lights woven into his chrome-colored hair.

"There's a reason we should never have given women the right to vote, let alone play at politics themselves."

"It's funny you should mention that, sir," said Jus Clo, taking a step towards his boss's desk, taking care not to tread on Mol Gat's fingers as he crawled across the carpet to pick up an errant hair clip.

He had sprayed his own extravagant hairstyle with an aerosol-based glue, and then dunked his entire head into a vat of multi-colored glitter.

The end result resembled something akin to the aftermath of an explosion in a Wiletime tree ornament factory.

"I actually had an idea for how we might be able to toss a dark stain upon President Tor Val's as yet untainted reputation," he announced with a smile.

He paused, in a way he hoped looked more dramatic than scared.

Saf Tah sighed. "Let's hear it, then," he growled. "And I

hope it's better than your idea to name a sexually trans-mitted disease after her, then release a comedy song about it!"

Jus Clo clutched his stack of files to his chest and tried not to let the hurt show in his eyes. "Oh, it's much better than that idea, sir. I stayed up quite late last night working out all the little details, and I think you'll find-"

"Get on with it!" bellowed Saf Tah.

Jus Clo jumped at the cry, quickly lowering his collec-tion of files to crotch level in an attempt to hide the fact that he had just peed himself a little.

"Yes sir!" he squeaked, awkwardly trying to blow his glitter-coated bangs out of his eyes without making offen-sive noises. "Of course, sir!"

Three seconds into his next dramatic pause, the aide thought better of it, and swiftly continued.

"We 'leak' the news to the press that Tor Val... is having an affair!"

Mol Gat gasped out loud, pausing mid-stretch as he reached out to set the Vice President's haircare pot back on his desk. "She is?"

"Of course not, you moronic mound of monkey turds!" roared Saf Tah. He pointed accusingly towards Jus Clo. "He made it up!"

Mol Gat gasped again, turning to face his smug colleague. "You did?"

Jus Clo nodded. "I did indeed," he said proudly. "And just think what the press will say when they get hold of that little tidbit of scandalous information..."

Mol Gat's eyes glazed over for a split second. "I, um... I can't imagine," he admitted a moment later.

"Well, I can!" thundered the Vice President. "They'll say exactly nothing, you simpering sack of shit. Tor Val is a widow. Her husband died on the journey over here ten years ago. She can have a relationship with whomever she damn well pleases!"

He slammed his mirror back down, causing the circle of glass inside the frame to crack into several pieces. "In fact, I wouldn't put it past the goddamn press to make a meal out of it and push her approval ratings even higher."

Jus Clo retraced his earlier step, eager to put more distance between himself and anything even vaguely throwable.

He was trembling so much that the tight silver curls of his freshly permed hair were practically vibrating.

Saf Tah fixed him with an angry stare. "Is that the best you've got?"

"Er..."

"Ooh, um... I had an idea as well, sir," Mol Gat put in, sounding much more confident than current circumstances suggested he should. "We've still got that ancient video footage of the Etheric Empire advancing on the Leith front line in their war. If we put that footage on TV, and played it backwards, it would, um... it would look as though the Empire soldiers were all cowards, running away from the enemy!"

Mol Gat blinked as a heavy plastic hair brush bounced off his forehead.

"Fools!" Saf Tah rumbled. "No, if we are to find a way to stop Tor Val from handing this world over to the new dictatorship on the block, we'll need to get a little more... personal."

He pressed a button positioned underneath his desk, and a hidden door clicked open halfway along one of the room's well-stocked bookcases. An unsmiling figure stepped through, removing his pair of mirrored sunglasses and slipping them into the inside pocket of his coat. Then he ran the palm of his hand over the sleek, smooth surface of his shaven scalp.

"Gentlemen," Saf Tah said to his two stunned aides. "I would like you to meet the President's head of security and my new best friend, Hip Win."

Federation Base Station 11, Nathan Lowell's Office

"Who was Dollen, really?" asked Jack once he and Tc'aarlat were seated in Nathan's office. "Aside from a pus-filled, suicide bombing bell-end, that is."

Tc'aarlat chuckled at the insult. As they'd passed behind the bar, he had grabbed an unopened bottle of single malt scotch and he was now holding it up to the light, admiring the warm glow of the amber liquid sloshing around inside.

"His real name was Nuckel Thuntang," replied Nathan. "He's been on the Etheric Empire's radar for a while now. We couldn't believe our luck when you brought him right to us."

"Yeah," said Tc'aarlat. "Real lucky."

"But, nothing went off when you took us through security at the docks," Jack pointed out. "No alarms. Nothing."

"You're right," agreed Nathan. "No alarms. We had them silenced just before you passed through the scanners, but we got a good look at his bomb vest."

"Wait!" cried Tc'aarlat, lowering the whisky bottle. "You

mean you *knew* he was wearing that thing the whole time we sat drinking and chatting with him?!"

Nathan nodded. "There was a chance he would try to ditch the explosives before you left after your delivery," he explained. "Or, the situation could have played out the way it did."

"We had to wait for him to make a move, or the best we could pin on him was transporting dangerous material. Once he'd planted the device, or tried to blow himself up, we had him on terrorist charges."

Tc'aarlat rubbed his mandibles together. "You lot sure have a twisted way of doing things," he said, plunging one of his long nails into the cork in the top of the whisky bottle and pulling it out with a *shtunk*!

He raised the bottle to his lips, spread his mandibles, and took a long drink.

"Yeah!" he growled once he swallowed. "That's the fiery pits of Hell burn I've been looking for! Which is exactly where I'd like to send every single one of those *Dark Tomorrow* fuckers!"

Nathan noticed Jack sigh heavily and close his eyes. "I believe you have something of a history with that particular group don't you, Captain Marber."

"Does he?" asked Tc'aarlat, pausing as he raised the bottle to take another swig of scotch. He turned to Jack. "Do you?"

"You could say that," said Jack darkly. He sat in silence for a moment, lost in a distant memory. The other two men waited for him to be ready to speak.

"It was a lifetime ago," he said eventually. "Back when I was a platoon sergeant in the *Empire's Special Assault*

Marines. We were on a mission to locate and kill a group of *Dark Tomorrow* commanders who were gathering for a meeting in the Tuko region of a planet called Garalis."

Tc'aarlat's eyes narrowed. "You were in the Federation's military?

"You knew I had a sordid past. Drop it." Jack fixed Tc'aarlat with a hard stare.

"How can I drop it? You set out to kill them!" the Yollin continued unperturbed.

Jack nodded. "We had no choice. We'd tried unsuccessfully to capture them, cut off their access to weapons, and turn their followers against them - but none of it had worked. This was the last resort."

"We got to the location - a family home on the outskirts of Baglavan City - the day before the terrorists flew in from all across the system, and secured a perimeter, staying hidden from our targets at all times."

"Did you get them?" asked Tc'aarlat.

Jack shook his head. "They arrived as planned, and I was ready to detonate the wireless charges we'd sunk into the walls and foundations of the house. The plan was to bury the bastards in rubble and leave them to rot."

"What happened?"

Jack sighed. "One of the commanders turned up with two kids in tow. I hadn't anticipated any of them bringing non-combatants along, especially not children. But, the decision was made to proceed as planned. I was ordered to detonate the explosives and kill the lot of them."

"And, I'm guessing you didn't."

"I wouldn't," said Jack. "I couldn't. I was there to execute terrorists, not kids. That's not what I signed up for."

"But they weren't kids, were they Jack?" Nathan interjected.

Once again, Jack shook his head. "They were Alstublafts; an alien race that just look like children. They were on the kill list as well. I hadn't read the briefing documents properly, just skimmed over them en route."

"But... someone else must have known who they were," Tc'aarlat suggested.

"They did," Jack confirmed. "My commander tried to take the detonator switch from me and complete the mission himself, but I knocked him out and threatened anyone else who came near with my sidearm."

"The platoon was forced to storm the house instead," said Nathan, picking up the story. "They got most of the terrorists, but a few key figures escaped. Figures who have since gone on to plan and commit atrocities across the galaxy."

"I was court-martialed, dishonorably discharged and sent to jail for six years," Jack added directly to Tc'aarlat. "I got out about six months before we bumped into each other in that bar on Phosos."

"Which is why you were looking for a new career," said the Yollin, almost to himself. "A career with no responsibilities."

Jack lowered his gaze and didn't respond.

"And why you're now overweight and so out of shape."

Jack sat upright, scowling. He opened his mouth to respond angrily, but Nathan grabbed three glasses from a side table before that could happen.

"Let's have a drink before that stuff all disappears," he said, looking pointedly in Tc'aarlat's direction.

"Hey, not my fault you two are slow," said Tc'aarlat, pouring out three generous servings from the remaining two thirds of the whisky in the bottle.

Jack took his drink and cradled it in his hands, eyes fixed on the floor. "What a fuck up," he said. "First, I let those *Dark Tomorrow* bastards escape from right under my nose, and then I go and deliver one right to the heart of the Etheric Empire."

Nathan downed his own drink in one, then sat back and considered the freighter captain for a moment.

"How would you like the opportunity to put all that right?"

8

Alma Nine, Taron City, Government Buildings, Presidential Suite

Bay Don reached for her cup of mogneti and took a swig, pulling a face when she realized the drink had gone cold.

The third one this afternoon.

Ever since the President had announced her plans to align with the Etheric Empire, Bay Don had been fighting off calls and visits from both news reporters and press journalists alike. No matter which media outlet they represented, they had all tried to gain access to Tor Val's office with pretty much the same argument...

This story is in the public interest.

The population has a right to know what its future holds.

The President owes the people an explanation.

Bay Don downed the rest of her mogneti, grimacing once again as she set the cup aside. Tough shit, journos. Tor Val had said she didn't want to be disturbed, and that meant no-one got past her trusted assistant.

And that decision didn't just apply to news hungry correspondents. She'd blocked three separate attempts by Saf Tah's staff to gain access to Tor Val, and endured a torrent of abuse from the Vice President himself during a particularly unpleasant call.

All of which simply made her more determined to deny entry to anyone.

Standing, Bay Don made her way across the President's outer office and flicked the switch on the kettle, hoping there was enough water inside for at least half a fresh cup of mogneti, ideally above room temperature.

She glanced at her boss's office door while she waited for the tell-tale sound of bubbling from the appliance. Tor Val had asked her to hold all calls and reschedule the afternoon's appointments so she could work. She watched the red light repeatedly flick on and off on the communication hub, indicating the President was making calls of her own.

But to whom, and for what purpose, Bay Don couldn't know. She just hoped it was all working in the President's favor.

Bay Don had been Tor Val's personal assistant ever since she had taken over the role of colony leader following her husband's death during the initial journey to Alma Nine. Back then, Lad Val had been chosen as President Elect by settlers traveling on board the interstellar ship, *Dessia*, named after the Malatian goddess of hope.

The trip from Malatia to the colonist's new home had taken several years and a strong leader was vital to maintaining the optimism necessary for the taxing journey ahead. In a free and open election, the *Dessia's* passengers had voted for astronautical engineer Lad Val over his closest rival, Saf Tah. And the result had been a popular one.

Lad Val and his family, wife Tor Val and their daughters Ran Val and Mas Val, were seen as the ideal family unit. Young, vibrant, honest - they were the figures of hope the settlers needed after receiving so much negativity over their decision to abandon their own planet and seek their future elsewhere in the galaxy.

Then, just weeks before their arrival at Alma Nine, the ship's solar array had malfunctioned.

Power cells quickly began to drain, threatening everything from power to the *Dessia's* engines to the life support system itself. While millions of microscopic nanobots worked around the clock to provide the transporter with an artificial gravity field, they couldn't create breathable air or fuel. Nor could they operate outside, in the vacuum of space.

The solar panels were going to have to be repaired manually, and the best qualified person for the job was Lad Val himself.

He had been on the design team for the *Dessia*, and he was the only person on board with extra-vehicular activity experience. And so, he and a trainee engineer had climbed into two of the ship's half-dozen spacesuits, clipped on tool belts and safety tethers, then climbed through the main airlock and out onto the exterior of the craft.

The repair attempt was big news, especially now that it was Alma Nine's future President tackling the job. Ran Val and Mas Val were interviewed about their heroic dad by fellow students in the onboard classroom, and the teachers even arranged a mini field trip to the starboard side viewing area once the spacewalk had started so pupils could watch Lad Val and his assistant at work.

Tor Val, already proud of her husband's success in the presidential elections, was there to watch the repair effort as it happened. She was given a front row seat near the large external windows.

Bay Don had been a classroom assistant at the time. She sat with Ran Val and Mas Val as their father exited the Dessia. They watched him fix the loose connection from the solar panels to the motor which kept them at the optimal angle to the closest star.

And that's when the *Dessia's* engines unexpectedly came back online. They jolted the spacecraft and caused Lad Val to lose his grip on the hand rail he was using to hold himself in place.

The students gasped as Lad Val was thrust backwards, away from the side of the ship, jerking to a sudden stop as the rolled-metal safety line stretched taut.

For a moment, everything seemed to happen in slow motion. The carabiner at the near end of the tether maintained its grip on the hand rail, Lad Val flailed his arms in a vain attempt to arrest his momentum, and the material of the future President's spacesuit ripped apart.

While there was no sound from the two men outside the craft, everyone watching from inside was screaming. The engineering assistant reached out with his gloved hand, fingers opening and closing, but it was already too late.

Lad Val drifted away from the side of the ship, his safety line waving uselessly from the rail and the tear in his suit allowing his precious supply of breathable air to rapidly escape.

Mas Val threw herself at the window, hammering on the thick glass, pleading for her father to return. Her sister simply crumpled to the floor, eyes rolling back in their sockets.

Bay Don didn't know which of the girls to help first.

Then, a teacher pushed her way through to Ran Val, freeing Bay Don to dart forward and wrap her arms around Mas Val's shoulders. The girl was simultaneously screaming and sobbing as her father floated further and further from the *Dessia*.

Tor Val climbed shakily to her feet, stunned. She and her daughters could only watch in horror as Lad Val somehow found the strength to raise a hand to his heart, then extend it towards his inconsolable family before his air finally ran out and his teal face turned dark green inside his helmet.

His sightless eyes remained fixed open as he drifted further and further away from everything and everyone he had loved.

It took two days for the ship's course to be changed and for rescuers to devise a way to retrieve Lad Val's body from the vacuum of space.

Lad Val's return to the *Dessia* was only temporary. In accordance with Malatian tradition, his body was placed into a casket made of organic material. Following the funeral service, this pod would be ejected out into space where it would navigate to the closest gas cloud and explode, reducing the pod's occupant to his or her constituent elements, returning the deceased individual to the universe.

This process was known as *The Journey Back*.

Toward the end of the service, Bay Don had once again sat with the two young girls while Tor Val, dressed in traditional purple mourning attire, stood to deliver a speech. In it, she honored her late husband and announced that she would be stepping into the role as President in his place.

Many of the gathering had turned to study Saf Tah's reaction to this news but his expression remained impassive. Only those close to him would later bear witness to the full ferocity of his rage at his quest for power being thwarted yet again.

And so, Tor Val became the first - and so far, only - President of the new colony of Alma Nine, rewarding Bay Don for her efforts in comforting her daughters at a time of need with a position as her assistant.

In the intervening years, Bay Don had been at Tor Val's side almost constantly. Through the difficult period of establishing a new home for the colonists, during a heavily contested re-election process, and now she would be there for her friend as she guided the planet into this exciting new phase of galactic citizenship.

The kettle clicked off as steam revealed the presence of boiling water inside, just as Tor Val's office door swung open to reveal an extremely tired looking President. Beyond, her normally immaculate desk was strewn with paperwork, with stacks of files set out on the carpet like an ocean of information surrounding a busy wooden island.

"Heading home, Ma'am?" Bay Don inquired, accepting

the loss of yet another cup of steaming mogneti. She took Tor Val's briefcase to carry it for her.

Tor Val nodded. "Having dinner with the girls tonight," she said with a weary smile. "Mas Val is home from her studies for a few days' vacation."

Bay Don raised her eyebrows, pleasantly surprised, as the pair set off down the corridor. "It's been a while since all three of you got to spend some time together, hasn't it?"

"Almost four months," replied Tor Val. "I'm looking forward to the chance of discussing topics that won't result in utter political turmoil, like homework, grades and boys!"

"You know you *are* going to have to meet with Saf Tah at some point tomorrow, don't you?" Bay Don pointed out.

"Doesn't mean I have to look forward to it!" chuckled Tor Val. "The man's grumpy enough at the best of times. Now he knows I've kept him out of the negotiations with the Etheric Empire, he'll be out for my scalp."

Bay Don chuckled. "What, and give up that precious twinkling mohawk of his? I doubt it!"

Tor Val wrapped an arm around her assistant's shoulders and pulled her close. "We can do this, you know. Together, we can take Alma Nine kicking and screaming into the future."

"*You* can," countered Bay Don. "There's no *we* in all this."

"Don't you believe it," said Tor Val with a mock scowl. "I couldn't have done any of this without you watching my back."

The two women reached the rear exit of the government building, and Bay Don hurried to open the door for her boss. "Have a good evening with the girls," she said. "Say 'hi' from me."

"Will do," responded Tor Val, "but Mas Val will expect to see you before she heads back to school."

"I'll pop around tomorrow after work," Bay Don promised, handing Tor Val her briefcase.

Tor Val turned as a sleek, black limousine pulled up at the door and the shaven-headed figure of Hip Win climbed out of the passenger seat. He opened the rear door to allow the President to climb inside.

The President hesitated. "This isn't my usual car," she pointed out to her head of security. "And that's not Rol Tak, my usual driver."

"Rol Tak is unwell," Hip Win explained, "and your usual car is undergoing its annual service. I have personally checked this replacement vehicle, and vetted the new driver."

Tor Val nodded. "That's all I needed to hear."

Bay Don watched as the President climbed into the back of the car, her shape barely visible behind the limo's tinted glass. With an almost inaudible hiss, the vehicle pulled away and sped off.

As she turned to head back to her office and her long awaited cup of mogneti, she noticed Hip Win pull out a portable communicator and dial a number. The conversation he had with whoever picked up was very short indeed.

All he said was: "It's on."

Alma Nine, Taron City, Highway 59, Tor Val's Car

Gan Roj glanced in the limo's rearview mirror to check where Tor Val was directing her attention. As hoped, she was engrossed in one of the several pieces of paperwork she had removed from the open briefcase on the seat beside her.

So engrossed she hadn't noticed that they were traveling on a highway heading out of the city center, in the opposite direction from her home.

Gripping the steering wheel with his left hand, he worked to pull two items from the right pocket of his coat. The first was a bottle of prescription painkillers, the only brand that now made any kind of difference to the agonizing cramps in his stomach.

They were an incredibly powerful drug, not prescribed to patients unless, like Gan Roj, they were in the excruciating final stages of his particular disease.

There wasn't much hope of him becoming addicted to the medication. Not in the short time he had left at least.

The other item was his communicator. Checking again that Tor Val wasn't watching, he rested the device against the steering wheel and tapped the icon showing the logo for his bank. A few screens later, he was logged into his personal account.

The money was there, as promised. He was now a millionaire.

Not that he'd ever get to spend a penny of it himself.

He emptied the bottle of pills into his mouth, ignoring the sour chalky flavor as he began to crunch down. Then, flicking back to the home screen of his communicator, he launched the photos app and brought up his favorite picture of his wife and children.

Blinking back his tears, Gan Roj pressed his foot down hard on the limo's accelerator pedal.

9

Federation Base Station 11, Nathan Lowell's Office

"Spies?!" exclaimed Jack incredulously. "You want us to work for you as spies?"

"That's one way of putting it," Nathan replied.

"What other way is there?"

"I prefer to think of it as covert intelligence operatives."

Jack frowned. "Same difference."

"Possibly," said Nathan. "But, whatever name we give it, you'll be helping the Etheric Empire to rid the galaxy of those who set out to control or harm innocent people, including all terrorists with affiliations to *Dark Tomorrow*."

Jack sat back in his chair, running the offer through his mind. The reason he'd enlisted for the Special Assault Marines in the first place was to help those who couldn't protect themselves. That all came to an untimely and unpleasant end following the botched operation on Maralis. Now he was being given the opportunity for a second bite at the cherry.

A nasty-ass terrorist cherry.

"You're already traversing the systems, hauling freight," Nathan continued. "What better cover than visiting areas of interest to collect and deliver cargo?"

"Once we've located a target, would we be expected to take on these bastards ourselves?" he queried. "Because, as much as Tc'aarlat and I try to keep ourselves in shape, there are still only two of us."

Nathan smiled, refilling the trio's drinks. "You'd just be the forward team, seeking out information and sending that back to me. Once we were confident you had located a serious threat, we'd send one of a variety of assets at our command in the Etheric Federation to further assess and resolve the situation."

"So, we wouldn't get to fuck up any bad guys personally?"

"Not unless you requested to do so," replied Nathan. "Then, you'd have our full backing, covertly, of course, which means no one will know."

Jack nodded. "Sounds good to me."

"Can I ask a question?" Tc'aarlat put in.

"Sure," said Nathan. "Would that question be whether you would receive extra remuneration on top of your regular haulage fees for undertaking espionage missions on our behalf?"

Tc'aarlat blinked silently for a moment. "Might be..."

Jack disguised his chuckle by taking another sip of whisky.

"You would be paid a handsome retainer fee, plus bonuses for delivering intelligence which leads to the inca-pacitation, capture or approved execution of enemy combatants."

Before Tc'aarlat could comment, Nathan added:

"Plus, we would vastly upgrade your ship and provide you with suitable weaponry for your future assignments."

Tc'aarlat exchanged a glance with Jack, then smiled. "Looks like we're in," he said cheerfully.

The three men raised their glasses and chinked them together before downing their remaining contents.

"There is one other issue," began Jack, taking his turn to pour out another round of golden goodness. "Now that we've lost Dollen, we're down a crew member. Although the company started with just the two of us, we've gotten used to having a dedicated navigator on the bridge."

Nathan took a sip, then put his glass aside and produced his tablet again. "Funny you should say that," he commented, his fingers dancing across the touch screen. "I had a message about that very subject just after we left the bar."

There was a knock at the office door. Nathan quickly spun his chair towards it and stood to deactivate the electronic locking mechanism. "Right on time..."

The door opened and two women entered the room. One of them was a tall, confident, statuesque blonde. The other woman was much shorter. She had dark hair tied back in a ponytail, brown eyes and appeared more timid looking.

"Gentlemen," proclaimed Nathan. "Allow me to introduce you to your new navigator, Adina Choudhury..."

Tc'aarlat was on his feet in a flash. He hurried over to take the hand of the blonde woman, which he stooped to kiss with a chivalrous bow.

"Allow me to be the first to welcome you to the crew of

the *ICS Fortitude*, my dear," he cooed. "I look forward to working with you and, of course, getting to know you better."

"Why, thank you," the blonde replied, retrieving her hand from the Yollin's grasp. "Although I'm Ecaterina Romanov, Nathan's mate."

Tc'aarlat frowned as though he didn't understand her words.

Ecaterina turned to allow the smaller woman to step further into the room. "*This* is Adina."

Jack crossed the room to shake Adina's hand. "Delighted to meet you," he said with a smile.

"Whoa, whoa, whoa!" cried Tc'aarlat, his mandibles wide and quivering. "Hang on just a minute."

"Is there a problem?" queried Nathan.

"Yes," Adina snapped. "Is there?"

All eyes turned to look at Tc'aarlat, who was suddenly thankful he hadn't yet found a way to approximate the human bodily function known as 'blushing.'

"No," replied Tc'aarlat, trying his best to avoid Adina's accusing stare. "Of course not. It's just that haulage is a... man's game..."

"A *what?!*" cried Adina and Ecaterina together.

"I didn't mean it like that!" Tc'aarlat said hurriedly. "It's just that, there's an awful lot of heavy lifting involved."

"Most of which is done by computer operated machinery," Jack pointed out. "How are you with tech systems, Adina?"

"Great," Adina replied. "I've been working in the research and development labs here for just under six years now, both on hardware and software projects."

"In fact, it was Adina's recent upgrade to the automatic docking program that facilitated the unloading of your own ship just a few hours ago," Nathan disclosed.

Jack crossed his arms. "Well," he said with a smirk in Tc'aarlat's direction. "I'm impressed."

"As am I," protested the Yollin. "I'd just hate for anything bad to happen to someone so..."

Adina raised her eyebrows. "Someone so *what?*"

"Yeah," agreed Ecaterina. "I'd be interested to hear this."

Tc'aarlat's eyes grew wider as he scrambled desperately through his vocabulary for an adjective that wouldn't be rewarded with a slap in the face. "...dainty?"

Adina had twisted Tc'aarlat's arm up behind his back before he even saw her move.

"How is this for dainty?" she growled.

"Ow!" he yelled, his mandibles clicking in agony. "*OW!* Get off me, woman!"

But Adina held firm.

"Mist!" Tc'aarlat barked. "Do something!"

Ecaterina took an involuntary step forward as the Raal hawk leapt off her perch - only to land on the shoulder of Adina's leather jacket. The bird cooed and nuzzled her new friend's ear with the side of her beak, cawing softly.

"Well," said Jack after a moment. "Looks like Mist has cast her vote, and I make it two to one. Welcome aboard, Adina."

Adina finally released Tc'aarlat's wrist and the Yollin quickly stepped away, rubbing at the aching muscles in his arm. His eyes narrowed as he glared at his feathered sidekick.

"Traitor!"

. . .

Alma Nine, Taron City, Weather Control Center, Main Laboratory

Yan Mil brushed his long, unkempt hair from his eyes and peered down into the microscope on his desk. Holding his breath in eager anticipation, he focused on the single nanobot hovering, almost motionless at the center of a small, glass box.

"Syringe," he said flatly, holding out his left hand. Zeb Lok, the white-coated figure sitting beside him, passed over a tiny hypodermic needle then turned back to watch the view from the microscope's lens on his own monitor.

"Introducing the graviton now," announced Yan Mil.

Gathered behind the pair of scientists, a clutch of laboratory assistants held their collected breath as their boss inserted the syringe into a pre-drilled hole on the side of the box and carefully pressed the plunger with a trembling hand.

A tiny, spinning particle shot out from the tip of the fine needle and began to sink through the air towards the bottom of the container. But, before it could reach the lower glass plate, a light flashed on the back of the nanobot.

"The bot knows the graviton is there," hissed Yan Mil. Everyone else continued to watch the experiment in fascinated silence.

Moving at an incredible speed, the bot darted forward extending a pair of crab-like pincers from the front of its minuscule body. It snatched the graviton from its downward trajectory and drew it back inside its body, the claws re-angling to keep the particle from escaping.

"OK," breathed Yan Mil, "here's the part we're waiting for..."

The nanobot rotated 180 degrees, revealing a collection of tubes and pipes extending from its undercarriage. From several of these openings fired a fine mist of chemicals which rose mixed together near the top of the glass box, forming what appeared to be a small cloud.

There was an almost inaudible crack of thunder, and then the cloud began to release a tiny torrent of rain.

Everyone gathered in the laboratory cheered and launched into spontaneous applause. Everyone except Yan Mil, that is. He simply continued staring into the eyepiece of his microscope, the relief that many months of endless hard work had culminated in the result he had predicted so long ago.

He did, however, allow himself a brief smile when a bolt of lightning no thicker than one of his own silver hairs shot out of the cloud, striking the end of the syringe's needle, creating a burst of light similar to that of a camera flash.

"It's a complete storm!" he proclaimed proudly. "Zeb Lok, pass me the connecter from the particle barometer..."

He held out his left hand once again, expecting his assistant to comply. Then he frowned. Whatever had just been placed in his outstretched palm was certainly not the barometer cable he had requested. Whatever it was, it was round, soft and felt smooth to the touch.

Lifting his head from the microscope, he stared at the object now sitting in his left hand. It was a parsel fruit.

"Zeb Lok..." he began, staring at the piece of fruit in surprise. "Why have you given me a-"

"Because you skipped lunch again, dear," interrupted a female voice.

Finally, Yan Mil lifted his gaze higher, his eyes widening even further. There, sitting in the seat where Zeb Lok should have been, was his wife, Vix Mil. He looked down at the parsel fruit, then back up at his wife.

She leaned in, giving him a kiss on the cheek.

"Er..., hello darling," Yan Mil said, still confused. "I... I wasn't expecting..."

"You weren't expecting me to be here," Vix Mil finished. "I know. Just like I know you haven't eaten today, hence the parsel fruit."

Yan Mil carefully placed the fruit onto his desk, beside the glass case he'd been working in. "But, how did you..." He sighed as what must have happened sank in.

"Zeb Lok has been telling tales on me again, hasn't he?"

Hearing his name mentioned, the scientist's assistant hurried to the other side of the laboratory to discuss the results of the experiment with another of his colleagues.

"Yes, Zeb Lok was the one who told me that you'd missed your lunch again," Vix Mil admitted, "but he only did so because he wants to help."

"By calling my wife to snitch on me?"

Vix Mil chuckled. "Actually, I was the one who called him," she said with a smile. "So, if you decide to blame anyone for keeping a close eye on you, blame me."

"Yes, but-"

"But nothing," replied Vix Mil, her expression becoming more serious. "If you don't remember to eat regularly, you won't have the strength to cope with all the late nights you've been pulling over recent weeks.

"You haven't been home in three days. I should never have allowed you to set up the apartment upstairs for when you decide to work late. And if I don't see you, I can't make sure you're looking after yourself.

"Now, are you going to eat that parsel fruit, or do I have to cut it up and feed it to you like a naughty child?"

Yan Mil did his best to ignore the sound of suppressed laughter coming from his subordinates. "Yes, alright dear..." He took a large bite from the treat, using the cuff of his lab coat to wipe an errant dribble of juice from his chin.

"Mmmm!" his commented as he chewed. "That's a ripe one."

"I brought two," Vix Mil said. "I made you some of your favorite soup." She tapped a nearby piece of scientific equipment. "I trust you'll be able to heat it up in one or other of these weird looking science gizmos."

"Yes," said Yan Mil before taking another bite of his fruit. "But not that particular gizmo; that's a mass spectrometer."

Vix Mil shrugged, smiling. "They all look the same to me," she said, patting the device with her hand.

"You're hurt," exclaimed Yan Mil, gesturing to a dressing on one of his wife's fingers.

Vix Mil shook her head. "I slipped and cut myself chopping vegetables for the soup. It's nothing."

Looking around the lab's other equipment, she added: "I presume you do have something you can use for heating food here somewhere, or are they all magical homes for families of fairy imps?"

"Nah, we keep the imps in the basement where they can't escape," said a voice.

Husband and wife looked up in unison as a tall man with hair styled into a high quiff approached. He held a glass of bubbly liquid in each hand, which he handed to Yan Mil and Vix Mil respectively.

"Thank you, Jon Rey," said Yan Mil, setting the drink down on his desk.

"What's the occasion?" Vix Mil inquired, first sniffing the contents of her glass, then taking a sip.

"Yan Mil hasn't told you?" inquired Jon Rey, surprised. "He's done it. He's finally been able to upgrade one of his original nanobots to be able to execute two functions at the same time."

"You have?" cried Vix Mil excitedly. "That's wonderful!" Jumping down from her stool, she wrapped her arms around her husband and hugged him tightly. "I'm so happy for you, my darling; I know how long you've been working on this project."

Yan Mil hurriedly extricated himself from the embrace, his eyes flicking across the lab to the group of assistants. "Not in front of everyone, dear..." he hissed.

"Oh hush, Yan Mil!" scolded Vix Mil with a smile. "They won't mind seeing their boss being congratulated by his own wife. You've achieved something wonderful, after all. You've successfully turned a plain, old nanobot into a fully-functioning female."

Yan Mil's mouth opened and closed for a few seconds before he could find his voice. "I've... I've done *what*?!"

Vix Mil winked conspiratorially to a chuckling Jon Rey.

"Well, you did say you'd been able to upgrade one of them to the point where it could multitask, didn't you?"

"Yes, but-" Yan Mil sighed, allowing himself a smile as he finally got the joke. "You can tease all you want, but this is a big step. Once I've reprogrammed all the nanobots with this updated software, we won't have to split them into two separate flocks any longer - one half for maintenance tasks and the other to manage meteorological issues.

We'll be able to dedicate the entire swarm to control the weather over much larger areas of land and sea. Perhaps even the entire planet."

"It's a huge step forward," added Jon Rey. "This is the first time the nanobots Yan Mil created for our journey to Alma Nine have been able to operate this way. For a while, we thought we'd have to start again from scratch. The government has allocated a huge budget for the development of an entirely new swarm. Now, that money can be used elsewhere."

Vix Mil threw her arms around her husband again. "Well done, my love!" she exclaimed proudly. "I always knew you would change the world one day - and now you've done it twice!"

Jon Rey took the opportunity to leave them to their embrace, crossing the lab to rejoin his colleagues.

"If only my day had gone as well," she sighed.

Yan Mil pulled back, studying his wife with an expression of concern. "Why?" he asked. "What happened?"

Vix Mil looked around to check what she was about to say wouldn't be overheard. Like her husband, her job was connected to the government, and required a certain amount of secrecy.

Their careers differed in that, while Yan Mil focused his talents on emotionless microscopic robots, Vix Mil worked with real people. In particular - offenders who had recently been released from prison. It was her job to help assimilate former criminals back into everyday society.

Technically, she wasn't allowed to discuss the cases she handled away from the office, but it was accepted that everyone in her department needed to blow off a little steam from time to time in order to avoid an unhealthy buildup of stress.

So, those in charge understood that staff would share details of their work day with their significant others, and were happy for them to do so, so long as that information went no further.

Vix Mil shook her head slightly as she began to explain. "For the past week, I've been working with Hen Wic. He was released early for good behavior, and I'd already managed to find him an apartment, and arranged for him to attend a job interview."

Yan Mil shrugged, blank. "Hen Wic?"

"You remember. He was caught threatening jury members in that big fraud case a few years back. The one that resulted in the resignation of half a dozen government officials."

"Oh, yes. Of course," said Yan Mil, the memory making itself known from the recesses of his mind. "This thug hasn't been menacing you, has he?"

"No, not at all," Vix Mil reassured him. "He's been nothing but polite since he was released, and seemingly full of remorse for his actions."

"I sense a 'but' coming..."

"I'm afraid so," said Vix Mil. "He was seen lurking near the home of the judge who passed sentence on him. That's a clear violation of his parole, and so I had no option but to report him to the relevant authorities, and he's now back behind bars ready to serve the remaining seven years of his sentence."

"And you're upset by this turn of events?"

"Of course," replied Vix Mil. "I really believed he'd turned over a new leaf and was ready to make a fresh start. It saddens me so much to have to arrange for him to be incarcerated once more."

This time, it was Yan Mil who initiated a warm hug. "It sounds as though this Hen Wic brought everything on himself, my sweet," he soothed. "You just did your job. A job, I might add, that you do extremely well. You help a great number of people piece their lives back together. You cannot blame yourself for those felons who do not wish to change their wicked ways."

Vix Mil sighed again. "I know," she said. "It's just such a waste of potential."

Yan Mil took his wife's chin in his fingertips and turned her face so that he was looking deep into her eyes.

"Do not concern yourself with this wrongdoer, my cherub," he soothed. "You did your best to assist him with his chance for rehabilitation, but he did not *want* to be helped."

He leaned in and kissed his wife softly on the lips.

Vix Mil closed her eyes, and kissed back.

And then the pair realized that everyone in the lab had fallen silent. As Yan Mil and Vix Mil looked up from their kiss, the staff members erupted in cheers and awarded the pair with a round of applause.

"Yes, well..." mumbled Yan Mil, clearly uncomfortable. "I really ought to be, you know... getting back to, er..."

"I should be going, too," giggled Vix Mill, planting a final peck on the end of Yan Mil's nose. "I know you still have a lot of work to do."

She stood from her stool, and retrieved her purse from the counter. "Don't work too late," she insisted, wagging her finger in a mock scolding gesture. "I'll pick up a bottle of something far too expensive for a work night on my way home, and we can celebrate your latest achievement over dinner later tonight."

Pausing only to wave girlishly to the weather control assistants, she hurried out of the lab. By the time the door swung shut behind her, Yan Mil was already peering back down the eyepiece of his microscope.

Alma Nine, Taron City, Weather Control Center, Main Entrance

Mak Git stepped further back into the shadows beneath the trees as the woman appeared in the small lobby of the weather control center. He watched as she pressed her thumb against a device held out by a uniformed security guard, then she stepped out into the early evening air.

Hurrying down the building's steps, she glanced briefly to her left. But Mak Git was certain his black clothing he was wearing would ensure she didn't spot him.

He took the opportunity to pull a crumpled photograph from his pocket and study it in the dim light. He looked up at the woman as she turned and set off down the street away from him, then back down at the picture.

That was definitely her. The woman he'd been sent to find.

That was Vix Mil.

Slipping the photograph away, Mak Git produced a short, gleaming blade from a different pocket. Then he stepped out from his shadowy hiding place, and began to follow his prey.

Federation Base Station 11, Guest Quarters

"Good morning Captain Marber, this is your 6am alarm call. You have a hand to hand combat training session scheduled to begin in half an hour."

Jack sat up in bed and groaned. Every muscle in his body throbbed, including several he had completely forgotten he owned now he was no longer undergoing military level exercise.

"Thank you, Turing," he said to the station's E.I.

Swinging his legs off the bed, he padded over to the suite's bathroom and stepped into the shower, turning down the controls in an attempt to soothe his aches and pains with a blast of ice cold water.

The past two days had passed in a blur. Once he, Tc'aarlat and Adina had agreed to undertake intelligence gathering missions for the Etheric Empire, an intensive period of preparation had begun.

The trio had each been given a brand new weapon - a high-tech pistol known as a 'Modified Jean Duke's Special'.

Like most people with military training, Jack was aware of Jean's reputation as an excellent gunsmith in addition to her work as an armorer and creator of attack and defense systems, but these pistols were beyond incredible.

Hand-crafted from the finest materials, each gun featured a dial which would allow the user to choose a setting from one to eleven, ensuring just the right amount of destructiveness for any given situation. These custom mods also included the ability to stun on the first three settings. It didn't launch a projectile until the number four setting, after which it became more and more deadly.

The first three levels would allow the user in order to send a wave of energy against a target. The projectiles fired were called pucks, that were accelerated at railgun speeds, with the top setting, level eleven resulting in the annihilation of something as big as a building, providing the user was powerful enough to hold the weapon at that setting.

Plus, the guns were isomorphic, with each individual weapon coded exclusively for the designated owner's DNA. No-one else would be able to fire these weapons if they somehow managed to get their hands on them.

Jack suspected something vastly more unpleasant than the frustrating click of a misfire would be the result if anyone ever had the opportunity to put this feature to the test.

His skin began to burn as the freezing water flowed over his body, easing his muscle cramps and jolting him awake more than any dose of caffeine ever could.

That said, he would still treat himself to an 'angry coffee', as he liked to call his beverage of choice before setting off for the rigors of the day, adding four shots of strong espresso to his cup with just a dash of boiling water.

The shower over, Jack stepped back out into his temporary bedroom and toweled himself dry before launching into his usual regime of stretches.

This was something he'd picked up while serving in the Marines as a way of ensuring he remained supple enough to handle any overtly physical surprises at a moment's notice.

His EM training hadn't prepared him for the many styles of fighting Nathan had put him and his crew through over the last couple of days.

They had received instruction in just about everything from close quarters combat to an extreme form of Krav Maga. The result - aside from his protesting muscles - was a reminder that he needed to be ready for anything now that he was stepping into the perilous side of life once more.

He flicked on the coffee machine, listening to it hiss and spit while he dressed in figure-hugging black sweats in preparation for the morning's exertions.

He knew that Tc'aarlat and Adina would both be wearing the same for their scheduled sessions but, while his new navigator would carry off the outfit with effortless style and athletic grace, his Yollin partner would once again resemble a badly-wrapped stack of broken bricks.

The image brought a smile to his face as he snatched up the cup of steaming black java, downing it in two swift gulps. Then, with a brief pause to study his reflection in the mirror fixed to the back of the door, he left the room and set off for another tough but satisfying day of exhaustion and agony.

ICS Fortitude, **Bridge**

The *ICS Fortitude* fired its forward thrusters, slowing as it approached the gate.

Adina concentrated hard on the screens of the navigation panel, quickly making the necessary calculations required to manually input the pitch and yaw settings required for smooth transfer to another part of space.

Acting confidently, she reached across the desk to flick the necessary switches, and tap a series of commands into the cargo ship's computer system.

Suddenly, an alarm sounded and lights began to flash all across the bridge.

Adina glanced up at the main screens, quickly realizing that the freighter was unexpectedly pulling to the left. Had those idiots loaded the cargo unevenly yet again?

She spun back to her control panel, her fingers dancing across the several different keyboards as she fought to correct the error.

But the alarms refused to silence.

Now, the edge of the gate was looming large in screens all around the bridge, the image growing bigger by the second.

There was a deafening screech as the port side of the ship made contact with the side of the gate, sloughing off decades of faded paint and smashing external cameras, antennae and doors to airlocks alike.

Six seconds later, the *ICS Fortitude* exploded, completely destroying the gate and killing everyone on board.

"Gott Verdammt!" cursed Adina, slumping back in her seat as the virtual reality simulator began to reset itself around her.

The door to the simulation room opened and Ecaterina stepped inside, reading the damage report displayed on the screen behind Adina's chair.

"Botched the gate transfer procedure, huh?"

"Third time in a row," sighed Adina. "But at least I didn't rupture the fuel cells and irradiate a nearby solar system this time."

Ecaterina winced. "Yikes!"

"Is all this really necessary?" asked Adina. "You promised the ship is having a new Entity Intelligence installed. Won't that handle all these tricky maneuvers?"

"Ordinarily, yes," replied Ecaterina with a nod. "But you need to be able to work the bridge manually in case the EI becomes corrupted, or even shuts down completely."

"OK," Adina said, gritting her teeth and clicking the command for the computer to launch yet another random simulation. "Here goes nothing."

Ecaterina reached over to hit the pause icon on the screen. "Before you do that..."

She reached into her pocket and produced a clear pill bottle. Inside were dozens of tiny black tablets, each with a small yellow dot on one side.

Adina took the bottle and stared at it. "My meds?"

Ecaterina nodded. "Safely produced in the Federation's own pharmacy labs," she disclosed. "No more buying dodgy drugs from obnoxious little parasites in dark alleyways, OK?"

Adina's eyes widened. "But, that means-"

"Don't panic," Ecaterina said, cutting her off. "No-one knows who they're for. My position on board does have certain privileges, you know."

Adina wrapped her arms around her friend, hugging her tightly.

"Thank you!"

"No problem," Ecaterina smiled. "Now, get back to work and see if you can at least get one crew safely through a gate without blasting them into billions of screaming atoms!"

Federation Base Station 11, Alexi Romanov Lecture Theater

Tc'aarlat stood on the stage and swung the lure in circles above his head, keeping the line at a steady fifteen feet as it twirled.

Mist was perched on the back of a seat near the rear of the auditorium, her sharp eyes following the fake wings fixed to the sides of the lure, waiting for her master to give her permission to strike.

Squinting, Tc'aarlat could just about see the hawk's claws flexing, ready to release her grip on the seat and take flight.

He waited a few more seconds, then clicked his mandibles together and gave a shrill whistle.

Instantly, Mist was airborne, wings spread wide and beak pointed to the spot in the air where she had already calculated the prey would be at the split-second she arrived.

As always, her estimation was spot on. She stabbed at the lure with her beak, causing it to wobble as it continued on its circular journey.

A second whistle from Tc'aarlat saw her bank to the right and swoop back to land on the leather pad affixed to his shoulder and receive a chunk of muri meat as a reward.

Mist lifted one foot in order to clamp the cube of flesh under her claw, so that she could tear strips of the morsel with her beak to devour.

The Yollin reached up to scratch the side of her head, the bird rewarding him with a soft currr.

Mist hadn't exactly appeared delighted to spend the past few days cooped up in a small guest room with her owner.

It was bad enough spending time on the *ICS Fortitude*, but at least she could fly around any of the cargo decks which happened to be free of freight and get some exercise.

She could barely even expand her wings to their full span in Tc'aarlat's tiny room.

Jack and Tc'aarlat had been shown the lecture theater during their initial tour of the Base Stations' facilities. At the time, a university class about the event horizons of black holes had been in full swing. But Tc'aarlat had spotted the potential of the vast room as a place to exercise Mist.

So, once he was settled, he had inquired about the possibility of using the space when it wasn't being used for educational purposes. A request which had been quickly granted.

He and Mist were listed on today's schedule between a beginners' class on quantum mechanics, and a lengthy reading from and discussion about the life and work of famed Yollin spelunker and folk singer, Unshak'lak.

Tc'aarlat had promised he and his hawk would have vacated the room long before that session started.

For his own sanity more than anything else.

But, as useful as the lecture theater was for Mist to stretch her wings, it still wasn't ideal.

"I know girl," cooed Tc'aarlat, reeling in the line of the lure. "You've not exactly had a chance to get out and feel the fresh air on your feathers lately, have you? But at least big rooms like this are better than spending all day on the cramped bridge of the ship."

"Which actually isn't quite so cramped any longer," said a voice behind him.

Tc'aarlat turned to find Nathan heading his way down the lecture theater's left aisle, striding past row after row of empty seats towards the equally deserted stage area.

Mist hopped from leg to leg excitedly as the man approached. This was the human who frequently carried treats in the deep pockets of his coat.

And today was no exception.

Nathan produced a ball of compacted Yollin wist maize and rolled it between his fingers. The sphere of grain was soaked in honey, smeared with salt, and then baked until it was hard.

The result was a common treat given to many of the indigenous animals of Yoll, although the snack had also proved to be popular with the now co-resident humans as an alternative to sugary breakfast cereals.

Yoll's cereal manufacturers had printed new packaging in an effort to market what they considered animal feed back to these strange-habited arrivals.

Nathan tossed the maize ball to Mist, who snatched it in her beak, and began to crunch down hard on it.

Right in Tc'aarlat's left ear.

"Thanks for that!" He groaned, jerking his shoulder to dislodge the noisy eater. With a disgruntled craw, Mist flapped as far as the edge of the stage's wooden lectern and continued to devour the tasty morsel.

"So," said Tc'aarlat, stepping forward to shake Nathan's hand. "You were saying something about the bridge on the *Fortitude*?"

Nathan nodded. "It's ready," he beamed. "E.I. installed, new high-resolution camera system up and running. The works. And it's not just the bridge. The whole ship's good to go."

Tc'aarlat's mandibles pulled wide in surprise. "Already?" he queried, warily. "I thought you were going to upgrade both main engines?"

"We have," Nathan promised. "And we've made one or two other improvements which we think you'll enjoy. Want to go see?"

Tc'aarlat grinned. "Does the Pope shit in the woods?"

Nathan blinked, blank.

"What?" demanded Tc'aarlat, frowning. "Isn't that one of your human figures of speech? I'm sure I've heard Jack say it before."

"It's possible you may be confusing it with something else," Nathan suggested politely.

Tc'aarlat shrugged. "Whatever," he said. "I'm not even

sure what a Pope is, to be perfectly honest. From what Jack's told me, I'm guessing it's quite powerful. Something like a fertile female bistok, perhaps; sharp teeth, covered in thick fur, and fighting to protect its young. Am I close?"

"Near enough," replied Nathan, doing his best to conceal his smirk. "What say we go check out the ship. I've arranged for Jack and Adina to meet us in the hangar."

Tc'aarlat whistled for Mist, who returned to her perch on his shoulder pad just as the back doors to the theater opened and a large crowd of people began to file in and sit down.

"Wow," said Tc'aarlat as he and Nathan made their way toward the backstage exit. "Who knew dreary songs about big holes in the ground were so popular."

11

Federation Base Station 11, Combat Training Center

A foot clad in a thick-soled leather shoe made contact with Jack's stubbled jaw.

Hard.

His head snapped round to the left and, in an effort to minimize damage to his spine, Jack leapt into the air, twisting his entire body in the same direction.

As he landed, the heel of a hand slammed into his back, sending him sprawling across the thin rubber mats covering the training center's floor.

Jack rolled, spinning round and jumping back to his feet just in time to block the fist headed in his direction. Reaching out, he grabbed the offending arm at the elbow, locking it in place, and bringing his other hand up to strike his opponent's nose.

There was a sickening crack! and Ricky Smith staggered backwards, wiping a rivulet of fresh blood from his upper lip with his sleeve. "Ooh," he smiled, his eyes sparkling. "That was smooth!"

Both combatants paused for a moment while Ricky's nose repaired itself, the splintered bones realigning themselves and damaged tissue making good.

"I'd be out for at least day from that if I hadn't spent time in the pod-doc," commented one of the Federation's New Rangers. "Nice move. I'm glad I accepted Nathan's invitation to come here and help you train."

The New Rangers, the next generation brought up with the ideals of the original Rangers, Barnabas and Tabitha. And the work ethic. Even with being enhanced or Were, training was critical for sustained superior performance.

Jack held out his hand, palm up, and flicked his fingertips upwards once, twice - gesturing for Ricky to attack him again. "Plenty more where that came from," he grinned.

"Promises, promises!" Ricky chuckled.

Jack expected the Ranger to charge at him but, instead, he struck a casual pose, hands on hips, as if both unafraid and unprepared.

"Reckon you can handle this, do you?"

Jack allowed himself a smile. "Well, if you insist…"

Snarl!

Jack sighed.

"There's a werewolf behind me, isn't there?"

Ricky nodded, thoroughly amused. "There is," he confirmed, standing easily on the balls of his feet, his earlier pose of indifference gone. "Word of advice Captain Marber - don't allow yourself to become distracted in the midst of a battle."

Jack dragged his concentration away from the Ranger

before him and listened for the sound of long claws scraping against the surface of the floor mats.

Carefully deducing the exact moment the werewolf began to pounce, Jack hurled himself to one side, hitting the ground and rolling away from the immense, grey-furred beast.

Caught off-balance, the werewolf turned, his mouth wide and long strings of saliva spraying in Ricky's direction. The second ranger nimbly jumped out of the way of the incoming strings of expectorate, an expression of disgust washing over his face as the floor was spattered with slimy spit.

"Would you stop that bullshit!" Ricky snarled.

As the second Ranger finally found his footing and rocketed forward, Jack dropped to the floor, first parting his legs wide, then scissoring them back together with as much force as he could muster.

He caught the werewolf's head tightly between his thighs and began to pummel its snout with punches. The werewolf howled in frustration, its jaws snapping together as it tried to meet each new blow with a painful bite.

Realizing he couldn't pull himself free, the second Ranger instead opted to lunge forward, scrambling over his victim and pushing him onto his back. Jack's eyes widened as the wolf's hot breath seared the now exposed skin of his throat, and he fought to pull his knees up to his chest, and plant his feet against the creature's vulnerable underbelly.

Thrusting his legs upwards, he allowed the momentum of the latest charge to tip him further backwards, sending the wolf up and over his head where it landed in an ungainly heap.

Jack was on his feet in seconds, as was the Were.

The two fighters circled each other, neither daring to take their eyes away from the other for a split-second.

The werewolf threw back his head and bellowed.

"RRROOOAAAAAARRR!"

Jack cricked his neck noisily from one side to the other. "Well, here goes nothin'..."

Rising up onto his toes, Jack began to yell what he hoped sounded like a terrifying battle cry as he raced towards the second Ranger.

"YYYAAAAAAAARRRRRRGGGGHHH!"

Wiping the sweat from his brow with a towel, Ricky winced as the werewolf lashed out with one of his massive paw's razor sharp claws slicing a trio of deep gashes across the side of Jack's face.

Jack hit the ground both awkwardly and hard, his right foot twisting the wrong way around as the ankle bone snapped, a jagged white point ripping through the skin. Blood gushed from the wound, pooling on the mats around the damaged extremity.

"Ooh," exclaimed Ricky, grimacing. "That's gotta sting!"

The werewolf glared down at the twisted body of his opponent, stomping in his direction. Jack felt the thudding footsteps reverberating through the floor and made an effort to push himself up by his hands.

"OK," he groaned as the shadow fell across him. "No more Mr Nice Guy. Now, I'm taking the gloves off!"

Then he collapsed, face first, onto the floor.

Ricky hurried over to tug at the second Ranger's furry

leg and get his attention. "I think he's had enough for now," he said.

The shaggy head growled, but backed off.

Ricky nodded. "At least give him chance to get up again..."

He glanced down at Jack's broken and bleeding ankle and added. "If he can."

As he watched, the piece of broken bone jutting through Jack's skin began to retreat back inside the torn flesh, and his foot turned as the ankle proceeded to mend itself.

"Hey! You've been in a pod-doc, too!"

Jack rolled himself painfully onto his back and looked up at him. The gashes on his cheek were also now busy repairing themselves.

"My platoon was hit by an IED while on patrol on some pathetic excuse for a planet in the Venford System," he explained. "Two of my guys didn't make it. I was one of the lucky ones, and only had to spend three weeks in the nearest pod, on a base four light years away."

His foot now facing its usual direction, Jack took Ricky's proffered hand and stood, tentatively testing his injured ankle by putting weight onto it. It hurt, and was likely to do so for quite a while, but at least he was able to walk again.

"So," he commented, looking up into the coal-black eyes of the werewolf Ranger. "Best, two out of three?"

Before the werewolf could reply, Turing's voice echoed around the room. "Excuse me, Captain Marber. I'm so sorry to interrupt your training session like this..."

"It's no problem," replied Jack, taking the towel from

TOM DUBLIN & MICHAEL ANDERLE

Ricky and using it to dab at what remained of the scratches on his cheek. By now, they were little more than angry, red scars. "Go ahead."

"Thank you, Jack," said Turing. "Nathan has asked if you would kindly meet him and the other members of your team at dry dock F2 as soon as possible."

"Looks like this session's over, guys," Jack said to his sparring partners. "Tell Nathan I'll be there shortly, Turing."

"I will."

Reaching up, Jack patted the werewolf on his shoulder. "I'll let you off this time, big fella," he grinned. "But only because I'm needed elsewhere. Count yourself lucky."

Tossing the towel over his shoulder, he turned and limped away in the direction of the showers.

"Take it easy, hopalong!" the now-human second ranger called after him.

Alma Nine, Taron City, Channel Three News, Dressing Room 1

Cal Car took a sip from his cup of mogneti and winced. The stuff from the first-floor vending machine again. How many times would he have to tell the studio assistant that he hated the stuff? It was the freshly brewed mogneti from the green room, or nothing.

Pouring the stewed black liquid into the sink, he checked no-one was lurking outside the partially open door then produced a slim metal flask from his jacket pocket and took a long pull.

The liquor burned as it made its way down his throat,

causing him to cough before quickly slipping the bottle away. His producer didn't like him drinking before a news broadcast, but if the channel's lesser employees couldn't follow a simple request about where to get his mogneti, he wasn't going to stick to the rules either.

"Fifteen minutes," announced a female voice from the doorway.

"Thank you," said Cal Car, glancing over to see which of the three production assistants had been sent to tell him how long he had until the broadcast would begin. Bah! It was the one who always wore long, shapeless sweaters. He couldn't remember her actual name, so he referred to her as The Frump.

Not to her face, of course. At least, not since the old breakfast presenter had been fired for taking bets on the breast size of the busty, new fashion reporter. She'd found out about it, and complained directly to the channel's owner - threatening to go to the press if he didn't act to reprimand the culprit.

So, the early morning anchor had been swiftly dismissed. And he'd left without giving Cal Car his well-deserved winnings.

Almost certainly 36DD.

As for The Frump, he'd likely never know thanks to her baggy wardrobe. The statistics the two remaining production assistants, Grin-On-Legs and Wiggles, were still a work in progress.

Flicking a switch, the bare bulbs surrounding his mirror lit up instantly revealing the imperfections in Cal Car's skin. Scowling, he grabbed a compact from his make-up kit and began to smear the teal-colored powder evenly over his face.

After almost a decade in front of the camera, he prided himself on still looking as fresh as the day he'd first arrived at Channel Three. All those years of hard work as a print journalist had paid off.

And yet, ten years and a handful of industry awards later, he still wasn't reporting on the big stuff, despite repeated requests. He wanted to expose juicy political scandals, beam live from war zones, or go live from the stock market as financial crashes doomed the lower classes to years of poverty and despair.

But, what did he get? Updates on farming news, rumors of affairs between beautiful yet vacuous movie stars, and the latest success stories from Taron City's weather control center.

Stuff anybody with a pulse and a decent set of straight teeth could do.

"Ten minutes, Cal Car."

It was the Frump again. It was obviously her turn to shepherd him around the building tonight. With any luck, the task would fall to Wiggles tomorrow, so he could find an excuse to lag behind and watch that amazing ass of hers as she led him to the studio floor.

His make-up complete, Cal Car snapped the compact closed and set it aside. Standing, he pulled the tissues from inside his shirt collar and threw them into the trash as he made his way to the dressing room door.

Here we go again!

Then he set off to broadcast what he believed would be yet another uneventful program of unexciting news.

He didn't know just how wrong he was.

Federation Base Station 11, Dry Dock F7

Tc'aarlat, Adina and Nathan looked up as Jack hobbled along the side of the dry dock towards them, running his fingers through his damp hair.

"Combat training?"

Jack nodded. "Word of advice - never let one of the Federation's Rangers distract you when there's a werewolf in the vicinty."

Tc'aarlat shuddered. "I'm down for a session with one of the Rangers tomorrow," he croaked. "And I doubt I'll be able to get that image out of my head now."

"Lady, gentlemen," said Nathan in an effort to attract the trio's attention. "Allow me to introduce you to the *ICS Fortitude*, Mark Two."

He opened the door and stepped aside, allowing Jack, Tc'aarlat and Adina to step through and get their first look at their newly upgraded ship.

They stood in stunned silence for a few moments, staring up at the vast freighter. Eventually, Adina found the words to describe what was going through everyone's mind.

"What a pile of shit!"

12

Alma Nine, Taron City, Channel Three News, Studio 4a

"...which resulted in yet another bumper crop of parsel fruit this year, and record exports of the sumptuous snack to several other planets in the Ordanian Hub."

Cal Car flashed his trademark smile as the teleprompter script only he could see on the transparent screen covering the lens of the TV camera flickered for a few seconds, then vanished.

If those idiots in the control room made him ad-lib one more time, he would grab them by the-

The teleprompter returned and began to scroll once more, revealing the next block of text in the evening news bulletin.

"I'll be back with your daily sports update here on Alma Nine's premier news service, Channel Three News, but now it's over to Sim Ket for tomorrow's weather promise."

Cal Car held his smile in place until the red light on top of the camera switched off. Across the studio, Sim Ket began to detail what the following day's weather would be like all across the planet, down to the exact minute.

When Cal Car had started out in TV news, weather presenters were forced to study spreadsheets of air pressure readings and closely examine grainy satellite images in order to guess what might happen on the weather front in the coming days.

The results were on par with those of gaudily dressed fairground mystics who claimed to be able to put grieving relatives in touch with their recently deceased loved ones.

But, now the colony's groundbreaking weather control system was up and running, all TV meteorologists had to do was read from a script received directly from the control center, and they could promise what a certain day's weather would be like weeks in advance.

It made the job so simple even a child could do it and, judging by the barely-old-enough-to-vote weather presenter the channel had recently hired, it seemed the industry was already heading in that direction.

"What's the deal with the teleprompter," Cal Car asked into his lapel microphone as the make-up girl dashed over to refresh the soft mat powder coating his famous face.

While she worked, he grabbed a hand mirror from the shelf beneath his desk and used it to check his reflection, pulling back his lips and studying the shine on his extremely costly teeth.

Pleased with what he saw, Cal Car ran his fingers through his thick mane of expensively styled shaggy silver hair. There was just no way that new babe on the studio reception desk would be able to resist his charms, or the king-sized vibrating water bed he recently had delivered for his penthouse apartment.

But, first, he had yet another glitch to get to the bottom of. "I asked about the teleprompter, Jun Ret!"

"Yeah, sorry about that," the news producer's voice replied via his earpiece. "We're still ironing out the glitches in this new system. Bear with us while we-"

"Bear with you?!" Cal Car interrupted, sending the make-up artist scurrying away with a wave of his hand. "I've been bearing with you for weeks. If this crap doesn't get sorted soon, I'll have my agent contact-"

"And you're back in five, four, three..."

Cal Car slid the mirror back under the desk, fixed his smile in place, raised an eyebrow and waited until the light on top of the camera lit up once more.

"Thank you, Sim Ket! Now sports, and in battleball, the Malatian Princes beat the Ch'arrack Destroyers fifty-two to forty-eight in a close-run game last night at the-"

Cal Car paused as the screen in front of him suddenly went dark.

"I'm sorry, we seem to be having some technical difficulties this evening. We'll get those sports results to you just as soon as we can. In the meantime..."

He rested a finger on his earpiece, listening hard for whatever pathetic excuse the production team was going to make this time.

But, nobody spoke to him. Instead, everyone in the gallery seemed to be holding an urgent discussion in hushed tones.

And some of them were crying.

What the fuck?

Cal Car's trademark smile faltered slightly as the one-way screen covering the camera lens remained devoid of well, anything at all.

He became very aware that millions of viewers were waiting for him to say something, if they weren't already flipping over to the second-rate outfit that was Alpha News in their thousands, that was.

"Once again, ladies and gentlemen, please bear with us while we deal with this unexpected technical issue. We promise to get the sports... update... to you..."

His voice trailed away as two words began to flash on the teleprompter screen...

BREAKING NEWS

Then...

REMAINDER OF SCRIPT ABANDONED

And, finally...

URGENT!

Cal Car gasped. This was it. He was finally getting his wish. He was about to report to the world on a live story.

"If you're just tuning in," he announced, as more information began to scroll up into his line of sight, "this is Cal Car and the Channel Three News team, bringing you a breaking story tonight."

Whoever was in control of the teleprompter was clearly typing out his script in real time, judging by the poor grammar and numerous typos now filling the screen.

Once again, he would have to dig deep into his plentiful stores of professionalism in order to save the day. Only this time, the channel's owner was bound to see the benefit of transferring him over to the galaxy-wide network.

Goodbye, parsel fruit and battleball!

Working to keep his excitement under control, Cal Car quickly switched from his trademark smile to his well-practiced deadly serious expression.

"Reports are coming in from the Sipar region of Taron City that Alma Nine's President, Tor Val has been-"

The rest of the sentence stuck in his throat.

Cal Car's hands began to tremble.

"No!" he said, suddenly hoarse. "It's not true." He pressed his fingers hard against his earpiece. "This can't... Tell me it's not true!"

His producer came back on the line. "It's true, Cal Car," he croaked. "The Vice President's office has just confirmed it."

Stunned, Cal Car lowered his hand and stared blankly into the camera lens.

"Th-There has been an accident," he said quietly. "A terrible, terrible accident."

He remained speechless for a second or two, then...

"The President, Tor Val, is dead."

Federation Base Station 11, Dry Dock F7

Tc'aarlat ran the thick skin of his fingers over the chipped yellow paint covering the hull as he waited for the starboard side access door to hiss open.

"So much for being upgraded," he commented. "It hasn't had so much as a paint job."

Nathan turned to him. "This isn't 'Pimp My Space Ride'", he pointed out. "The improvements we've made for you are on the inside of the ship."

"But-"

"And, we left the exterior looking like a battered old freighter because we want everyone to believe it's a battered old freighter."

He lowered his voice and spoke conspiratorially. "Spies tend to work best when undercover!"

Tc'aarlat scowled, his mandibles clicking together as the others laughed. "In that case," he grumbled, "maybe it would be best not to continually refer to us as spies. Don't we get code names or something?"

"I was thinking the same thing," said Nathan. "All you have to do is come up with something.

"How about Titanic Tc'aarlat and his two plucky yet also completely subservient sidekicks," suggested the Yollin.

Nathan scowled. "All you have to do is come up with something... else."

"That's right," Tc'aarlat growled. "You humans carry on ignoring anything the weird alien guy says."

Jack shrugged as Tc'aarlat began to sulk. "If you insist..."

Adina turned to Jack. "Is he always this full of joy?"

"Not always," smirked Jack in reply. "Sometimes he has a grumpy day."

Mist gave a shriek that may have been agreement, and nibbled at a lump of hardened skin at the top of Tc'aarlat's right ear.

The side door finally locked into its open position with a clunk, and Nathan led the group inside.

Jack and his team wandered through the upper cargo bays, examining the fresh dull-metal pillars which were reinforcing all of the cargo bays.

"These look pretty sturdy," he commented, slapping his palm against one of them.

Nathan nodded. "It's a new alloy we've developed. The stuff is reasonably lightweight but it's incredibly strong and stands up to a hell of a pounding. We've also lined the interior of the entire hull with it."

"We'll be able to haul much heavier cargo now," said Jack. "Although we're likely to see a substantial loss of speed and maneuverability as a result."

"Not any longer," Nathan relied. "We've replaced both main engines with gravitic drives. Trust me - no matter what you're carrying from now on, this thing will go like a rocket on speed."

Jack nodded his approval. "Nice!"

"The auxiliary engines, bow thrusters and so on have all been upgraded to gravitic thrusters. Non-reactive fuel, magnetic currents and electrical potentials provide enough acceleration to get you out of trouble and can, at a push, be used for main thrust in the unlikely event of a problem with your main engines."

"Sounds like you've thought of everything," said Tc'aarlat with a grudging smile. "A bitch in time saves nine!"

Jack opened his mouth to correct the Yollin, then closed it again. "You know what? Forget it."

Nathan grinned. "I think you're gonna like this next bit..."

The tour continued swiftly through the cargo bays until they reached the wall at the rear of a hangar in the lower deck.

Jack took a step back to admire the new metallic lining

of the loading doors. "They look pretty sturdy now," he commented.

"They do," agreed Nathan. "But they're not the rear doors."

Jack's brow knitted. "What?"

"Put your hand against the metal," he suggested. "Anywhere will work."

Cautiously, Jack stepped up to the door and pressed his palm against the door at shoulder height. The area around his palm glowed a brilliant blue and then, with a loud hiss, the rear doors began to slide down, disappearing into some hidden compartment below them.

"False doors," explained Nathan. "Touch sensitive to each of your palm prints, no matter where you put your hand, or which one you use. And beyond..."

Jack's eyes grew wide as rows of ceiling lights sprang into life, illuminating the silver-walled room beyond. The space was clean, bright and fresh - a world away from the scuffed flooring and dented panels of the main cargo area.

And, sitting in the middle of this sterile space...

"Holy mother of God!" Jack breathed.

Tc'aarlat rested a trembling hand on his shoulder. "You said it brother!"

There, in front of them, was a sleek, black spacecraft. It was about the size of a large Earth automobile and had dark, tinted windows.

Nathan took a step across into the ship's docking area, gesturing for the others to follow. Two strips of landing lights flashed in lines from the real back doors of the hangar.

"Meet The Pegasus," he announced. "A short-hop shuttle for use in, well... any situation you deem necessary. It won't take you between planets, but I'm sure you'll find a use for it."

Just then, a voice spoke out. "Nathan, I have an urgent message for you from Ecaterina."

"Thank you, Turing," Nathan replied.

He turned to the others. "I'll be back with you in a moment," he promised. "I'll meet you up at the bridge. Still got one or two new toys to show off to you."

As Nathan hurried away to take his call, Tc'aarlat reached out to run his hand over the gleaming black paint covering the hull of *The Pegasus*, but hesitated.

"I don't even want to get fingerprints on this thing!"

Adina grinned. "It is a little flashy!"

"Flashy?!" spat Tc'aarlat, unable to tear his admiring gaze away from the cruiser. "I'd have sold two of my kidneys to own something like this when I was younger."

"Hopefully, that won't be necessary," said Jack. "Come on, let's get up to the bridge and see what they've done up there."

Tc'aarlat's mandibles drooped in disappointment. "Really?"

Rolling his eyes towards Adina, Jack reached out and grabbed the Yollin's arm. "The pretty spaceship will still be here when we get back," he promised.

The trio stepped out of the hangar, the bright lighting fading quickly as the false loading doors slid smoothly back into place.

In less than a minute, The *Pegasus* and its home had vanished, and looked as if it had never been there at all.

Adina studied Tc'aarlat, surprised. "Are... are you crying?"

"Of course not!" Tc'aarlat insisted, wiping his eyes. "It's probably allergies. Or something."

"Sure!" Adina replied with a smile. She hooked her arm through his and urged him on. "Let's catch up with Jack."

Jack paused just outside the bridge to examine the wall beside the door. "They've left the bullet holes following our recent get-together with those Skaine pirates," he pointed out.

"And the smears of blood on the floor," Tc'aarlat added. "Maybe they haven't done as much up here."

He stepped up to the automatic door, waiting for it to slide open, before adding. "Although I may have spoken too soon..."

Adina and Tc'aarlat stepped onto the bridge to find Jack already trying out his brand new captain's chair.

"It doesn't squeak at all!" he exclaimed, spinning round in a circle.

"I bet mine still does," moaned Tc'aarlat as he slumped into his own seat. "Not even a new cushion for my bad back!"

"I'm guessing this is where I sit," said Adina, taking a seat at the navigation console and examining the array of buttons and switches in front of her. "This doesn't look too complex."

"I'm glad you agree, Miss Choudhury," announced a familiar male voice.

The front screens lit up a brilliant white and a vast face smiled down at them.

The face of Captain Jack Marber.

Tc'aarlat squealed and fell off his seat, Mist flapping into the air and landing on the headrest of his battered old chair.

"How in the name of the entire universe, did you get up there?" he demanded.

Jack continued staring up at his own face. "That's not me!"

"Indeed I am not," confirmed the face. "Allow me to introduce myself. I am the *ICS Fortitude*'s new Entity Intelligence. My name is Solo."

"So, why do you look like Jack?" Adina queried.

"Well, Miss Choudhury," Solo began.

"Please, call me Adina."

Solo smiled. "Very kind, Adina. I was about to explain that my outward appearance is only an avatar. I can change it to reflect just about any life-form, human or otherwise."

"Then, why pick that ugly mug?" demanded Tc'aarlat as he climbed back into his seat.

Solo turned to look down at the Yollin. "I merely presumed Captain Marber's loyal crew would respect his particular physiognomy and respond positively to it."

Tc'aarlat sighed. "Not you as well. I'm not a member of the crew; I'm his partner."

Solo looked apologetic. "Oh, I'm so sorry," the E.I. responded. "I had no idea the two of you were romantically involved."

"Not like that!" yelled Tc'aarlat. "I'm his business partner!"

Jack gave a Adina a sly wink. "Maybe it would be best if you were to change your appearance, Solo," he suggested.

"Very well, Captain Marber-"

"And none of this 'Captain Marber' nonsense. You can call me Jack."

"Very well, Jack. How's this..."

The trio watched as Solo's face warped into the stern Yollin features of Tc'aarlat himself.

Mist let out a shriek and flapped hastily out of the bridge.

"Oh Lord, no!" croaked Tc'aarlat. "That's worse than before!"

"Try something else," said Jack. "Someone a bit less... immediate."

"OK," replied Solo. "What about this one?"

This time Solo's avatar melted and reformed into that of a middle-aged woman with ash-blond hair. She had a full mouth and kind, blue eyes.

"Oh, I like her," said Adina.

"Fine by me," said the Yollin with a mild shrug. "Who is she?"

Jack stared up at the screen, an expression of surprise etched across his features. He swallowed hard. "Where the hell did you get that face?"

"Do you know her?" Adina asked.

Jack continued gazing up at the woman on the screen, nodding. "I did once," he replied. "I haven't seen her for a very long time, though."

Tc'aarlat slapped Jack on the shoulder, his mandibles twitching. "What's wrong, big man?" he asked, chuckling. "Your secret past catching up with you, is it? Someone you hooked up with who you'd rather forget?"

The Yollin smiled to himself. He'd been waiting for an opportunity to engage in some of the playful banter he'd witnessed in bars and at sporting events ever since the humans had arrived.

This was his chance to try out what he'd learned about male repartee.

"I haven't met too many human women," the Yollin continued, nodding towards Solo's new visage, "but that one looks like she's a bit of a *goer*, if you know what I mean?"

He glanced over at Adina and attempted to wink - something he'd often seen humans do when they were partaking in similar conversations. Yollin eyelids, however, weren't quite as supple as those possessed by Earth folk and he wasn't quite able to pull off the move.

To Adina, it looked as though Tc'aarlat was attempting to suck one of his eyeballs deep inside his own skull.

Jack sat silently as the Yollin continued with his teasing.

"Hey, there's nothing to be ashamed of, Jack. Lots of men like spending time with older women. They may not have the sexual energy and inventive imagination of the latest models, but what they lack in raw passion, they more than make up for with experience."

Adina did her best to hide her smile. "Tc'aarlat, I don't think-"

"I bet that one taught you a few tricks you hadn't seen before, didn't she? They really go to town, these older types. Some of them haven't seen action for quite a while, so they're not only eager, they're *grateful* as well."

He nudged Jack with his elbow. "Come on then, player! Tell us what you got up to with this little minx!"

Jack sighed. "Well, quite often there was food involved..."

"Ooh, saucy! Liked to make you breakfast, did she?"

"And lunch, and dinner," finished Jack. "Mainly because that little 'minx', as you refer to her, is my mother."

Tc'aarlat's face froze, his mandibles wide. Slowly, he turned to look up at Solo, who was smiling warmly down at the trio.

"And a lovely, kind woman she looks, too," croaked Tc'aarlat, turning towards the bridge door in the hope of a quick exit.

But, before he could scurry away and bury his head somewhere cold and dark, Nathan reappeared. And he didn't look happy.

"Is everything OK?" asked Adina.

Nathan shook his head. "I'm afraid not," he said. "A political situation we've been keeping a close watch on has taken an unexpected turn. We're going to have to bring our brief time together to an abrupt end."

Jack's expression hardened. "You mean?"

"I do," said Nathan. "It's time for a real mission."

13

Alma Nine, Taron City, Government Building, Front Steps

A gentle breeze ruffled the upright strands of silver hair in Saf Tah's mohawk as he stepped up to the podium and faced the hushed representatives of the press. The usually bright white lights woven into his hairstyle had been swapped for more muted, purple bulbs to reflect this more somber time of grieving.

Although some of the keener eyed reporters had already noted that the Presidential seal on the front of the podium was now ringed in Saf Tah's political colors of red and green, as opposed to Tor Val's navy and lemon.

"Ladies and gentleman," Saf Tah began once he was certain all of the cameras from the major networks had begun their live broadcasts, "I am speaking to you from outside Alma Nine's government buildings, although I truly wish that I wasn't."

He paused to wipe a tear from the corner of his eye.

"As you will no doubt be aware, last night our cherished

President, Tor Val, was tragically killed in a horrific automobile collision, along with her driver, Gan Roj."

Near the center of the small group gathered behind the Vice President, Bay Don pulled Tor Val's two crying daughters in closer, holding one in each arm as tightly as she could.

Saf Tah continued...

"Tor Val's death leaves a terrible hole in not just the lives of her family and close friends - among which I was honored to be counted - but in the life of every citizen of this world, whether they are one of the brave settlers who came here from Malatia all those years ago, or among the very first generation to be born on Alma Nine."

Mol Gat ticked two of the items off the checklist in his notepad. Saf Tah was sticking to the speech he and his fellow aide had prepared, and was hitting all the key points. If he kept this up, there wouldn't be a dry eye on the entire planet.

"Investigations are underway as to the cause of the fatal crash," Saf Tah promised, eyes flicking from one camera lens to the next, "although at this stage, the incident appears to have been nothing more than a blameless accident."

Tor Val's head of security, Hip Win, stood motionless near the back of the group behind the Vice President, his mirrored sunglasses betraying nothing of his current emotion.

"No matter what the cause of the tragedy, the result is the same: Tor Val has left us and, like her husband on our journey to this world, we must prepare for her to undergo The Journey Back."

The press's sensitive microphones picked up a devastated sob from Tor Val's older daughter, Mas Val.

"It is with this dreadful news in mind that I hereby instigate an official three-day period of mourning, starting tomorrow. This period will end following Tor Val's funeral on the third day."

The assembled guests and journalists greeted this announcement with a polite round of applause. Saf Tah waited for silence before continuing.

"Tor Val's body pod will be launched from Taron Park, from where it will be guided into the depths of the Ordon Nebula, where she will be returned to the star dust from whence she came, and reunited in death with her husband, Lad Val."

A second smattering of applause did little to drown out the sound of crying from Tor Val's two daughters.

This caught Saf Tah's attention, and he turned, reaching out his hands towards the girls. Both turned towards Bay Don, as though asking for permission to accept the gesture, to which their friend simply nodded.

Ran Val was the first to step forward and take one of the proffered hands, closely followed by her sister. Saf Tah drew them close and wrapped his arms around them. The girls buried their faces against his shoulders.

Saf Tah held the embrace while cameras clicked around him like the sound of early evening insects. As the volley of photographic sounds faded away, he turned back to the microphones, eyes red, and spoke once more.

"These are two of the bravest, most caring young ladies you will ever meet," he proclaimed.

Jus Clo quickly looked up from the tablet on which he'd been closely following the Vice President's words.

"Bistok's bollocks!" He hissed to the figure standing beside him. "He's off script!"

Mol Gat let out a series of strangled coughs as he tried to attract his boss's attention, but it didn't work. Instead, Bay Don reached out to hand the aide a tissue, forcing him to have to pretend to blow his nose.

"I urge everyone," Saf Tah continued, "not just the media, to give Tor Val's brave, brave daughters..."

He paused, searching through his memory for either one of the girls' names, but came up blank.

"...here the space they need over the coming days and allow them to grieve in private."

This received another short round of applause, much to the relief of the Vice President's aides.

"Phew!" Mol Gat wiped his brow with the tissue, before realizing he had just faked filling it with the contents of his nostrils. He quickly stuffed the tissue into his pocket, hoping the TV cameras and photographers hadn't spotted his blunder.

Jus Clo rubbed his thumbnails with his fingertips - the traditional Malatian gesture for luck - and hoped the final part of Saf Tah's speech would be as well received.

"In my own personal effort to help Tor Val's distraught daughters as much as I can," said Saf Tah, "I have decided to remove a pressing burden from their young shoulders; one which must be weighing extremely heavily at this moment in time."

The two girls glanced at each other, confused.

Saf Tah cleared his throat, and spoke the final words of his address.

"An hour ago, I issued a decree which amends the constitution of Alma Nine, allowing me to take on the role of President with immediate effect, instead of expecting either of these poor, grieving girls to struggle to fill such an important position."

The podium lit up as dozens of camera flashes fired at once. In news studios all across the planet, TV anchors and political commentators began to dissect Saf Tah's announcement.

Outside the government building, Bay Don stepped forward to take the arms of Tor Val's daughters and lead them away from the urgently shouted questions of the reporters:

Is such a decree legal, Mr Vice President?

Can you really just announce yourself as Alma Nine's new ruler?

Surely tradition dictates the presidency must stay within Tor Val's immediate family?

Saf Tah, why aren't you calling an election?

How do you girls feel about what the Vice President has done?

As Bay Don and her clearly distressed charges disappeared inside the building, Mol Gat stepped forward, hands raised. "The, um... Vice President will be happy to answer any, um... questions you may have at a later-"

Boom!

Suddenly, the atmosphere exploded with a deafening crash of thunder, and streaks of forked lightning shot across the sky like tongues of white-hot fire. Rain began to pour down, quickly drenching everyone at the press conference, causing cameramen and sound operators scattering in a vain attempt to get their delicate equipment under some sort of cover.

Saf Tah gazed up at the banks of thick black clouds, the rain causing his mohawk to wilt.

"Why didn't you tell me we were due for a thunderstorm?!" he demanded.

Jus Clo flicked through the weather promise app on his tablet. "We're not, sir! This is completely unexpected!"

Boom!

Mol Gat covered his ears with his palms as another burst of thunder detonated directly above their heads.

Torrential rain began to flood the street, the water level rising so quickly that fleeing reporters' feet kicked up waves of spray as they dashed back to their respective vehicles.

"No!" bellowed Saf Tah. He and his two aides were now the only figures left out in the open. "Storms cannot be unexpected. We have the most advanced weather control system in the galaxy!"

Mol Gat shrugged. "Um..."

Before he could say anything else, another spear of lighting crackled out of the rapidly darkening sky and struck the wooden presidential podium, causing it to erupt into flames.

The two aides grabbed their boss and dragged him away from the burning lectern, but not quite quickly enough. A spark of fizzing electricity still playing around the metallic bodies of the abandoned press microphones arced through the air, striking the chain of purple lights woven into the Vice President's hair.

There was a bright flash and a noise that sounded like WUMPH! as Saf Tah's scalp was instantly consumed with fire.

Thinking quickly, Mol Gat threw himself at the Vice President, pushing him to the ground and plunging his flaming head into the deepest puddle within reach. The hairy blaze was extinguished with a hiss.

Jus Clo momentarily froze, horror etched across his features as he watched a stream of bubbles escape from Saf Tah's submerged mouth and nose. Then, pulling Mol Gat away from their employer, he gripped what little remained of the Vice President's hair and heaved his head out of the water.

Saf Tah gasped repeatedly, gulping down lungfuls of freezing cold air.

Jus Clo stretched out a hand, aiming to help the VP back to his feet, but Saf Tah scuttled backwards through the downpour, fearful that his aide might cause him further harm.

A large shadow fell over them both. Saf Tah and Jus Clo looked up to find the imposing figure of Hip Win standing before them, his bald scalp slick from the rain.

Thrusting out a hand, he shoved Jus Clo backwards, sending him tumbling into the flat flowing river that had now taken over the street. With his other hand, he lifted the stunned and disoriented Vice President, threw him over one of his vast shoulders, then stomped in the direction of the building's entrance doors and safety.

Bobbing from the huge security operative's giant

strides, Saf Tah raised his frazzled head and hissed a final command to his two sodden assistants.

"Find out what happened to weather control system RIGHT FUCKING NOW!"

ICS Fortitude, Bridge

"OK," said Jack, reaching out for a bank of switches slightly to his left. "Are we ready to release the dockside clamps?" His fingers hovered over the controls.

"Excuse me, Captain Marber," Solo interrupted. "Would you like me to handle the departure from here?"

Jack looked up at the face still filling the main view screen. "You can do that, even with this old tech?"

Solo nodded. "The entire bridge has been completely refitted," she said. "Then, the old control panels were put back in place and connected to the new technology underneath. I can, should you so wish, completely take-over the docking and un-docking process."

The E.I.'s face faded from the screens, replaced with the view of space outside the ship.

"Oh," said Jack, dropping his hands into his lap. "Er... you do that, then."

"Of course, Captain."

It was now just over two hours since Nathan had told the team they were to prepare for a swift departure. Jack and Tc'aarlat only needed a few minutes to collect their meager belongings from their respective rooms, but Adina had requested extra time as she had to head back to her apartment and pack, with a little help from Ecaterina.

It would also be a useful opportunity for Ecaterina to

present Adina with what advice she could about coping with her wolf side. Ideally, the pair would have time to work through various techniques, but the urgency of the mission meant these would have to wait until the team returned.

She also wanted to pay another brief visit to her Uncle Yousuf. She didn't know when she'd next be returning home, and whether he would be able to remember who she was when that day came.

And, of course, the vast cargo bays of the *ICS Fortitude* had to be loaded by teams of dock workers under Nathan's command, although neither Jack nor Tc'aarlat had yet been told what the freight consisted of.

Nathan said he would explain everything once they had set off on their journey.

Jack knitted his fingers together and looked from Tc'aarlat to Adina and back again. "Right then," he said. "I guess I'll just sit here and... supervise."

"And I may as well go and unpack," said Adina. She grabbed the handles of two large suitcases and wheeled them out through the bridge doors and along the corridor beyond.

Two minutes later, she poked her head back in.

"Er... any idea where I live now?"

Alma Nine, Taron City, Weather Control Center, Yan Mil's Apartment

Zeb Lok hammered on the door of the building's penthouse apartment for the fifth time in as many minutes.

"Yan Mil!" he shouted. "Open the door, please!"

Behind him, the elevator doors opened with a ding.

"Any luck?" asked Jon Rey as he stepped out onto the small landing.

Zeb Lok shook his head. "Nothing. I've knocked, called and even sent messages from my computer. He simply won't talk."

"This is ridiculous," grumbled Jon Rey. "I understand he's heartbroken about losing his wife, but locking himself away doesn't achieve anything. We're all here for him."

"Not if we can't get in to see him," Zeb Lok pointed out.

"Are you sure he's OK?"

"Who knows?" said Zeb Lok with a shrug. "I've heard him moving around in there, but he's not responding to anyone."

He turned and knocked on the door again. "Yan Mil. It's me, and Jon Rey."

"Let us in so we can talk with you," pleaded Jon Rey.

Once again, there was no reply.

"We may have to go in there without his permission," suggested Jon Rey. "I presume the building's maintenance team has a master key."

"They did," said Zeb Lok. "It went missing just before Yan Mil locked himself inside his apartment."

"You think he has the key with him?"

"It's a possibility."

Jon Rey sighed. "You should get back to work. I'll stay for a while and see if I can get him to open up."

Zeb Lok nodded, pressing the button to call the elevator. "Good luck," he said, "but I wouldn't hold my breath."

14

***ICS Fortitude*, Crew Quarters**

Following the directions she'd been given, Adina found her way to a short corridor with two metallic doors on each side. She'd been told that the cabins on the left were occupied by Jack and Tc'aarlat, so she turned to choose one of the two remaining rooms.

The first door she opened revealed a cabin crammed with trays of canned food, bottles of water and more toilet paper than she'd ever seen in one place in her life.

"I guess I won't be sleeping in here," she said to herself as she closed the door again.

The only remaining room was more habitable, but only slightly.

The cabin featured a narrow cot which hinged down from the far wall, a small hand basin and what appeared to be a repurposed school locker for use as a closet.

Scattered around were objects she presumed had belonged to her predecessor, Dollen. Or, as Jack now called him, *That Sphincter-faced Turd Gargler*. This amounted to two trash bags filled with unwashed clothing, a handful of personal grooming items and what appeared to be a modified electric animal prod of some kind.

She made a mental note to keep that when it came time to ditch the stuff.

Dumping the smaller of her two cases onto the bed, she unzipped the lid and flipped it open. Sitting on top of her pile of hastily folded clothes was the bag of pills she had 'bought' in the alleyway.

Ecaterina had asked the pharmacy guys back on Base Station 11 to check them out and they'd discovered that, while much lower than the strength Adina had asked for, the DNA suppressants did not contain any additional or potentially harmful ingredients.

She had been allowed to keep the pills in addition to the newer prescription provided by Ecaterina, though she would have to take double the dosage for them to have the same effect.

Fishing two of the tiny tablets out of the bag, she tossed them into her mouth and swallowed them dry. While there was a glass sitting next to the faucet on the hand basin, she didn't know what Dollen had previously used it for and decided that a few seconds of disgusting taste was preferable to dealing with whatever germs she might pick up by using the traitor's cast off.

"What are those for?"

Adina spun to find Tc'aarlat standing in the open doorway.

"Nothing!" replied Adina, silently admonishing herself for sounding a little too defensive. "They're just... pills."

"Ah..." said Tc'aarlat, nodding. "Just pills. Yeah, I take those from time to time. They're great, those *just pills*."

"What is your problem?"

Tc'aarlat tried his hand at perfecting his human-like shrug again. "Nothing," he answered. "I've just never seen pills like that before."

Adina scowled. "Yeah well, you didn't notice a suicide bomber right under your nose either, so I'm not going to lose any sleep over it."

"Hey!" Tc'aarlat retorted. "I was just trying to make conversation."

"If you *must* know, I get travel sick," said Adina, praying the Yollin would buy her lie. "Well, I did back home, so it could well happen out here in space, too."

"Perfect," commented Tc'aarlat with a twitch of his mandibles. "Not only do we have to put up with a new crew member, but now she's going to vomit everywhere."

"Not if I take my meds, I won't," snapped Adina, stuffing the bag of tablets onto the shelf of her locker and slamming the door shut. "What are you doing here, anyway? Don't you have some co-piloting to do?"

Tc'aarlat jerked a thumb over his shoulder towards the door on the opposite side of the corridor. "I just came to get Mist a couple of treats from my cabin. Is that OK with you?"

Adina glanced at the Yollin's shoulder pad, noticing for the first time that the Raal hawk wasn't with him for a change.

"Mist's a beautiful bird," she said. "Where is she now?"

Tc'aarlat's expression softened slightly, a faint smile

playing around his mouth. "I left her on the bridge with Jack, just to annoy him."

"Annoy him?"

This time, Tc'aarlat did smile. "Yeah, he hates her. Calls her a flying rat." He spotted Adina's concerned expression and added: "It's OK, though. The feeling is more than mutual. Mist thinks he's a piece of garbage, too. I like to leave them alone now and again in an effort to get them to bond."

Now Adina was smiling, too. "Think that'll work?"

"They'll either learn to get along or kill each other trying," grinned Tc'aarlat. He turned and reached for the handle of his cabin door. "Let me know if you need anything."

"Actually, there is one thing you could help me with," said Adina. "Where are the bathrooms on this thing?"

Tc'aarlat turned back again. "Bath*room*," he said, "singular. Down the end of the corridor, turn right. One toilet and one shower stall, which I *really* hope Nathan included in the upgrade to the ship. Fucking water pressure's so weak you have to walk around in the thing to get wet."

"I'll bear that in mind," said Adina, turning back to her case. She pulled out a bra and held it up. "So, can I get a little privacy?"

Tc'aarlat's eyes widened in horror at the sight of the underwear. His mandibles tapped together and he was suddenly very glad he hadn't chosen to learn the human function of blushing.

"Yes!" he said, turning to his right and deliberately averting his gaze. "I'd better get back to the bridge, anyway. Jack and Mist might well have killed each other by now."

Just then, Solo's voice echoed out around the ship. "Tc'aarlat and Miss Adina, Nathan Lowell has initiated a video call to the ship, and wishes to discuss the details of this mission with you."

"Coming!" called Adina, stepping out of her cramped quarters. She closed the door and began to follow Tc'aarlat back towards where Jack was waiting. They were almost there when she realized she was still carrying her bra.

She shrugged and hung it over the corner of a sign on the wall which read 'Authorized Personnel Only'. "Well, that is the rule where people accessing my underwear is concerned."

Then she hurried to join her new crew mates on the bridge.

Adina entered the bridge to find Jack leaning back in the captain's chair with his foot resting on Tc'aarlat's co-pilot seat. The Yollin was hunched over, changing a dressing on Jack's ankle.

"What?" Adina exclaimed. "I know Tc'aarlat said he was leaving you and Mist alone to either bond or kill each other, but I didn't believe she would attack you."

From her perch high on the corner of one of the bridge's security cameras, Mist let out an indignant caw.

"Mist didn't do this to me," said Jack, wincing as Tc'aarlat pulled the old bandage away from his skin. "This was thanks to a fucking werewolf."

Adina caught her breath. "Really?"

Jack nodded. "The Second Ranger took it upon himself to toss me around like a pox-ridden rag doll."

"Why?" asked Adina, taking her own seat at the navigation desk.

"It was supposed to be combat training," explained Jack. "Although it turned out more like *the big, bad vampire and over-sized mongrel have a bit of violent fun at the out-of-shape soldier's expense.*"

"Ignore him," Tc'aarlat chuckled as he wound a new dressing around Jack's leg. "He's just pissed because they beat him to a pulp."

"You would be, too," exclaimed Jack. "It fucking hurt!"

"You're an enhanced human who was given boosted recuperation abilities in some magic Kurtherian fish bowl," said Tc'aarlat. "Couple of days and you won't even remember this."

"Oh, I'll remember it alright," moaned Jack. "And if Ricky Smith thinks-"

His brow furrowed.

"Hang on..."

Tc'aarlat worked to tie off the bandage. "What?"

"You deliberately leave me alone with your blasted bird to try and force me to get along with it?"

Tc'aarlat threw an accusing glance in Adina's direction, but she wasn't paying attention. He turned back to Jack. "First of all, Mist is a *she*, not an *it*," he pointed out. "And, yes I do. It's about time you two got to know each other better. Who knows, you might even grow to like her."

Jack lifted his eyes to meet Mist's for a moment. It was clear that the Raal hawk was just as unhappy with Tc'aarlat's impromptu match-making sessions as he was.

"The day I decide to like your bird, is the day you serve her up to me, roasted, with mash potatoes, carrots and all the trimmings. Come on, it's got to be Thanksgiving *somewhere* in the galaxy, right?"

Mist began to make a growling noise at the back of her throat.

The Yollin slapped Jack's ankle, pushing his leg off the seat and causing his foot to slam down onto the metal floor.

"OW! What did you do that for?"

Tc'aarlat shrugged, this time getting the move exactly right. "Your foot was on my seat." He sat down, busying himself with checking the positions of the buttons on his console.

"Oh, don't start sulking just because I joked about eating your stupid sidekick!"

Tc'aarlat didn't reply.

Jack spun in his chair - taking a second to fully appreciate the lack of squeak - and looked at Adina.

"Adina, you know I was just joking, don't you?"

Adina didn't reply either.

Slowly, Jack turned back to face the front screens. "Well, this is going to be a pleasant trip, isn't it," he said to himself. "It had better not take too long to get to... actually, does anyone happen to know where it is we're going?"

Solo's face appeared to fill the screens once more. "I have been given co-ordinates within the Ordon Nebula, Jack. However, the journey shouldn't take too long. We have a lot of distance to cover, but I'll be utilizing two Federation Gates to get us there. Barring unseen delays, our estimated time of arrival is in just over an hour."

"Great," said Jack, reaching over to grab his tablet. "Thanks, Mum."

The bridge fell silent while everyone allowed the faux pas to sink in.

Jack closed his eyes, dropped his head down to his chest, and sighed. "Oh, baby Jesus and all the baby saints. Tell me I didn't just say that."

Adina began to giggle.

"I told you earlier: Solo looks like my mother."

Tc'aarlat tried to remain serious, but his shoulders were soon shaking with barely suppressed chuckling.

"It was an easy mistake to make, Okay?!"

Adina tossed her head back and began to laugh loud and hard. Tc'aarlat gave up any pretense not to be enjoying the situation and laughed along.

From her perch, Mist cried chee chee repeatedly in what sounded very much like a human expression of amusement.

Even Solo appeared to be tittering.

Jack felt his cheeks burn. "Look, I didn't mean..."

But, it was no good. He had to admit to appreciating the comical turn of events and, before long, he was joining in with the laughter.

"I haven't done anything like that since the ninth grade, when I accidentally called the school principal 'Granddad'!" Jack sniggered. "He was only in his 40s, and wasn't impressed."

"You think that's bad," said Adina, wiping tears from the corners of her eyes. "I once sent a naughty text to an ex-boyfriend after a night out, telling him that I was, er... let's say *thinking* about him and included a snapshot of the action. The only problem was, I was so drunk I accidentally sent it to someone in my contact list with the same name. *His dad*!"

Tc'aarlat's mandibles shot wide open in surprise. "No!"

Adina nodded, covering her face with her hands as she recalled the embarrassing memory. "Yep. And he replied to me, too!"

This time, it was Jack's turn to look shocked. "How the hell did you get out of that?"

"I didn't," replied Adina with a smirk. "He was cool about it, although I did delete both of them from my contact list after that."

Once again, the ship's bridge echoed with the sound of laughter - just as the image on the screens changed, and Nathan appeared from his office.

"Sounds like you guys are getting along," he commented with a smile.

"You could say that," said Jack. "Although, that could be because Tc'aarlat and I have been around a lot longer than our new navigator here. Apparently, she has a thing for older men."

A pen bounced off the side of Jack's head.

"Hey! You're making me sound like some sort of grave robber!"

"Maybe that could be our team name," Tc'aarlat suggested. "*Adina and the Coffin Dodgers.*"

This kicked off another round of helpless laughter among the trio.

Nathan waited patiently for the merriment to die down. "My apologies for having to change the subject to the task at hand, but our scanners show you are approaching the first of your two Gates, and it will be much easier to discuss your mission while we are all in the same sector of space."

Adina clicked a link on her tablet that brought up a star chart. "Where we're going is that far away?"

"You'll be heading through the Ord Gate, and into the Ordon Nebula," Nathan explained. "A vast cloud of gas and dust from which stars and planets are still in the process of forming."

"Doesn't exactly sound hospitable," said Jake.

"Parts of it aren't too bad," said Nathan. "But there are areas of the Ordon Nebula I wouldn't wish my worst enemies to visit."

"Like the Ordanian Hub," Tc'aarlat put in.

Jack turned to him. "You've heard of this place?"

Tc'aarlat nodded. "Everyone who's ever been involved in the less than legal aspects of life has. Like Nathan says, it's not exactly a vacation spot."

Nathan uploaded a graphic to the ship's view screens, depicting a small solar system. "There are five planets in the Ordanian Hub, all orbiting a dark energy star," he said, zooming in to the center of the image. "Each one is home to some breed of criminal. Thieves, murderers, people traffickers - you'll find them all here, and much more besides."

Tc'aarlat's mandibles tapped together. "The people who hang out there make the Skaine look like schoolgirls."

"And that's where you're sending us on our first mission?" demanded Adina.

"Thankfully, no," Nathan replied, sliding a handful of papers out from a manila folder on his desk. "You're headed to Alma Nine, a small planet on the outskirts of the nebula and home to an alien species from a world called Malatia."

The on-screen map moved to focus on a small, blue dot on the far right hand side of the display.

"The Malatians arrived just over ten years ago, terraformed the planet and made it their home."

"Why the move?" asked Jack. "Are the Malatians colonists?"

"Before long, they'll be refugees," answered Nathan. "Their home world is living on borrowed time, destined to be destroyed when the star it orbits goes supernova at some point in the next thousand years. The group living on Alma Nine has established just one of dozens of other world colonies, and they are by far the most successful."

"So, what's the emergency?" queried Tc'aarlat. "Why are you sending us there now. And what, exactly, are we supposed to be delivering?"

Nathan laid out the current political status on Alma Nine, explaining about Tor Val's successful leadership, and how she had reached out to the Etheric Empire shortly before her death in a traffic accident.

"So, she dies right after announcing that she wants to join the Federation?" said Adina. "Sounds like quite a coincidence."

"Exactly our thinking," said Nathan. "That's why you guys are headed there. You're carrying several miles worth of crowd control barriers; railings to line the route of Tor Val's funeral procession through the streets of Taron City, the colony's capital."

"All well and good," commented Jack, "but that doesn't explain how we can get close enough to the big players to find out what's been going on behind the scenes. Not everyone treats their delivery crews the way you do."

"We've already thought of that," said Nathan as a printer embedded in the bridge's control desk began to produce the first of three postcard sized pieces of paper. "You are also the official delegation from the Etheric Empire, there to pay your respects to Tor Val and her grieving subjects. Solo should be printing out your invitations now."

Jack took the invitations and passed one each to Tc'aarlat and Adina.

"Hang on," said Adina, scanning the ornate script providing details of the time and location for the service, "we're going to a funeral? I wish you'd told me that before I started packing. The only black dress I have with me is more suited to a night out than a somber memorial."

"That's just as well," smiled Nathan. "The Malatian color for mourning is actually purple."

Adina threw her hands up. "Well, that's me out, then. I don't own anything purple - aside from an old pair of sweat pants I wore when I painted my apartment."

"She's got a point, Nathan," Jack said. "I can't say my wardrobe boasts any purple clothing, either. We're not exactly going to look respectful."

"Relax," insisted Nathan. "We've got you covered. You'll find suitable outfits in your size waiting in the storage compartment of *The Pegasus*."

"That sweet space cruiser?" said Tc'aarlat, excitedly. "We get to turn up in that baby? We'll be the envy of everyone there."

"We're going to a funeral, Tc'aarlat," Adina reminded him. "Not a movie premiere!"

Tc'aarlat utilized his well-practiced shrug once again. "It's all about image at these events. We're the official representatives of the Etheric Empire - the most powerful alliance in this part of the universe. We have to look the part."

Jack frowned. "Is this the same Etheric Empire you said was full of, what was it now... shit for brains piss-gargling hobo-huggers?"

The Yollin's mandibles froze wide open as his eyes flicked up to Nathan's face on the view screen. "Hahahaha-ha!" he exclaimed loudly. "Nice one, Jack. Good to see the ass-kicking you got at the hands of that werewolf hasn't affected your sense of humor!"

Nathan's video feed slid to one side of the screen allowing Solo to fill the other half. "I'm so sorry to inter-rupt your briefing, but I wanted to let you know that we've arrived at the first Gate."

"I'll leave you to it," said Nathan, sliding his paperwork back inside the folder and setting it aside. "Contact me when you arrive at Alma Nine, and we'll discuss the finer details of your mission from there."

The video link ended and the view of Nathan's office disappeared, revealing the team's first view of the Gate they were about to pass through. The gold and green metallic hoop seemed to simply hang in space out in front of them.

"Whoa!" cried Adina. "They're much more impressive up close than the ones I tried to get this ship through in the simulations."

Jack turned, his brow furrowing. "Tried?"

Adina smiled, winningly. "Tried, and succeeded!" she

beamed, before spinning to face her own control panel and studying the readouts.

"Can I please ask you all to secure your seatbelts and safety harnesses without delay," said Solo.

Jack looked down, surprised to see his new seat had a pristine grey seatbelt attached. "Is that really necessary?" he asked.

Solo scowled. "Yes, Jack, it is. You will find that I insist on safety first, and I will not take this ship any further until you are all securely fastened into your chairs."

Tc'aarlat threw Jack a look. "What the fu-?"

"I mean it!" Solo assured them. "While you are on board this vessel, you are *my* responsibility. And it is a responsibility I intend to take very seriously. Now, fasten your seatbelts."

"It's just like dealing with my mum," said Jack with a sigh. "Come on, we'd better do as she says or we'll be here all day."

Solo watched as the trio clicked and clunked their safety belts and harnesses into place. Mist flew down from the camera high in the corner and took her usual place on Tc'aarlat's shoulder.

"OK," said Jack. "*Now* can we pass through the Gate and continue with our important mission?"

"Of course, Captain Marber," replied Solo with a sweet smile. "Hold on tightly, everyone. Here we go..."

15

Alma Nine, Taron City, Government Building, Front Steps

Bay Don pulled her coat tightly around herself and hurried down the steps of the government building, taking care not to slip in the six inches of snow that had amassed over the past 12 hours.

The afternoon's weather report had promised clear skies, sunshine, and just enough rain to keep local gardeners satisfied.

That clearly wasn't how it had turned out.

Dipping her head in an attempt to stop the icy wind from biting her face, Bay Don turned towards the blizzard and stamped purposely along the now pure white street.

Funeral arrangements for her boss - and friend - Tor Val were taking up the majority of her time now. The day to day affairs of government seemed to have faded into the background, like distant music played at a gathering where introductions and polite conversation were the order of the day.

Where once Bay Don's desk had been home to an endless stream of urgent messages and documents requiring the President's signature, there were now letters of condolence, requests for statements and passive aggressive cards stealthily demanding to know why certain members of society were not among the numbers invited to the impending state funeral.

Yet, somehow, Tor Val's assistant found the strength to push them all aside, instead focusing the majority of her energy on ensuring the well-being of Tor Val's two distraught daughters.

Both Mas Val and Ran Val now clung to their mother's trusted employee, trusting in her ability to keep both the prying press and well-intentioned citizens at bay while they tried to grieve.

Bay Don remained acutely aware that both girls had been through all of this before, when their father had died so valiantly, and publicly, during the colonists' journey to what they hoped and prayed would be a new home, and a fresh start.

Now, the girls had no-one left to turn to. No-one, that was, except for Bay-Don herself.

Arriving at the entrance of the weather control center, Bay Don stomped the snow from her boots, then swung open the large glass door and stepped into the heated lobby. A wave of warmth swept over her, and she quickly pulled down the zipper on her padded coat as she approached the guard.

"Bay Don to see Yan Mil," she said, accepting a tablet from the uniformed sentry and pressing her thumb to the fingerprint scanner on the screen. Instantly, her name and photograph appeared, confirming her identity and allowing her access to the laboratories hidden deep below ground on the lower floors of the facility.

The guard grunted what may have been a welcome as Bay Don made for the bank of elevators at the rear of the entrance hall. She pressed a button, glancing back at the wild, unpredicted weather outside the building's doors while she waited for the car to arrive.

She had tried to call the weather control laboratories on many occasions for the past two days, but had constantly received a busy signal. Although it wasn't technically her job to keep tabs on what the scientists were doing, the thought of Tor Val's funeral taking place in the midst of a storm was extremely upsetting.

It was time to find out exactly what was going on.

The elevator arrived, and Bay Don stepped inside, pressing the appropriate button for the main labs. As she was carried deep into the building's lower levels, she pulled back the hood of her coat and ran her hand across the short layer of now damp hair on her head.

She'd only ever seen snow from a distance before, on the peaks of distant mountains far to the east of Taron City. Dangerous increases in temperature meant her home world of Malatia hadn't seen snow for several generations by the time she was born. As a result, she had grown up believing snow to be a romantic, almost magical substance.

As she stood in the warmth of the elevator simultaneously shivering and steaming, she realized that she had very quickly come to change her mind.

Snow was shit. Cold, wet shit. And, the sooner the

weather control system was up and working again, the better.

With a ding, the doors slid open and Bay Don took a step forward to alight from the car, then froze.

The entire laboratory was in a state of utter chaos.

ICS Fortitude, Bridge

"Excuse me, Captain Marber..." Solo's voice rang out as her image appeared on the view screen. "My apologies for interrupting while you are reading."

Jack looked up from his tablet where he had been studying the political history of Malatia, and how many of the planet's partisan prejudices had followed the world's colonists to their new home on Alma Nine. He placed the tablet aside and stretched.

"Interrupt away, Solo, this stuff's about as exciting as navel lint. And, I've already told you, please just call me Jack.

"If you insist, Jack" Solo replied, "although I do believe the use of your official title more appropriate when discussing mission elements."

"Mission elements?" asked Adina, looking up from the same historical document on her own tablet.

"Yes," confirmed Solo. "We are now in the final stages of our approach to the planet of Alma Nine, and have been hailed by their docking computer, requesting confirmation of our identity. Am I free to respond?"

"Yes, of course," Jack assured the E.I. "There's no need to check with me for things like that. I more than trust you to handle it."

"Thank you, Jack," said Solo with a smile. "I appreciate your confidence in my abilities. I merely wondered if telling them you were a covert team of espionage agents posing as the crew of a cargo freighter may undermine what you're trying to achieve. But, if you'd prefer honesty, I'm happy to-"

"No!" cried Jack, jumping to his feet. "Don't tell them that bit. Just the name of the ship, and that we're here to deliver their railings."

"And that we're the official representatives of the Etheric Empire for the president's funeral," Adina reminded him.

"Yes, that too."

Solo's image nodded slightly. "Yes, of course. I shall remain discrete in all further communications."

With that, the screens returned to show the vast multi-colored clouds of dust and raw elements the *ICS Fortitude* had been traveling through ever since passing the second Gate three hours previously.

Now, barely visible among the space dust, a small grey and green planet could just about be seen, growing larger with each passing minute.

Glancing up at the screen, Jack crossed to Adina and leaned down to whisper in her ear, "You're a bit of a computer boffin, right?"

Adina's brow furrowed. "I wouldn't say *boffin* exactly, but I know a bit about tech systems, yes."

"You don't suppose something went wrong with Solo, do you?" Jack continued. "It's just that she doesn't seem to be, how can I put this... fully installed."

Adina smirked. "She's certainly one of the more quirky

pieces of Entity Intelligence software I've encountered," she admitted. "If you like, I'll try to take a peek at her core data without her knowing."

"Without who knowing what?" asked a voice.

Jack and Adina turned to find Tc'aarlat standing behind them. He had excused himself from the bridge around thirty minutes earlier, and had now returned dressed a little differently.

"What in the name of all things holy are you wearing?" demanded Jack.

Tc'aarlat grabbed the edge of the floor-length purple cape he had tied around his neck and twirled on the spot, allowing the soft, silky material to billow out impressively.

"What, this old thing?" he grinned, mandibles quivering. "It's just something I threw on to lounge around in."

Adina chuckled. "It's certainly... flamboyant," she commented.

"And, it matches these," said Tc'aarlat excitedly. He tossed the cape back from his shoulder to reveal a purple shoulder pad, made from the same leather-looking material as the new cuffs fastened around his wrists.

"Go on, be honest... How do I look?"

Jack looked the ensemble up and down. "Like an extra from a bad pirate movie," he grinned. "All you need is the parrot."

Tc'aarlat glanced over his shoulder and whistled. A few seconds later, Mist flew onto the bridge and landed on her master's shoulder.

"You were saying..."

"Just a shame she clashes with the purple," said Adina.

"Got it covered," Tc'aarlat replied. He whistled again,

and Mist stood perfectly still for a moment, allowing the burgundy coloring of her feathers to morph into the exact shade of purple of the Yollin's outfit.

"Purple!" cried Jack as the realization hit him. "That's what you've been given to wear for Tor Val's funeral."

"Exactly," Tc'aarlat confirmed. "I've hung both your outfits on your cabin doors, if you want to-"

Suddenly, the ship plunged down a short distance, almost as though they had fallen into some kind of hole. A second later, the movement happened again, and the bridge began to shake and judder.

To Jack, it felt like the turbulence he had often experienced while flying on operations with his Marine platoon.

Tc'aarlat stumbled back hard against the wall, Mist crying out as he fell.

Jack spun, clutching the back of his chair. "Solo! Urgent update!"

Solo's face reappeared, briefly blocking the view of Alma Nine below. "I'm studying the data now, Captain," she said, "or would you prefer me to call you Jack in situations such as this?"

"I don't care what you call me!" Jack roared. "Just tell me what the fuck is going on!"

"Certainly Captain," responded Solo calmly. Her face faded from the screen as she continued to speak, allowing the three crew members a clear view of the planet below as it rushed towards them.

"Basically, we're crashing."

Alma Nine, Taron City, North West Suburb

It took Pol Tod almost ten minutes to realize her hands were shaking.

She had vaguely been aware that she was gripping the steering wheel much more tightly than she usually did, and she was conscious that she was purposefully driving below the sign-posted speed limit. But the tremors coursing down her arms and through her fingers came as a surprise.

Checking there wasn't another vehicle behind her, Pol Tod flicked on her blinker and pulled over to the side of the road. Shifting into 'park', she held up her hands and watched them trembling for a few seconds.

Then, without warning, she burst into tears.

In eleven years as a first responder, no emergency had ever affected her as the one she had attended yesterday evening. The things she had seen would never leave her memory. And, if the bad dreams she had suffered the night before were anything to go by, she was destined to experience savage nightmares for a long, long time to come.

Reaching into her purse, Pol Tod grabbed a handful of tissues and did her best to bring her sobs under control. She angled the rearview mirror to study her reflection, but quickly wished she hadn't.

Her bloodshot eyes were circled with dark rings - the result of working a typical shift after an entirely sleepless night.

The headlights of an approaching car dazzled her, and she reached up to move the mirror back to its usual position. A few seconds later, the car passed by - and Pol Tod was crying all over again.

The vehicle now shrinking into the distance was a limousine - just like the one she'd been called to last night.

Except that this one wasn't a mangled mess of twisted metal and body parts.

Pol Tod had been the first paramedic on the scene, less than eight minutes after the president's car had veered off the highway and slammed into the side of a high school building.

She'd noticed there didn't appear to be any skid marks or other signs the car had been braking when it plowed through the crash barrier and left the road, but she pushed the detail from her mind as she'd scrambled down the shallow verge to reach the battered vehicle, hoping the occupants had somehow survived the disastrous impact.

It was quickly clear that neither of them had.

The driver - a large man in a chauffeur's uniform - had been thrown through the windshield, the razor-sharp metal of the buckled hood almost completely decapitating him before the school wall had brought the vehicle to a sudden and violent stop.

Determining there was nothing she could do to help him, Pol Tod had turned her attention to the passenger in the back seat. Whether down to the dim light of the evening, the fact that the woman was covered in blood, or a combination of the two, she hadn't recognized Tor Val as she fought to get through the crumpled rear door to reach the victim.

Then, as she had been pulling to open the door a few inches wider, the woman had opened her eyes and groaned.

Quickly doubling her efforts, Pol Tod had managed to move the door just wide enough to squeeze through the narrow gap she had created and climb inside.

"It's OK," she had said as soothingly as possible. "I'm here to help. There's an ambulance on the way."

The injured woman had murmured something Pol Tod hadn't been able to understand at the time, but would later work out were the names of Tor Val's two daughters. Then she had closed her eyes once more.

Never to open them again.

Pol Tod was still performing CPR when one of the recently arrived ambulance crew had taken hold of her bloodied hands and gently pulled them away from Tor Val's motionless chest.

"It's too late," the man had whispered. "She's gone."

Later, at the hospital, Pol Tod had recounted the events of the evening over and over to law enforcement officers before pushing her way through the hordes of shouting paparazzi gathered outside and setting off for the remaining few hours of her shift.

Tor Val was dead, and nothing would ever be the same again.

16

Alma Nine, Taron City, Weather Control Center, Main Laboratory

Lab assistants ran around the room like farm animals fleeing a hungry, ax-wielding butcher.

Every computer screen flashed with urgent warnings of torrential rain, gale-force storms, icy snow blizzards or potentially lethal hail. A bank of over-heated printers spewed out lengthy paper chains of data, the bulk of which simply gathered in piles on the floor, unnoticed and unread.

And, completing the pandemonium, radio and television channels barked hastily prepared and completely conflicting soundbites of advice on how to protect yourself and your loved ones against this unexpected onslaught of atrocious weather.

"Excuse me..."

Bay Don stood in front of the closing elevator doors and tried to attract the attention of one of the distracted lab technicians. If the woman had heard her, she gave no indication and simply dashed past her, reading from a tablet and wearing an expression of pure dread.

"EXCUSE ME!"

Raising her voice, she reached out and grabbed the arm of the next stampeding scientist to stray in her direction. She read his name tag as he slowed and turned to face her.

"Jon Rey," she said, maintaining her grip on his arm in case he showed any desire to continue scurrying about the room in a protracted panic. "Please can you tell me what's happening with the weather?"

Jon Rey stared at her as if she had just asked him to juggle handfuls of sand underwater. "Can't you tell?" he questioned. "It's gone crazy!"

"I can see that," replied Bay Don, "and feel it, as well. What I mean is, why isn't the weather under control?"

"What? Who *are* you, and why are you down here?"

Bay Don pulled aside the front of her coat, revealing her official government pass, dangling from a lanyard around her neck. "I am, or rather *was*, Tor Val's personal assistant," she said, flatly. "And I really need to know what's going on."

Jon Rey glanced down at her hand, causing her to remove it from his arm. Despite her concerns, the lab assistant didn't take her release as an excuse to immediately break for freedom. "We're desperately trying to figure that out," he admitted. "No-one really knows."

Bay Don's eyes flicked around the room, looking from person to person. "Where's Yan Mil?" she demanded. "Surely he must be able to explain why things have gotten so bad all of a sudden."

For the first time since they had begun their frantic conversation, Jon Rey's eyes softened. "You don't know."

It was a statement more than a question.

"Know what?" asked Bay Don.

Turning to look around the laboratory himself, Jon Rey spotted the person he was looking for and called out, "Zeb Lok, I need you for a moment."

Glancing up from a sheaf of papers at least as thick as the manuscript for a high fantasy trilogy of novels, Zeb Lok's eyes widened in surprise.

"Bay Don!" he cried, quickly striding over to shake her hand. "No-one told me you had an appointment."

"I don't," Bay Don replied. "I didn't know I was coming myself until I set off. I've been busy with the committee arranging Tor Val's funeral."

"You're on the funeral council?"

"Sadly no," said Bay Don. "Although they are letting me sit in to confirm any details they're unaware of. Favorite blooms, that kind of thing."

"Ridiculous!" spat Zeb Lok. "You've been her best friend for years. You're more like a sister to her than a secretary."

Bay Don felt her eyes well with tears. She blinked hard in an effort to stop herself from crying - something she had been doing without warning several times a day ever since the accident.

"My relationship with Tor Val is a discussion for another day," she said. "But I need to know that the weather will be back under control in time for her funeral. I can't, no... I *won't* let her final journey through Taron City be marred by climate chaos. It has to be sorted by then."

Zeb Lok and Jon Rey exchanged a glance. "We can't

TOM DUBLIN & MICHAEL ANDERLE

guarantee that," the senior lab assistant admitted. "I'm sorry."

"But, why not?"

"Because we don't know what's gone wrong ourselves!"

"We're trying everything we can to bring the system back under control," Jon Rey explained. "But, without knowing what caused this problem in the first place, we're just shouting into the dark."

"Then, what about Yan Mil?" queried Bay Don. "He designed this system, surely he'll be able to work out what has caused it to malfunction."

The two men shared another look. "This is why I called you over," said Jon Rey. He turned back to Bay Don. "Excuse me, I must return to work."

Zeb Lok waited until Jon Rey had left, then he took Bay Don aside, lowering his voice. "Yan Mil can't be here at the moment," he said softly. "He's upstairs, in his apartment."

"Upstairs?" questioned Bay Don. "But wh-"

"His wife is dead."

Bay Don's hand shot up to her mouth. "Vix Mil?"

Zeb Lok nodded. "I'm afraid so."

"Wh... What happened?"

"She was mugged," replied Zeb Lok. "Heading home from the lab after paying a visit to Yan Mil. Some guy with a knife jumped her and stole her purse. The medics say she might have survived if she had received prompt treatment, but she wasn't found for several hours. She bled out."

Now tears did fall down Bay Don's cheeks. "Why didn't anyone tell me?"

Zeb Lok rested a hand on her shoulder. "It happened the evening of Tor Val's accident. We figured you'd had enough bad news for one day." He gestured around the room. "Then all this shit started, and I guess no-one thought to bring you up to date. I'm sorry."

"I'm not blaming you," said Bay Don, pulling a handkerchief from her coat pocket and using it to dry her eyes. "How is Yan Mil?"

"That's just it," replied Zeb Lok. "We don't know. He locked himself in the apartment he occasionally uses when he works late, and hasn't come out. We've tried calling, knocking on the door, video calls. He just asks us to leave him alone."

Bay Don sighed. "I understand that, but he can't-"

WUMPH!

Everyone in the room clamped their hands over their ears as the air around them seemed to solidify for a second. Then, as if pressed down upon by some invisible hands, they began to fall to the ground.

Screams and cries for help added to the already oppressive levels of noise flooding the room.

Bay Don and Zeb Lok hit the floor at the same moment.

Bay Don tried to force herself up with her hands, but found she couldn't move. It was as if someone was standing on her back, forcing her down.

"Wass... ging on...?" she murmured, suddenly scared that she was unable to even speak properly, so great was the pressure bearing down on her.

"Ah... dunno..." answered Zeb Lok, trying hard to re-angle his head so he could look around the rest of the laboratory. But, he couldn't move either - and all the other people seemed to be suffering in exactly the same way.

All he could see was the bank of television screens upon which the rolling news channels were being broadcast. Television screens which now erupted with plumes of electrical sparks as they collapsed in on themselves.

Shards of glass and pieces of plastic rained down on the scientists lying beneath the sets. The terrified lab techs tried to slide themselves away from danger but, like everyone else, were completely unable to move.

Around the rest of the room, computers imploded, table legs buckled, and glass containers shattered. Pipes burst, spraying jets of water across the trapped employees.

Within seconds, the room began to flood, adding to the sense of panic. There may have only been a few inches of water on the ground but, now that everyone was being pressed to the floor and unable to even lift their heads, that's all that would be needed to cause them to drown.

Bay Don struggled to inch her fingers closer to her pocket in an attempt to reach her communicator. If she could just manage to press the emergency call button, she might be able to summon help.

Just then the ceiling collapsed.

Alma Nine, Taron City, Channel Three News, Dressing Room 1

Shards of glass rained down as the dressing room's mirror - and all the lightbulbs surrounding it - exploded.

Although Cal Car had no idea at all what was happening, he was thankful that whatever invisible force was pressing him hard against the floor had knocked him off his chair face down.

The sharp pieces of glass could embed themselves in the back of his head and neck with his blessing, so long as none of them attempted the lacerate his well-known face.

His passport to his TV career.

Cal Car's mentor - a much-loved, experienced news anchor he'd had the good fortune to work under back on Malatia - had paid the ultimate price as a result of superficial damage to his face.

As an attempt to reverse the natural signs of aging, the anchor had opted to secretly undergo cosmetic surgery, paying well above the going rate to find a doctor he could trust not to go running to the press.

Following a supposed vacation, the anchor had returned to air with skin so taut and blemish-free he could barely form any facial expression besides the now constant look of mild surprise.

As viewing figures slumped, the anchor became a figure of ridicule on social media sites with satirists and members of the general public alike poking fun at his new, static appearance.

The more the anchor denied he'd been under the knife, the faster new cruelly-edited pictures of him flashed from screen to screen as people shared the fake photographs with their friends and family.

It wasn't long before the news channel he had worked at for decades decided to let him go, citing the anchor's failing health as the reason for replacing him with a younger, more flexibly-faced newscaster.

The truth, however, was that the man was now a laughing stock. And the handful of loyal viewers who refused to join in with the mockery said they missed his

former, wiser face. The face of experience. The face they knew they could trust.

Cal Car had lost contact with his former inspiration when he boarded the spaceship *Dessia*, determined to become a popular television personality in the Malatian's newest colony.

The last he'd heard, the former anchor was eking out a meagre living by writing erotic novellas about a brilliant journalism professor and his harem of willing, nubile pupils.

As much as Cal Car suspected he would be able to pen any number of similar pieces of smut, he had no desire to test out the theory. And so, as the ceiling above him creaked and groaned threatening to give way, he kept his priceless face pressed into the dressing room's aged carpet.

Alma Nine, Taron City, Central Hospital, ER

Pol Tod tried her hardest to ignore the screams coming from all around the emergency room as she dragged herself, inch by inch, under the bed of the patient she had just been treating.

The man on the trolley above her was balding, obese, and had been cursing loudly as she had tried to explain that his years of heavy drinking and eating nothing but fast food had been major factors in this, his third heart attack.

She had been futilely extolling the virtues of a healthy diet and regular exercise when some overwhelming force had pushed her to the floor.

Her patient had cried out in pain at first, but his cater-wauling had swiftly faded away until, as far as she could tell with the deafening cacophony from all around the department, he finally fell silent.

Pol Tod managed to pull herself beneath the metal frame of the hospital bed. She wasn't 100% certain why she felt the need to take cover, but the sound of smashing glass when whatever this was had first started was accompanied by a dimming of light in the room.

If the large fluorescent tubes fixed to the ceiling where somehow being torn from their fittings and cast down on the people below, she wanted to get out of harm's way.

Of course, her first thought was for the safety of the ER's patients but, as she was unable to get to her feet, she opted to keep herself safe so she would be able to return to providing care if and when whatever was causing this opted to let the bizarre and terrifying situation end.

She fought to keep her panic under control. Ever since the night she had battled to save Tor Val's life, the medic had suffered from regular bouts of uncontrollable anxiety.

She hadn't slept since, hadn't eaten and was suffering with agonizing migraine headaches.

Her work began to suffer.

After discussing negative reports concerning mistakes she had made in the field - the first ever such accusations that had been made against her - her superiors had taken the decision to reassign her to a position in the ER. The move they claimed, was a temporary one and would help ease the unbearable pressure she was clearly working under.

In reality, they wanted Pol Tod somewhere where they could keep a close eye on her.

Concentrating on her breathing, Pol Tod finally felt the

potential panic attack begin to subside. Yes, whatever was happening was scary, but she appeared to be safe and unhurt, despite her inability to move very far.

Just then, the man on the bed began to groan again. He was alive! Pol Tod was making a mental checklist of tests to run on the injured individual when all this was over when, with a screech of breaking metal, the bed frame she was hiding under collapsed.

The full weight of both the bed and its vastly overweight occupant slammed down on top of her.

Pol Tod had endured her last panic attack.

17

ICS Fortitude, Bridge

The ship bucked and pitched like a rodeo steed, the thankfully recently reinforced metal hull screeching as it protested loudly to the sudden, unnatural movements.

And, all the while, Alma Nine grew bigger and bigger ahead.

Jack, Adina and Tc'aarlat gripped their respective consoles tightly in an effort not to be tossed around the bridge like a dried pea inside a referee's favorite whistle.

"What. The. Fuck?!" demanded Jack, trying to make himself heard over the sound of the ear-splitting alarm. "Solo, I'm talking to you!"

The E.I.'s avatar appeared on screen, looking as calm as ever.

"I'm sorry, Captain Marber," she said. "I'm not certain I understand the question. Which element of our current situation are you referring to?"

"ALL OF IT!" yelled Jack, ducking as Mist's water dish was dislodged from its spot to the right of Tc'aarlat's position and flew across the bridge. It hit a metallic storage closet fitted to store ammunition for the group's new collection of weapons and shattered into several pieces.

"Why is the ship behaving like this?" Jack roared.

"I shall be pleased to answer your query," replied Solo, "but first I must ask each of you to return to your seats and fasten your safety belts or harne-"

"SOLO!" all three crew members bellowed together.

The E.I. made a noise that, to the untrained ear, may have sounded like an exasperated sigh. Tc'aarlat made a brief mental note to ask Solo to teach him how to do it.

"The *ICS Fortitude* is currently being struck by a string of what appear to be gravitational waves," Solo explained.

Adina twisted the upper half of her body to look up at the screen, but not daring to release her grip on the navigation console. "What?! That's impossible!"

"I'm afraid I must disagree," countered Solo, "it is an entirely possible situation. If two black holes or two neutron stars were to collide nearby, the result would be the exact phenomenon we are now experiencing."

Tc'aarlat took up the interrogation. "And, have they?"

Solo blinked. "Have they, what?"

"Have two black holes or two neutron stars collided nearby?!"

Solo was silent for a brief moment, then replied: "No, there is no evidence to support that scenario."

"Then it's impossible!" repeated Adina.

Solo faded from view. Now, the entire view screen was filled with the image of the planet below. Continents and coastlines were clearly visible, and getting closer by the second.

"Well, something's causing this," shouted Jack. "And, if we don't figure out a way to- SOLO, SWITCH OFF THAT *GOTT VERDAMMT* ALARM!"

Solo spoke without returning to the screens. "But, then how will you be aware that we are engaged in a potentially dangerous predicament, Captain?"

"WE'LL DO OUR BEST TO REMEMBER! NOW SWITCH OFF THE ALARM BEFORE I FIND WHICH-EVER ONE OF YOUR CIRCUIT BOARDS IS CONTROLLING IT AND BLAST IT INTO OBLIVION!"

The Captain turned back to his colleagues. "IF WE DON'T-"

The alarm quickly silenced, leaving just the groans and screeches of the ship itself to contend with.

"If we don't find a way to deal with this, our career as spies is going to be very short indeed!"

"Anything in mind?" questioned Tc'aarlat "Before that mind ends up as little more than a reddish smear on the planet's surface, that is."

"I have," announced Adina. "It's risky, but it's the only thing I can think of."

"Go for it," Jack responded.

Adina took a quick, calming breath then called out. "Solo, on my command, please rotate the ship 90 degrees to starboard."

"Yes, Adina," the E.I. responded.

Tc'aarlat frowned. "That's it?!" he barked. "Your risky idea is to make a quarter turn to the right?!"

Adina nodded. "Whatever's causing these gravitational waves, we're flying straight into them. And they're pounding us. If Nathan's team hadn't reinforced the ship's structure, we'd have been torn apart by now."

Tc'aarlat's mandibles spread wide. "So, what will-"

"Let her speak!" Jack commanded.

"I know that," responded Tc'aarlat. "I just think it's a clear case of too many cocks spoil the broth!"

Jack shook his head, sighing. "Go on, Adina..."

"Obviously, I'm guessing..." Adina continued.

Tc'aarlat opened his mouth to comment, but the warning look he received from Jack made him reconsider.

"...But if we can somehow work *with* the movement of the waves, we might be able to harness the energy they're producing and use that to our advantage to help us land safely."

Despite the situation, Jack found himself smiling. "You're suggesting we *surf* down to the planet's surface?"

Adina grinned. "Essentially, yes."

Jack shook his head slightly. "That's the most utterly insane maneuver I've ever heard anyone suggest, let alone attempt. But, we're about to come to a very sudden and extremely violent stop, and it's the only idea we've got."

He winked to Adina. "Do it!"

Tc'aarlat increased his grip on his console and screwed his eyes closed. "Oh, shit!"

"OK, Solo..." began Adina. "Begin the turn... now!"

The ship began to shudder even more as the barely audible bow port side thrusters fired. On the screens, the view of the fast-approaching planet shifted slightly to the left.

"I think now's a good time to take Solo's advice about the safety belts," Jack shouted as he reached back for his newly-fitted chair, strangely disappointed that he was only going to enjoy it for what was promising to be a particularly short trip.

Beside him, Tc'aarlat strapped himself into the co-pilot's seat - once he'd swept the long, purple cloak aside and prevented it from blocking access to the strong steel buckles.

Reaching up, he lifted Mist from his shoulder and held her firmly to his chest. "It's OK, girl," he soothed to the trembling bird. "Everything's going to be alright."

SQUAWWW!

Tc'aarlat scowled down at her. "Yeah? Well, what was I supposed to tell you? The truth?!"

Adina fought to reach for the harness fitted to the back of her own chair, and clicked the cold, metal clip in place. Turning to watch the coastline of whichever area of land was below them give way to a vast blue ocean edged with pure white spray, she allowed her thoughts to wander back to her Uncle Yousuf in his room at the care home.

If she were to die now, would the care home staff inform him, or decide it would be best for the old man simply to quietly forget the niece he had brought up like a daughter of his own?

Whichever choice they made, she smiled as she pictured him in her mind's eye. Here, he was young again, and the two of them were racing across the lush, green park at the center of the base station that was the only home either of them had ever known.

And they were laughing.

If this was to be her last ever thought, it was a good one.

Behind the bridge, the piercing report of metal

colliding with metal suggested the strengthened frame of the ship was beginning to fail.

"I hope *The Pegasus* is OK," Tc'aarlat said to no-one in particular.

Jack felt himself pinned back in his seat as the level of g-force began to climb. The 90 degree turn was almost complete, and there had been no let up from the wild bucking and pitching of the ship.

He pushed down hard with his legs, forcing his chair to turn enough for him to be able to see his two friends - one old, one new - and even that bastard bird.

His chair squeaked as it twisted round.

For fuck's sake!

"You did well, Adina," he said with a smile. "It was a strong idea, and it's not your fault that-"

Suddenly, everything fell still and silent.

The trio froze, each mentally checking that they hadn't just slammed into the surface of the planet and that this wasn't the split-second of calm before they were crushed and mangled beyond recognition.

"Holy Bistok shit!" hissed Tc'aarlat. "It's working!"

Alma Nine, Taron City, Weather Control Center, Main Laboratory

It had taken almost all of her strength, but Bay Don had finally managed to drag herself out from underneath the fallen plaster and debris and underneath the nearest work surface.

The metal legs holding the tabletop in place were bent and buckled, but the worktop seemed to be able to withstand whatever was causing these sudden bursts of pressure. Bursts which seemed to be rising and falling in severity, almost as if they were waves.

Something dripped into Bay Don's left eye, causing it to sting. Once again working hard against the intense downward force, Bay Don forced her hand up to wipe her face, concerned to find her fingers now coated with blood. She must have a cut on her forehead somewhere, unsurprising considering the carnage all around her.

Some of the other people scattered about the laboratory floor were in a considerably worse state. Many were groaning and crying out in pain as they lay beneath mounds of debris, twisted metal beams, and even office furniture which had until now been used on the floor above.

Worse, a couple of the scientists were silent, and making no attempt to move or free themselves from where they were trapped. Bay Don could only hope that they had merely been knocked unconscious by debris as the ceiling had collapsed.

She heard a muffled groan and re-angled her head to see Jon Rey lying on his back in front of the dented elevator doors. His right arm was twisted at an awkward angle and Bay Don could tell, even from a distance, that it was probably broken in at least two places.

Gripping one of the table's legs, she began to haul herself over towards him, when another of the acute waves of pressure hit the lab. Cries of pain and discomfort sounded from several of the injured assistants, and a shower of dust rained down from what remained of the damaged ceiling.

Bay Don felt the air around her grow heavier, pushing down on her spine and pressing her cheek hard against the cold, cracked tiles that made up the floor.

The wave lasted around 7 minutes, after which the pressure eased a little, but not completely. Finally, Bay Don was able to drag herself over to Jon Rey. The scientist was floating in and out of consciousness, thanks in part to the excruciating stabs of pain emanating from his arm but also due to - Bay Don retched as she caught sight of the injury - the broken test tube embedded in Jon Rey's throat.

Working hard to raise her hand, Bay Don's trembling fingers reached out to pull the jagged glass container free from Jon Rey's blood-soaked skin, but hesitated, wondering if removing the fragment would cause the wound to bleed further.

Jon Rey shifted slightly, a gurgling sound accompanying the stream of bloodied bubbles running from his mouth and down the side of his face to spatter on the floor beside him.

Bay Don had to make a decision one way or the other, knowing that the wrong choice could prove fatal for the scientist. Without the ability to lift her head any higher and study the lesion, whatever she did would be the result of little more than guess work.

More scarlet saliva bubbled from between Jon Rey's lips. Bay Don screwed her eyes closed and screamed inwardly. *Come on!* she ordered herself. *Do something. Anything!*

Opening her eyes again, she gripped the rim of the broken test tube and yanked it free from Jon Rey's throat.

. . .

ICS Fortitude, **Bridge**

"You beauty!" yelled Tc'aarlat, lifting Adina and spinning her around. "You did it!"

Adina blushed, returning to her seat. Solo had chastised the trio when they had decided to release their safety belts but they had chosen to ignore her protestations.

"How did you know that would work?"

Adina shrugged. "Honestly? I didn't. But, before we left, I was working on a magnetic force field addition to the armor the Queen's Bitches and Guardians wear into battle. This situation reminded me of how I eventually got that to work."

"We're very grateful," said Jack, typing furiously onto the screen of his tablet. "But that still doesn't tell us exactly what this situation is. I can't find any reference in the history documents Nathan gave us to suggest this is some kind of natural phenomenon on this planet."

He glanced briefly up at the screens. The ground below them, now easily identifiable as a major city covered with a blanket of crisp, white snow, was still rushing towards them. But their descent was now more controlled than before.

"Solo, any idea what caused this yet?"

Solo's face faded into view. "No."

Jack looked back up at the screen and noticed the avatar wasn't meeting his gaze. "Are you... Are you sulking because we took off our seatbelts?"

The E.I. turned her digitized head further to the side. "That would be a human reaction, Captain. As you are aware, I am *not* human and, as such, have neither the ability to sulk, nor the authority to tell you what to do. Even if it is merely a suggestion for your safety."

Jack puffed out his cheeks. "Put your safety belts back on, guys," he said flatly.

"What?" cried Tc'aarlat, "but she said-"

"Just do it!"

Grumbling, Tc'aarlat returned to his seat and worked at finding the clasp of his seatbelt underneath the heavy material of his cape once more.

CLICK!

"There!" he said, pulling at the twin straps that crossed his chest. "Now are you satisfied?"

Solo looked from Jack to Tc'aarlat, then on to Adina. Finally, she smiled. "Perfectly," she responded. "And to answer your question, Jack - I'm afraid I have been unable to ascertain a reason for these sudden gravitational waves.

"However, I have discovered they are not restricted to here in the planet's upper atmosphere. The effects are also being felt at ground level and, from what I can tell from news reports and emergency communications, causing a considerable amount of destruction."

Jack looked grave. "Any report of casualties?"

"Several, I'm afraid," replied Solo. "Would you like me to list them all for you?"

"That won't be necessary," said Jack. "Just get us down there safely, and we'll do what we can to help once we've landed."

"Of course."

Solo vanished, leaving the three crew members with their own thoughts.

"We need to find out what's behind this," commented Jack, "and, if at all possible, stop it from happening again."

"Especially as there are likely to be scores of foreign dignitaries headed this way for the president's funeral," Adina pointed out.

"I hadn't thought of that," admitted Tc'aarlat. "We won't be the only ones representing their home world or civilization at this funeral. There's likely to be all manner of important types there."

Jack looked serious as an unexpected burst of turbulence reminded them they had only just managed to escape the potentially deadly effects of the gravitational waves, and were now using the phenomenon in order to reach the ground and land safely.

"That is if they make it this far."

18

Alma Nine, Taron City, Weather Control Center, Main Laboratory

It took the medical team around 15 minutes to fight their way down the fractured stairwell and break into the basement labs once the unusual waves of pressure had finally stopped flowing.

In all, the city had been pummeled by these sudden surges in gravity for a little under an hour.

Bay Don sat back against the crumpled metal doors of the now useless elevator while a medic attended to the gash on her forehead. Thankfully, the wound wasn't too deep and, after a couple of stitches, the injury was able to be dressed, freeing the first responder up to help someone else.

She watched as Jon Rey was carried through the shattered doorway on a stretcher, injured but alive. Several evacuations had already been made, with the most badly injured transported to three of Taron City's hospitals - all of which were on high alert following the incident.

That just left the walking wounded, and those who hadn't survived.

As Bay Don climbed shakily to her feet, she glanced over to where three figures lay, unmoving, beneath lilac-colored sheets. Whatever had been the cause of the escalation in gravity had claimed its first victims.

And word was coming in that at least twenty more people had succumbed to the attack - if that was even the right word to use for what had happened - with hundreds of walking wounded.

On the opposite side of the laboratory, Zeb Lok clicked off his communicator and crossed to where Bay Don was standing. "I've just spoken to Yan Mil," he said. "He says he isn't hurt, but refuses to leave his apartment, or let doctors inside to check on him."

Bay Don shook her head disbelievingly. "I understand he's upset about his wife, but this is an emergency. Surely the entire building will have to be evacuated now."

"Apparently not," said Zeb Lok. "From what I'm hearing, this was the only floor where any of the structure gave way. Everyone injured on the upper levels were either hurt by flying glass, or by the force of being thrown to the ground.

And we have to continue our research into what has gone so wrong with the weather control systems."

The sound of scraping metal caused the pair to turn and look at where technical engineers were pulling one of the large mainframe computers from its chassis.

"Once we get our backup systems online, that is," Zeb Lok finished.

"I should get back to my office, if it's still standing," said

Bay Don. "We'll need to find a safe place for the funeral committee to reconvene."

"You think Tor Val's Journey Back will still happen?"

"It has to," Bay Don replied. "Everything is in place, and there will be well-wishers arriving from all over the galaxy at any time."

As she turned to leave, Zeb Lok reached out and rested his hand on her arm. "I really think you'd be better off going home to rest," he suggested.

"No," said Bay Don flatly. "Tor Val wouldn't have let something like this stop her from carrying out her duties, and neither will I."

Zeb Lok nodded. The president's personal assistant was, of course, right.

He waited until Bay Don had crunched through the broken glass covering the lab's floor and disappeared into the stairwell before heading back to work himself.

ICS Fortitude, Bridge

Solo brought the *ICS Fortitude* in to land safely within a large vacant lot near to the city center. The cargo ship's vast landing gear sank into the ten inches of snow already covering the ground, while an ongoing blizzard threatened to add to the drifts already built up against each and every wall.

The ship had been less than a mile above the ground when the effect of the gravitational waves had suddenly and unexpectedly disappeared. The *Fortitude* had dropped like a stone for a few moments before the engines had rallied and managed to stabilize the descent.

"This isn't doing my insides any good," groaned Tc'aarlat, clutching at his stomach as the tips of his mandibles ground together.

"Maybe snacking on your bird's pet treats all trip wasn't the best idea," suggested Jack.

"They're tasty!" argued Tc'aarlat, dipping his hand into Mist's bowl and snaffling another handful of maize nuggets. He popped one into his mouth and crunched down on it. "Want one?"

Jack held up his hand, shaking his head. "No thanks," he replied. "I've got a nice bowl of dog food set aside for dinner, and I don't want to ruin my appetite."

Tc'aarlat glanced over towards Adina as she snorted back a laugh. 'Hey, I don't know what kind of food these people will be serving us while we're here," he pointed out. "I don't want to spend the next few days hungry because I don't want to eat some plate of weird alien worms."

Jack blinked. "Alien worms?"

"Well, I don't know, do I?"

"No, you're right," said Jack, turning back to his console. "Best get your fill of pet snacks in while you've got the opportunity."

"Exactly," said Tc'aarlat, missing the point entirely. Tossing the remaining pellets into his mouth, he reached for more, only to receive a hard peck on the back of his wrist from Mist.

"OW!" he cried, pulling his hand away and rubbing at the red mark on his thick skin. "What did you do that for?"

"I don't think she's in the mood for sharing," Adina commented.

Adina peered at the view outside the ship on the view

screens. "I thought this planet had some state-of-the-art weather control system?"

"It does," said Jack. "At least, that's what the intel said."

"Maybe this is how they like things," suggested Tc'aarlat.

"What?" questioned Adina. "A freezing winter blizzard?"

"Maybe," Tc'aarlat replied. "It would certainly go well with all the shattered windows and crumbling brickwork on the buildings."

Jack snatched up his tablet and placed two fingers on the screen, spreading them apart. The image on the main view screens became magnified, focusing on an apartment block at the other side or the lot.

"I think that's new," he said, studying the camera feed. "There's broken glass and chunks of masonry on top of the snowdrifts over there. They haven't been covered up yet."

Adina grabbed a set of headphones and slipped them on. "I can hear sirens outside, too. Lots of them." She flipped a switch, transferring the sound from the external microphones from her headset to the bridge's speakers.

The ship was suddenly filled with a mixture of shouts, screams and what could only be the sirens of a range of emergency vehicles.

"This isn't good," said Jack as Adina muted the sound. "Maybe those gravitational waves hit down here, as well. Solo, are you picking anything up about that?"

"Yes, Captain," Solo responded as she appeared in screen, her head floating in front of the destruction outside. "Several local news stations are reporting on what is being described as a recent surge in gravity, and the private radio channels used by law enforcement officers are being used to dispatch rescue crews to several locations across the city."

"We picked the perfect time to arrive then," said Tc'aarlat.

"Actually, the Malatians aren't yet aware that we have arrived," said Solo. "I followed procedure and hailed several of their space traffic control centers, but received no reply."

"They're likely to have had other things on their minds," said Adina. She opened a metal cabinet near to the rear bridge door and retrieved three thick coats, handing one each to Tc'aarlat and Jack.

"So, what now?" asked Tc'aarlat, untying the cape from around his throat. "Any idea where we're supposed to go? Or do we need to just wander the streets asking who ordered 16 miles of crowd control barriers?"

"Let's hope it doesn't come to that," said Jack, slipping his arms into his coat. "My guess is we should head for wherever Tor Val's office was. There should be somebody there who can put us in touch with Saf Tah."

"The guy who had the president bumped off?" asked Tc'aarlat.

Jack raised a finger to halt the Yollin's train of thought. "We don't know that's the case," he warned. "We have to go into this with an open mind."

"It's obvious," Tc'aarlat countered, pulling on his own coat and zipping it up. "He wants to be in charge, she's pushing ahead in the polls, so the only way he can get the top job is to eliminate the competition. Bish. Bosh. Job done."

"*If* that's what happened, we still need to find evidence to prove it," Jack reminded him.

Tc'aarlat shook his head. "Give me ten minutes with the guy. I can spot a liar a mile away."

"Yeah," said Adina, pulling up the fur-lined hood of her jacket. "You did such a great job with your suicide bomber pal, after all."

"That was different," argued Tc'aarlat.

Adina's eyes narrowed. "*How?*"

Tc'aarlat's mandibles opened and closed for a moment. "Well, he... That is, the... I mean..."

He sighed. "Jack didn't guess he was a terrorist either, and he's supposed to be the one who's trained to find them!"

"What about weapons?" Adina asked. "Should we take them?"

"That might not be a bad idea," replied Jack, turning to one of the bridge's control panels and tapping a code into a built-in keyboard. "But, keep them out of sight."

A drawer slid open, inside which were the three Jean Dukes Specials Nathan had provided for them, set in outlines perfectly cut from a piece of protective foam.

"Make sure you get the right one," he reminded Tc'aarlat and Adina. "They're isomorphic, and will only work if held by the registered owner."

"I was just about to say exactly that!" said Tc'aarlat, surprised. "Great minds drink alike!"

"Come on," said Jack, leading the way off the bridge and along the corridor to the nearest exit. "Solo, have you had any response from the local officials yet?"

"I'm afraid not, Captain. Do you think it will take long to find someone in a position of authority?"

Jack tapped his personal access code into the keypad

beside the starboard side forward exit, and the trio watched as the door hissed open, allowing icy gusts of wind to blow in from outside.

There was a series of clicks as a dozen Malatian soldiers flicked off the safety switches of their weapons, all aimed directly at the three surprised crew members.

Jack slowly raised his hands, and gestured for Tc'aarlat and Adina to do the same.

"No, Solo," he said. "I don't think it will take us very long at all."

Alma Nine, Taron City, Channel Three News, Studio 4a

The report from outside the hospital where Tor Val had been taken after the accident was longer than the channel's usual pieces to camera.

Cal Car sat silently while the junior reporter on screen droned on and on about how the doctors and nurses on duty that night were coping with the emotional fallout from attempting to revive the late president, and how the hospital car park had become a sea of flowers, stuffed toys and handwritten messages of love.

Although he was barely paying the reporter any attention - he had already given up trying to remember her name - he kept his 'listening face' fixed in position in case whoever was mixing the vision up in the gallery decided to flick focus back to him.

He occasionally nodded his head as well, just to be sure he looked as if he was interested in what was being said.

Despite being the very thing he had wished for, broadcasting about a serious, worthy event such as Tor Val's death was proving to be excruciatingly boring. He never believed he'd find himself yearning for the days when the headlines consisted of thinly veiled propaganda from whichever government department's turn it was to appear to be successful.

Bumper crops, beautifully controlled weather, falling crime rates. The constant stream of good news may have lacked any real depth or opportunity for debate, but he was getting so tired of hearing minuscule details about the regularity of brake fluid top-ups, examinations of the surface of the road, possible reasons why Tor Val was heading away from her home and daughters, and whether the driver had drunk one beer or two during his dinner break that day.

It wasn't as if he could avoid the subject when he was away from work, either. Flags of Tor Val's colors flew at half-mast everywhere there was a vertical pole, and frequently where there wasn't. Popular TV and radio shows had been cancelled to make way for even more opinionated 'experts' to blather on about unimportant factors relating to the tragedy. Every front page of every newspaper was given away to the story, with bold print headlines yelling the latest tidbit of information - real or imaginary - at its suddenly increased readership.

And Cal Car was at the heart of it all.

Ha! he thought to himself. *I must remember not to make any flippant comments about hearts until all this nonsense is over and done with.*

"...and now back to Cal Car in the studio," said the reporter, jolting the news anchor out of his reverie.

Cal Car spun his chair back to face the camera. "Thank

you..." he began, making one last rummage through his memory for the reporter's name. But, no. It simply wasn't there. "...my friend. And now we go over to the weather control laboratories where Sim Ket has been hearing about efforts to solve the ongoing issues with the weather, and if these mysterious surges in gravity will be solved in time for Tor Val's funeral and Journey Back."

Fucking hell, she's even in the pissing weather report now!

As Sim Ket began his report, Cal Car allowed himself to return to his daydreams where he fantasized about sharing a new, frivolous morsel of celebrity gossip.

Those were the days.

19

Alma Nine, Taron City, Government Buildings, Vice President's Office

Saf Tah perched delicately on a hastily repaired chair in his office while his two executive assistants worked at clearing up the debris from around what remained of the vice president's desk.

The gravity surge hadn't proved to be as destructive to the government building as it had been at the weather control labs, but there was still a lot of damaged equipment and splintered furniture to be cleared away.

Jus Clo scooped the broken computer from the center of the floor and dumped it into a large metal trash can which sat beside two identical bins, both of which were already full.

"Such a waste," he sighed, peering down at what had once been a state of the art laptop.

"It, um... certainly is," agreed Mol Gat, tossing a shattered desk lamp in on top of the ruined machine. "I um... always liked that lamp."

"When you two have finished mourning over lost office supplies, I'd like to get back to work!" spat Saf Tah, wincing as a sharp dagger of pain shot through his groin.

When the gravitational waves had hit, Saf Tah had been locked in a passionate embrace with one of the more curvaceous secretaries from the agriculture department on the fifth floor.

Mol Gat and Jus Clo, having been banished to his outer office to ensure no-one burst in and interrupted the illicit encounter had heard a piercing scream as they had both been flung to the ground by the severity of the sudden attack.

Concerned for the well-being of their employer, and terrified of his reaction if they didn't hurry to his aid, the pair had somehow found the strength to fight against the intense force, and managed to open the door to the vice president's inner office.

There they discovered Saf Tah lying on the carpet, pinned beneath his pneumatic partner, struggling to breathe and sobbing like a child.

The lovers had, by all accounts, just been about to 'cement inter-departmental relations' when the gravity blast had thrust the unlucky woman down onto a considerably excited part of Saf Tah's anatomy, bending it in two and tearing a number of usually untroubled tendons.

It had taken the two assistants ten minutes to slide the Rubenesque beauty off their boss, and further fifteen to drag him to the vending machines at the top of the stairwell where they had purchased several cans of ice cold soda to use as aids in easing his excruciating pain.

Ever since, Saf Tah had walked with a pronounced

limp, and none of the government secretaries would type up any of the letters he dictated in support of their suitably offended colleague.

Jus Clo was still reeling from the string of obscenities hurled at him after he had submitted an expenses claim to Saf Tah for the urgently purchased cans of soda.

The last of the trashed office paraphernalia ditched into the bins, the assistants stood in front of their boss's chair for a moment. Then, upon receiving a particularly unpleasant glare, they both sat down on the carpet, cross-legged.

"OK," croaked Saf Tah, his voice still almost an entire octave higher than it had previously been. "Take notes..."

Mol Gat stood and hurried to the garbage cans to retrieve a crumpled notepad and a pencil.

"I want to know exactly what caused that gravity shit yesterday," ranted Saf Tah. "What it was, who fucked up, and why he or she is still walking around freely and breathing the same air as me."

Jus Clo raised his hand. "But-"

Saf Tah ignored him. "Next, get hold of someone on Tor Val's funeral committee and find out exactly what they have planned for her Journey Back. This may be the useless heifer's last hurrah, but it's *my* big day, and I don't want anyone or anything to ruin it. Do you hear me?"

"Yes, sir," mumbled the two junior men together.

"Finally, find out who-"

Saf Tah was interrupted by a sharp rap, followed by the door to the office swinging open and Captain Den Pow of the Malatian army marched into the room. The soldier snapped to attention and saluted smartly.

Gripping the back of his chair, Saf Tah eased himself slowly to his feet and returned the salute. "What is it, Captain?"

"We have intercepted three lifeforms, Mr Vice President," announced Den Pow. "They arrived in the midst of yesterday's emergency, and we believe they may have had something to do with the event itself."

Saf Tah's eyes grew wide. "Is that so?"

Mol Gat and Jus Clo remained seated on the carpet, their eyes flicking back and forth between the two men as the conversation continued.

"Where are these illegal invaders now?" the vice president asked.

"We have them locked securely in a holding cell at our barracks, sir."

Saf Tah smiled. "Very good, Captain. I shall come along and speak to these interlopers myself. That will be all."

Captain Den Pow saluted again, then turned and marched back out of the office, closing the door.

"Well, well..." Saf Tah cooed to himself. "It would appear your tasks have just been made that little bit easier, boys."

Mol Gat shared a confused look with his fellow subordinate. "Um... they have?"

"They have if the bastards behind yesterday's fuck up are already locked up, yes," Saf Tah continued. "Call for my car. I shall leave for the army barracks within the hour."

As the assistants clambered to their feet, Saf Tah sat back down - a little too hard. His chair, held together with little more than sticky tape and glue, collapsed causing the vice president to crash to the floor and land right on his damaged majority.

They say you could hear his scream three blocks away.

Alma Nine, Taron City, Army Barracks, Holding Cell

Jack sat with his back against the wall, watching Tc'aarlat as he paced tirelessly up and down the length of the cramped cell.

"How dare they treat us like this?" he barked, for at least the sixth time in the last 30 minutes. "We told them who we were: official envoys from the Etheric Empire, here to pay our respects to their president!"

"I'm sure they'll work that out soon enough," said Jack. "They've got our official papers. All they have to do is contact Nathan back on the base station, and he'll clear everything up."

"That's if they *can* get in touch with him," Adina put in from where she was lying on the cell's single metal bench.

Tc'aarlat spun to face her. "What do you mean?"

"Well, if Solo was right, and these guys couldn't radio back to us when we were falling through their lower atmosphere, I doubt they'll be able to make a call half way across the galaxy."

"You've got a point," admitted Jack. "If their communications equipment was damaged by the gravity surge, they may not be able to confirm our identities for a while yet."

"But, they *have* to believe us," grumbled Tc'aarlat, pacing again. "I *can't* stay locked up in here. Not with you two!"

Jack and Adina looked to each other, then back at the Yollin.

"What's wrong with 'us two'?" Adina demanded.

"It's nothing personal," Tc'aarlat replied. "It's just that

I'm used to having my own space. I come from a very quiet, unassuming family."

Jack laughed. "Yeah, that's one of the first things I thought when I saved you from the assassin on your tail all those years ago. *That bloke's very private and unassuming for a dangerous mobster.*"

Tc'aarlat paused his pacing again. "I've told you again and again - I was *not* a mobster! I just happened to work for them."

"Is there a difference?" queried Adina.

"There are *lots* of differences!" protested Tc'aarlat. "Far too many to go into right now, but trust me, there are plenty."

"If you say so."

The conversation was interrupted by a screech from a room on the opposite side of the corridor to their cell.

"Mist!" cried Tc'aarlat. "Hang in there, girl. I'm coming for you."

He turned back to his crew mates, tears in his eyes. "I can't believe they've got her locked up in a cage!"

"They've got *us* locked up in a cage!" Jack reminded him.

"Well, not for long!" spat the Yollin. Grabbing hold of the cell bars, he began to shake them and shout as loudly as he could.

"Hey! Whichever one of you green-skinned fuckers is in charge. I demand to be set free this instant or I'll kick your teeth so far down your throat, you'll have to stick gum up your butt to chew on it!"

"See," said Jack to Adina, "quiet and unassuming."

"And they're teal," added Adina.

"What?!"

"The Malatians' skin is teal-colored, not green."

"Is there a difference?"

"Oh, there are *lots* of differences," smiled Adina. "Far too many to go into right now, but trust me..."

"Ha ha, very funny!" scowled Tc'aarlat. "I don't care what color they are, I just want one of them to have the guts to talk to me, face to face!"

"I have the guts for that," said a voice.

Jack stood as three Malatian men were buzzed through the security door at the end of the corridor and headed their way. Adina rose from her bench and crossed the cell to stand with Tc'aarlat.

The obvious leader of the trio was limping, and had a string of red and green lights woven into his silver mohawk, the tips of which appeared to be burned away.

The front man stopped at the bars of the cell and faced off against Tc'aarlat. "So, you're our new guests?"

The Yollin sneered. "Guests? I wouldn't treat a rabid bistok this way! I demand you let us out of here right now."

Mohawk man smiled, but not with his eyes. "You're issuing demands? Of me?"

"You?" spat Tc'aarlat. "And who the fuck are you supposed to be?"

The man limped closer to the bars, but not so close that anyone could reach through and grab him.

"I'm your worst nightmare!"

This made Tc'aarlat chuckle darkly. "Hard man, eh?"

"Not anymore," announced one of the other men. "A chubby secretary broke his dick."

Saf Tah sighed. "Excuse me for a moment." Turning, he

punched Jus Clo hard in the face, then returned his attention to the three prisoners.

"Now, where were we?" he said, ignoring his assistant's muffled cries of pain.

Jus Clo had both hands pressed over his nose and mouth, trying in vain to stem the flow of blood from both.

"Do you have any idea who we are?" asked Tc'aarlat.

"But, of course," replied Saf Tah. "You're the aliens who attacked our planet with some type of gravity weapon."

Jack stepped up to join Tc'aarlat and Adina at the cell bars. "You think that was us?"

"But, of course!" said Saf Tah, matter-of-factly. "Or perhaps it's mere coincidence that an uninvited spacecraft appears in orbit around our planet at the exact moment Alma Nine's gravitational forces became weaponized."

"We had to fight off those gravitational waves ourselves," protested Adina. "They almost caused us to crash. We're here for Tor Val's funeral."

Saf Tah threw a self-satisfied smirk towards Mol Gat who beamed back, terrified he might be on the receiving end of his boss's next burst of anger. While he felt sympathy for Jus Clo, who was still cradling his now clearly broken nose, he wasn't brave enough to demonstrate that pity while the vice president was in mid-interrogation.

"The funeral does not take place for another two days," said Saf Tah. "And guests will not begin to arrive until tomorrow morning."

"We were asked to come early," Jack responded. "We're here to deliver your public safety barriers."

Saf Tah blinked, looking unsure of himself for the first

time since he and his entourage had arrived. "I don't believe you," he announced. "Anyone could say that."

"Yes," agreed Jack, "but not everyone would be in possession of both our official delivery docket, *and* our invitations to attend the president's funeral as emissaries of the Etheric Empire, would they?"

Adina fought to hide her smile as Saf Tah visibly paled. "Captain!" he roared, not taking his eyes off Jack. "Where are their papers?"

"Here, sir!" replied Den Pow, stepping out from his office and passing a handful of documents to Mol Gat, who handed them to his boss as if simply touching them could prove poisonous.

There was a moment of silence while Saf Tah flicked through the paperwork, occasionally glancing up at either Jack, Tc'aarlat or Adina.

The Yollin grinned and wiggled his fingers in a mock friendly greeting when it was his turn to be considered.

Without saying a word, Saf Tah handed the documents back to Mol Gat, then punched him hard in the face as well.

While both of the political advisors wailed and staggered about, holding their noses, Saf Tah relaxed his fist and slid his arm through the bars to shake Jack's hand.

He cleared his throat.

"Welcome to Alma Nine."

Alma Nine, Taron City, Outside Tor Val's Residence

Cal Car took a final opportunity to examine his hair in his hand mirror before slipping it into his pocket as the Channel 3 News theme tune began.

The past couple of days had been so hectic, he was worried the extra shifts he was having to work would have some effect on his appearance, and that would never do.

With seemingly endless TV coverage of the colony's display of grief for Tor Val, channels were trying every trick in the book to ensure theirs was the news service the public chose to watch.

Some anchors had taken to wearing only the official mourning color of purple, while others openly wept on camera while reading updates.

Then the higher-ups at Channel 3 had held a meeting, from which they emerged with a wonderful idea...

Get Cal Car to host the bulletin from outside the late president's official residence.

In the open air!

Bundled up in the thickest, warmest coat the station's wardrobe department could find, Cal Car shuddered - not from the cold, but from his proximity to the general public.

For the past 48 hours, there had been a constant stream of well-wishers making a pilgrimage to Tor Val's residence, each loaded down with flowers, cards, poems, teddy bears, candles and - in one of the day's more unusual tributes - a highly decorated prosthetic leg.

Beneath a hastily erected canopy was a table with a large book of condolence in which grieving citizens could write a personal message. The tome now being used was the sixth volume.

Tor Val's official colors were everywhere. Navy blue and lemon flags hung from every streetlamp, banners were displayed in the windows of almost every building, and many walls had been freshly painted as a show of support for the late president.

However, the colors did little to lift Cal Car's mood.

He had instructed his agent to complain about the network's insistence that he broadcast outdoors among the elements and the plebs, but his grumbling was short-lived. His showbiz representative merely had to remind him that the news industry's annual awards ceremony was on the horizon, and Cal Car had immediately withdrawn his request.

If he could become the face of the public's grief over Tor Val's death, he was almost certain to be nominated for one or more of the prestigious awards on offer. The 'Almy' for *Most Dedicated News Anchor* was so close, he could already smell the expensive polish he would use on it daily to keep it sparkling.

He'd already cleared a spot for it on the book shelf in his living room.

"OK, Cal Car," said the producer via his earpiece as the theme tune neared its end. "You're on in five, four, three..."

"Good evening, and welcome to Channel 3 News," he announced directly to the camera. "I'm Cal Car.

Today's top story - the endless streams of well-wishers and grieving visitors coming to pay tribute to the late Tor Val at her place of residence. Many of these people have queued all day out here in the cold and damp, just for the opportunity to lay a bouquet of flowers in front of the house, bow their heads, and offer up a prayer for their - nay, *our* - beloved former president.

Fen Ret has more..."

The light on top of the camera went out as the studio-bound producer cut to a pre-recorded segment in which a junior reporter had interviewed members of the public waiting for their turn to pay their respects.

This allowed Cal Car and the small production team a few moments to stamp their feet, blow into their hands, and gaze wistfully at the steaming mogneti machine just visible inside the nearby Channel 3 News van.

Whipping out his mirror, Cal Car examined his hair, scowling as he saw just how much the continuously falling snow had caused his trademark shaggy perm to wilt. His lovingly teased curls drooped and fell, hanging like the untended hair of a happily married man.

The new receptionist wouldn't give him so much as a second glance if she tuned in and saw him looking like this.

As he pocketed his mirror, he became aware of a figure standing close beside him. Uncomfortably close. He turned to find an overweight man with back-combed hair holding out a pad and pen, and grinning like a simpleton. The greasy skin of his face had been haphazardly painted in Tor Val's colors of navy blue and lemon yellow.

"I want your autograph, Cal Car," the man drooled, his eyes unblinking. "I'm your biggest fan!"

"Yes," said Cal Car with a sigh. He took the proffered notepad and quickly dashed off an unreadable signature. "Yes, you probably are."

It was going to be a long night.

Alma Nine, Taron City, Government Building, Presidential Suite

Bay Don carried three mugs of steaming mogneti over to her desk, and placed them down before Zeb Lok and Jon Rey.

"I'm so pleased to see you're OK," she said to Jon Rey as he lifted one of the mugs in his unbandaged hand and sipped at the drink.

"Thanks to you, I am," said Jon Rey, gesturing to the dressing covering his throat. "The doctors say if the medics had tried to move me with the broken glass still in there, I would likely have severed an artery."

Bay Don's cheeks flushed a deep sea-green. "I just did what anyone else would have done in the same position."

"Well, you're *not* anyone else," said Jon Rey. "You're the person who saved my life, and I'll never forget it."

"Speaking of lives," said Zeb Lok. "Have you received any figures?"

"Some," said Bay Don, putting down her mug and grabbing a sheet of paper from her desk. "As far as we're aware, we have 27 dead, and 112 injured."

"27..." sighed Zeb Lok. "That's terrible, but it *could* have been a lot worse, I suppose."

"It may well prove to be," said Bay Don. "We haven't yet gotten reports in from some of the outlying towns and villages."

"You won't need to," said Jon Rey.

Bay Don scowled. "Won't need to?"

Zeb Lok shook his head. "That's why we're here," he explained. "We've made a discovery - and this is where it gets weird..."

"*More* weird than the planet being hit by a series of rogue gravitational waves?" asked Bay Don.

"That's just it," replied Zeb Lok. "It *wasn't* the whole planet. The surge in gravity was localized to Taron City."

"But... But that's *impossible*!" exclaimed Bay Don.

"We know," Jon Rey assured her. "We thought we were dealing with some hugely powerful but rare natural phenomenon for this part of the galaxy. Something that hasn't happened in the ten or eleven years since we arrived. But now we're completely stumped."

Bay Don picked up her mogneti and raised the mug to her lips, but was too deep in thought to take a drink. "Could it be something unique about the land Taron City was built on?" she queried. "I know our architects ran a number of surveys when the location for the capital was first chosen, but I don't remember there being anything unusual in the results. Maybe they missed something."

"That's one possibility," said Zeb Lok.

"There's another?"

"I'm afraid so," Zeb Lok. Jon Rey nodded in agreement.

Bay Don looked from one man to the other. "What?"

Zeb Lok paused to take a sip of his mogneti. "It's possible Taron City was deliberately targeted."

"Someone did this on *purpose?*" Bay Don swayed slightly, suddenly feeling light-headed by the very idea that the gravity surge was a man-made event.

"We don't know," admitted Jon Rey. "At least, not yet."

"So, what can you-"

Just then the door to the outer office burst open, and Saf Tah strode in at the head of a group of people.

Two of them Bay Don knew - they were the vice president's personal assistants and advisors. For some reason, they both had bloodied bandages fixed over their noses and two black eyes.

Behind them were three aliens - two of which appeared to be human!

Bay Don only recognized the humans because they looked to be the same species as the extra-terrestrials Tor Val had spoken to via video links from the Etheric Empire. One was a tall male with pink skin, while the female was shorter. Her skin was the color of ripe parsel fruit.

The third creature had the same basic biology as the humans, but was encased in some kind of external crust or exoskeleton. And, there was a deep red feathered animal sitting on its shoulder.

Bay Don didn't have long to study the newcomers, however. Saf Tah was walking purposefully towards the door of the inner presidential office.

Tor Val's office.

She stepped in front of the vice president, stopping him dead. "Can I help you?"

"I'm commandeering the president's office," said Saf Tah. "Step aside."

Bay Don felt a knot of anger begin to form in the pit of her stomach. "I shall do no such thing," she proclaimed. "The president's office is out of bounds to... lesser officials."

Saf Tah's eyes narrowed. "How dare you?!" he rumbled. "These people are the official delegation from the Etheric Empire, and I have important business to discuss with them."

Zeb Lok quickly set his mug down, gesturing for Jon Rey to do the same. "We'll be going," he said with a nervous smile. "Lots of work to be done."

The scientists scurried out of the office without saying another word.

Bay Don stood firm, folding her arms. "If you've got people to meet, use your own office."

"My office was damaged by the gravitational waves," said Saf Tah.

"Then I'll book you a meeting room."

"I shall soon be the president of this planet!"

"Then, that's when you can use the president's office," insisted Bay Don. "And not a minute sooner!"

Saf Tah glowered. "Foolish girl!" he barked. Grabbing Bay Don's arm, he pushed her aside, sending her tumbling to the carpet. She fell against her desk, spilling her half-finished mug of mogneti.

Adina hurried over to help her up as the vice president turned to beam at a displeased Jack and Tc'aarlat. "This way, gentlemen..."

Jus Clo darted forward to open the door and hold it as his boss marched confidently inside.

"Reckons he's a real tough guy that one," Tc'aarlat hissed to Jack as he made to follow. "Let's see how tough he is facing off to someone more his size. I don't like men who treat women that way."

Jack placed a hand on his arm and held him back for a second. "Me neither, but we have to stay on his good side long enough to learn whether he's likely to be a risk to the Empire."

"But-"

Jack smiled grimly. "Once we know that, *then* you can fuck him up with my blessing. I might even join in. Just play along for now."

Tc'aarlat glared into the office, where Mol Gat was helping Saf Tah settle into the chair behind the president's desk. "You had me at fuck him up," he snarled.

The Yollin entered the office with Jack at his heels. As he passed Adina, he leaned towards her and whispered. "See what you can find out about this bullshit-blurting bozo."

Adina nodded, turning back to Bay Don with a friendly smile as Jus Clo shut the door to the inner office.

Bay Don grabbed a roll of paper towels from a nearby cupboard, and used a strip to soak up the spilled mogneti.

A number of documents on her desk were already soaked, and were now virtually unreadable.

Lifting them between finger and thumb, Bay Don dumped the dripping papers into her wastebasket.

Adina grabbed the paper towels and tore half a dozen or so from the roll, using them to wipe down the side of the desk where the drink had spilled over. "Is Saf Tah always like that?" she asked.

"Like what?" responded Bay Don, flatly.

"A condescending fuckwit with an ego twice the size of this planet."

Bay Don tried to hide her smile, but failed. "You're seeing his pleasant side at the moment," she pointed out. "He can get a lot worse than this, and frequently does with Tor Val."

She stopped, mid-wipe, her eyes staring off into some unseen distance.

"He *did* that with Tor Val," she corrected. "Sorry. I keep forgetting that she's... I just expect her to walk through that door, like she always did."

Bay Don was crying before Adina's arms had fully wrapped around her.

"I miss her so much," she sobbed. "I wanted to see her, at the hospital, after the accident. They wouldn't let me. They said she was too badly... That I shouldn't see her like that. I didn't get the chance to say a proper goodbye."

Adina blinked back her own tears. "I understand," she said softly. "I had a similar situation when my mom died."

"Was that an accident, too?" Bay Don asked.

Adina sighed quietly. "In a way, yes."

Bay Don pulled away from her new friend, grabbing a

sheet from the paper towel roll to dry her eyes. "The worst part is the way he just strides in here, acting like he's already in charge."

Adina nodded. "I noticed that."

She glanced over at the closed inner office door.

"Don't worry. He won't get away with that shit with Jack and Tc'aarlat."

21

Alma Nine, Taron City, Government Building, President's Inner Office

"As president of Alma Nine," preened Saf Tah, "I, of course, have to take the wishes and feelings of my citizens into account when-"

"You're *not* the president though, are you?" Tc'aarlat challenged.

Standing directly behind their boss, Jus Clo and Mol Gat exchanged a nervous glance.

"I may not yet be president in name," replied Saf Tah in an obviously patronizing tone, "but for all intents and purposes..."

"...you're still the vice president," finished Tc'aarlat. "Second place. Number two, you could say - in more ways than one."

Saf Tah glowered across the desk and opened his mouth to respond. Jack jumped in before he could.

"I believe your inauguration ceremony will take place shortly after the funeral of Tor Val."

"That is correct."

"And you don't feel that is in any way insensitive?"

Now it was Jack's turn to be on the receiving end of one of Saf Tah's fierce stares. "No, I do not!" he insisted. "What *is* insensitive is the way Tor Val entered into talks with the Etheric Empire without either the knowledge or permission of the office of the vice president."

"Did she *need* your permission?" asked Jack.

"Well, not as such," said Saf Tah, "but it would have been polite for her to include me in such important negotiations."

"Ah," said Tc'aarlat. "So your problem is that she hurt your feelings."

"Scaww!" cried Mist.

"Not at all!" Saf Tah countered, adding the Raal hawk to his list of furious glare recipients. "I merely believe it is important for law-makers from all political persuasions to be involved if a course of action is likely to affect the future of everyone on the planet."

"Ah... got ya!" exclaimed Tc'aarlat. "Everyone needs to be able to have their say where important decisions are concerned."

"Exactly!" beamed Saf Tah, his well-practiced political smile fixed firmly in place.

"Important decisions like choosing a new president," added Tc'aarlat.

"Yes, exact-" Saf Tah's smile disappeared. "You gentlemen are trying to put words into my mouth."

Tc'aarlat rested his mandibles on the desk. "Trust me," he growled. "Words are far better than what I really *want* to shove in there."

"Brave talk for a pair of visiting dignitaries," Saf Tah spat. "Guests on this planet. Especially considering you are currently outnumbered."

Mol Gat and Jus Clo both took a nervous step back.

"Enough!" barked Jack. "This is getting us nowhere."

"I agree," confirmed Saf Tah. "And, before we continue our discussion, I would like a moment to talk privately with my advisors."

Jack nodded his agreement, then pulled Tc'aarlat to his feet and guided him to the far end of the office.

"What are you doing?" he hissed. "I thought we'd agreed to leave this guy alone until we knew where he stood on joining the Empire?"

"I tried," Tc'aarlat replied.

"For less than five minutes!"

Tc'aarlat shrugged, jostling Mist. "What can I say? He's a Grade A cockwomble. He doesn't deserve our respect."

Jack sighed. "I know, but we can't go back to Nathan and tell him we didn't give our target the opportunity to pick a side, one way or the other. It'll be even worse if he thinks we bullied him out of continuing the talks where Tor Val left off."

Tc'aarlat took a deep breath. "Alright," he said. "I'll keep quiet and let you do the talking. But, if he rubs me up the wrong way again, I'll-"

The Yollin was unable to finish his sentence due to being pushed face first onto the office carpet. It felt as if someone had just landed a spacecraft on top of him.

Mist lay to the right of his head, silent and unmoving. A brief feeling of panic washed over Tc'aarlat but, once he realized the bird's chest was still rising and falling as she breathed, he allowed himself to relax.

There was a deafening crack as the large windows shattered inwards, showering their paralyzed, prone bodies with bits of broken glass.

"It's happening again," croaked Jack from beside him, trying to force himself up from the floor, but the pressure was just too great.

Screams and muffled cries for help echoed in through the smashed windows, along with blasts of icy wind and thick clouds of snow.

Concentrating hard, Tc'aarlat dragged his hands up to either side of his chest, pressed his palms down against the rough carpet, and pushed back hard against the surge in gravity.

It was an agonizing process, and one during which the Yollin promised himself that he would return to the weight training he had abandoned shortly after absconding from his organized crime employers.

"I'll never skip arm day again!" he groaned as he fought against the almost overwhelming downward force.

Once on his hands and knees, he grabbed a nearby wastepaper basket, tipped out its contents, and placed it carefully over Mist. "Stay safe, my friend," he whispered. Then, gritting his teeth, he crawled over to Jack.

Above them, the ceiling began to buckle, adding a flurry of plaster and dust to the plumes of snow swirling in from outside. The beams creaked and groaned as they began to lose their battle with the unrelenting pressure.

Tc'aarlat knew he had to get the others under cover in

case the floor above came crashing down on top of them all.

"How the hell are you able to move?" demanded Jack, barely able to move his own eyes to see Tc'aarlat shuffling in his direction.

"The benefits of owning an exoskeleton," answered the Yollin. "It's a bitch to moisturize but, for once, I'm actually pleased to have it."

Slogging his way across the room, Tc'aarlat grabbed Saf Tah's wrist and dragged him to the president's sturdy desk, tucking him safely underneath. He then repeated the process for the vice president's two aides.

"I knew it!" rumbled Saf Tah. The vice president was lying on his back, eyes fixed on the underside of the desk above. "I *told* you Tor Val was given a better desk than me, didn't I? It's blatant favoritism!"

"For fuck's sake," groaned Jack as Tc'aarlat returned for his friend. "Don't put me under there with them. I'd rather take my chances with the ceiling beams."

"I think we might be about to do just that," said Tc'aarlat as the sound of cracking wood was accompanied by another shower of painted plaster. "Which means there's only one way to do this..."

Tc'aarlat crawled over Jack's body and lay on top of him just as the ceiling gave way and crashed down on top of the room's helpless occupants.

Bay Don lay on her back beside the mound of splintered

wood that had once been her desk as the roof of the inner office caved in.

She knew instantly what had happened, and that the same would shortly happen to the ceiling now hanging perilously over her and Adina.

And there was nothing she could do to protect herself.

The result was a strange sensation of calm. Soon, she would be setting off on her own Journey Back to join Tor Val among the gas clouds of the Ordon Nebula. If there was anyone left on Alma Nine to launch her casket out into deep space, that is.

She heard a sudden agonized grunt from Adina, and tried to angle her head to see where the human was. But, she found it impossible to move.

At Bay Don's feet, Adina screamed inwardly as she concentrated on her spine and limbs, forcing them to transform into their werewolf form beneath her clothing.

She writhed in agony as her vertebrae separated from one another, the fibers of the soft discs that lay between each of the bones ripping apart before glueing the vertebrae back together in a more lupine configuration.

Dense fur cascaded down her thickened arms and legs, stopping at her cuffs and the tops of her boots, her shirt and overall trousers bulging as new, more powerful muscles filled the unsuspecting material.

Her semi-transformation complete, Adina climbed awkwardly to her feet, praying her werewolf ankles wouldn't give way under the intense pressure. Staggering over to a metal filing cabinet, half werewolf and half human, she quickly pulled out each of the drawers with her unchanged arms, casting them aside like dead weights until all that was left was the empty frame.

This she dragged across to where Bay Don lay, staring feebly up at the rapidly growing bulge in the ceiling. Dropping down to lie beside her, Adina pulled the steel-framed cabinet over them just as the supports gave way, showering the office with massive amounts of deadly debris.

Bay Don felt Adina's body changing back in the darkness beside her, the human's cries of pain barely audible over the clanging of wood and brick against the exterior of the filing cabinet.

"What *are* you?" she whispered.

Alma Nine, Taron City, Weather Control Center, Temporary Laboratory

Jon Rey felt the pressure begin to build on his shoulders almost an entire minute before the alarms went off.

"OK, everyone," he announced. "Gravity surge approaching. You know what to do."

All around the temporary laboratory, scientists abandoned their work and sprang into action, aiming to prepare the room for another gravity surge within the 30 second target they had set themselves.

With much of their usual lab destroyed by the first attack, plans had been made to move the most vital parts of the organization's equipment to a more secure environment. That way, the scientists would be able to continue their research into what was causing the gravitational waves to sweep across the city and what, if anything, could be done to stop it from happening again.

The first task had been to excavate an unused basement room, originally included with in building's blueprints as a combination bomb shelter and panic room. Built with several layers of brickwork, the floor, walls and ceiling were all fortified with sheets of strong metal, adding an additional layer of protection for anyone fortunate enough to be selected to occupy the room in an emergency.

Upon the colonists' arrival at Alma Nine, they had been made privy to stories concerning their nearest neighbors - the five planets making up an area of space known as the Ordanian Hub.

These planets orbited a dark energy star, and were populated almost entirely by thieves, vagabonds and murderers.

Never had the oft-used phrase 'birds of a feather flock together' been more appropriate.

The two largest worlds - Talth and Skolar Major - were rumored to be controlled by some of the most violent families in the history of organized crime. Believing themselves to be safe from even the most eager officers of the law, these Mobsters filled their planets with goons, hitmen, drug dealers, money launderers and every other type of lowlife individual they could make contact with.

The result was a political and financial ecosystem that - so far - appeared to govern and police itself with an astonishing level of success. Thugs and racketeers were dispatched by the heads of these families in order to establish Mafia outposts in other systems, feeding back the profits from their many questionable enterprises via a variety of smuggling routes.

Skolar Minor and Beema played host to organizations

embroiled in the seedy business of people trafficking. Regular slave markets and auctions provided well-to-do but immoral oligarchs with all the servants, unpaid laborers and prostitutes they could ever need.

The final - and smallest - planet, Chakk, was where these gangsters and wrongdoers went to kick back and relax. With an unofficial treaty ensuring no business transactions or plots for power or revenge were enacted, Chakk had quickly become the resort of choice for just about every outlaw in the Ordanian Hub. Many of the wealthier criminals had gone so far as to buy pieces of land and build their own vacation villas there.

This was the reasoning behind the Weather Control Center's newly excavated basement shelter. Each major building constructed in the early days of Alma Nine's colony included such a space, stocking it with canned food and water should the room be required in the event of an incursion.

But, as time progressed and the residents of the Ordanian Hub appeared not to even notice the new arrivals to the previously uninhabited planet, these extra safety measures fell out of fashion. Most were stripped of their supplies and some, like the one Jon Rey and his fellow scientists were now working in, had been blocked off completely.

In addition to the tungsten-lined walls, shelving units and benches built from an almost pure form of titanium were used to house the lab's replacement equipment. Computer screens were fitted with shatterproof glass, handheld tools were made from chromium, and any piece of sensitive apparatus was housed in a metal box with shutters ready to slam down and protect the delicate contents at a few seconds' notice.

Jon Rey hit the button to bring down these protective shields, sending the entire lab into a well-rehearsed safety routine.

The scientists hurried to their individually assigned bunks. Each of the cots were built from flexible metal tubes, deeply padded so as to avoid as much damage to flesh and bone as possible, and covered with a semi-circular mesh cage.

It was unlikely the roof of this temporary laboratory would cave in as the last one had, but it was better to be safe than sorry.

Jon Rey felt his body being forced down into the soft padding of his bunk. "Here we go. Good luck, everyone."

He reached over to lower and secure the fastener on the metal cage that would protect him in the event of falling debris - then a bolt of pain shot down his injured arm.

Twisting in an attempt to ease the discomfort, his fingers fumbled with the catch on the cage, causing it to miss its slot.

Suddenly, another wave of gravitational pressure washed across the lab. The cage, still unsecured, was forced down on top of Jon Rey, the hinges fixed to the other side breaking in two.

The scientist found himself trapped beneath a now flattened sheet of metallic mesh which pressed harder and harder into his skin as the surge in gravity grew stronger.

He screamed in agony as the sharp edge of the metal strands cut deep into the skin of his face, carving his flesh into dozens of small diamond-shaped chunks.

Blood poured from every wound, lubricating the razor-edged struts, allowing them to sink lower into Jon Rey's face.

His eyes burst from the pressure. Now blind, the shock of his injuries blazed through Jon Rey's helpless body. He began to shake uncontrollably, rattling the metal cage as it was forced even further down into his tender flesh.

Finally, metal hit bone with a nauseating crunch. For the briefest of moments, Jon Rey prayed the torture might be over, but then the shallow angle of his bunk came into play.

Whoever had designed these bunks had decided they should not lie perfectly flat. Instead, the decision was made to set the head of the couch six inches higher than the opposite end, allowing the occupant to rest at what was considered to be a comfortable angle.

It was to be the decision that would end Jon Rey's life.

Now the blood-soaked metal lattice could no longer sink into his diced flesh. The compressed cage gradually but forcibly began to slide down his body towards his feet, acting like a cheese grater and sloughing the meat cleanly from the skeleton below.

All the other scientists could do was lie perfectly still, sobbing while they listened to their friend begging for death as his barely living flesh was slowly and agonizingly carved from his bones.

22

Alma Nine, Taron City, Government Building, Presidential Suite

The door to the inner office exploded outwards on Tc'aarlat's third attempt at ramming it with his shoulder.

Breaking away the splintered pieces of wood, he clambered over the debris covering the floor of the outer office, eyes scanning the room for any signs of life.

"Adina!" he cried. "Bay Don!"

"Under here," came a muffled reply.

Jumping down from the mound of rubble, Tc'aarlat pushed a broken roof beam off of the upturned filing cabinet as Jack clambered out of the president's office and scrambled over to help.

Together, they lifted the battered steel frame to find the two women huddled together underneath.

"That was quick thinking," Jack commented as they set the cabinet aside. He looked down at the discarded drawers, each filled with dozens of thick files. "How did you manage to get those out in time?"

"It was Adina!" exclaimed Bay Don as Tc'aarlat helped her to her feet. "She-"

"We did it together," proclaimed Adina, flicking Bay Don a look pleading with the secretary not to go any further with her explanation. "It wasn't easy, but we managed it."

Whatever Adina's reason was for wanting to hide the truth, Bay Don wasn't sure. But, she owed this strange human with incredible abilities a huge debt of gratitude, and so she simply nodded in agreement.

"It all happened so quickly," she said. "I don't remember much about it."

"Well, I do!" exclaimed a voice. The group turned to see Saf Tah's two assistants helping him to climb over the mountain of wreckage from the ceiling and floor above. "You men saved my life."

"To be fair, it was mostly Tc'aarlat's doing," Jack admitted. "I could barely move."

Tc'aarlat shrugged. "Probably down to all that extra weight you're carrying," he offered.

"Hey!" cried Jack. "I'm not that-"

"Maybe Tor Val was right," interrupted the vice president. "If you good people are examples of the bravery and heroism of the Etheric Empire, then maybe Alma Nine *should* consider aligning with you."

With that he beamed, slapped Jack on the arm, and marched from the outer office, his two simpering aides scurrying to catch up.

"Wow!" breathed Bay Don. "I've never seen him smile before. I mean *really* smile, with his eyes as well."

"Amazing what staring death in the face can do to someone," said Adina. "Maybe he'll be easier to work with from now on."

"I wouldn't hold your breath," said Tc'aarlat. "Leotards don't change their spots."

"I think you mean *leopards*," Jack commented. "Leotards are something very different indeed."

Tc'aarlat frowned. "Really?"

"Yep," said Adina with a grin. "They're about as dissimilar as your new cloak and Mist."

Suddenly, Tc'aarlat's eyes grew wide. "Oh shit!" he exclaimed. "Mist!"

The others watched as he scrambled back over the debris and into the inner office once more.

Adina rested a friendly hand on Bay Don's arm. "Will you be OK?"

"I will," the Malatian replied, looking around at what remained of her once pristine office. "I've got some clearing up to do, but it will give me something to focus on."

"We'll be back to help you this evening," promised Jack. "But first, we need to get to the bottom of what's causing these gravitational waves."

"And how, exactly, do we do that?" Adina asked.

Jack took a deep breath before replying. "We find ourselves a scientist."

Alma Nine, Taron City, Outside Tor Val's Residence

Once the onslaught of gravitational waves had faded,

Cal Car gripped the railings outside of Tor Val's house and used them to drag himself shakily to his feet.

A lightning bolt of pain shot through his left shoulder as he pulled, causing him to cry out and slump back against the now warped metal struts.

"Are you OK?" asked his cameraman as he pushed himself up.

"I think my shoulder's broken," Cal Car replied, wincing as he reached up with his good hand to touch the sensitive area. "Still, it's not as bad as it could be after 20 minutes face down in the snow."

All around them, grieving visitors began to rouse themselves, helping each other to stand and tending to those who had been injured by their sudden fall to the ground.

Cal Car noted that one or two of the well-wishers weren't moving. Instead, they lay deathly still, a thin layer of snow beginning to coat their staring, unseeing eyes.

He turned to the Channel Three News van, hoping to use the comms system to call for assistance for the wounded - but all that remained of the truck and its technical contents was a mangled lump of twisted metal.

Sirens echoed in the distance as the emergency services began their task of ferrying those in need of treatment to the already packed hospitals, and retrieving the bodies of those who had not been as lucky.

"You're hurt!" cried a voice from behind Cal Car.

The news anchor turned to find Tor Val's older daughter, Mas Val, in the doorway of her home. The girl appeared stunned but, thankfully, unhurt as she hurried down the steps to where Cal Car was resting.

A pair of ambulances pulled up at the curbside, para-medics leaping out to help those stumbling around aimlessly.

"I'm fine," proclaimed Cal Car as one of the medics caught his eyes. "Look after the others."

"You are not fine," countered Mas Val, looking from the presenter to the camera operator and back again. "Come inside, both of you, and we'll get that arm strapped up."

There was a sudden hiss of static in Cal Car's ear as he moved. Reaching up, he pulled out his earpiece - broken and smeared with blood - and tossed it aside.

"I know you from somewhere, don't I?" said Mas Val as she and the cameraman helped the anchor to climb the steps to the building's entrance.

Cal Car nodded. "Possibly, if you've ever watched Channel 3 News."

"You're Cal Car!" exclaimed Mas Val. "Your broadcast was the one my Mom trusted more than any other."

The news anchor stopped, the pain of his shattered shoulder temporarily forgotten. "Really?" he asked, stunned. "That's... Thank you."

"She always tuned in," explained Mas Val as she continued to help Cal Car inside. "In fact, she always said if any journalist was ever to sit down and interview her, she'd like it to be you."

Despite his discomfort, Cal Car nodded. "She was a wonderful woman," he said earnestly. "She'll be greatly missed."

"That's very kind."

Cal Car took a deep breath, briefly wondering whether

his next sentence would get him tossed back out into the cold and wet, and possibly fired from his job.

Then again, he was likely to only ever get one chance at this.

"If you like, I could interview you and your sister about the great work your Mom did to ensure the future of Alma Nine..."

Mas Val was silent for a moment, then turned to Cal Car as they reached the doorway. "I don't think that will be a problem," she smiled.

Alma Nine, Taron City, Weather Control Center, Temporary Laboratory

Zeb Lok looked up as the three aliens he'd last seen in Bay Don's office entered the room.

"Can I help you?" he asked, crossing to meet them.

"Captain Jack Marber," said Jack, holding out his hand. "This is Adina Choudhury and Tc'aarlat."

"And Mist," added the Yollin.

"SQUAWWWW!" screeched Mist, directly into Tc'aarlat's right ear.

Zeb Lok glanced up at the bird, then back at her owner.

"She's in a bit of a mood with me because I left her trapped under a wastepaper basket."

"We represent the Etheric Empire," Jack explained, making a mental note to ask Nathan for some kind of official badge or pass he could show at moments like these. "Here for Tor Val's funeral and Journey Back."

Zeb Lok nodded, waiting for more.

"The Empire has some of the galaxy's most experienced

scientists at our disposal," said Adina, picking up where Jack left off. "If we can get a message back through to our base station, they may be able to help you discover the cause of these violent gravitational waves."

It had taken the trio almost an hour to trudge through the ongoing blizzard to reach the Weather Control Center, fifteen minutes of which was taken up with an argument between Jack and Tc'aarlat about why or why not this was the perfect time to take *The Pegasus* out for 'a test drive'.

"Thank you," said Zeb Lok, "but there's no need for you to contact your own scientists."

Adina raised her eyebrows. "There isn't?"

"Not since we solved the mystery ourselves midway through the recent attack," said Zeb Lok, heading back to his computer and motioning for the others to follow him.

"Be careful," he warned as they ducked under a series of thick power cables stretched overhead from one corner of the room to the other. "Our main lab was destroyed in the original blast. We were forced to rig this place up in a hurry."

"You say you've found the cause of the problem?" said Tc'aarlat.

Zeb Lok nodded unhappily. "We did it to ourselves."

Alma Nine, Taron City, Vice President's Residence

Saf Tah paced back and forth along the length of what, until recently, had been a sumptuous library cum study.

"Scheming, conniving scum!" he thundered. "Who do they think they are? Coming to *my* planet, all high and mighty, and *daring* to save my life."

Mol Gat look confused. "Um... I don't really understand, sir."

"Of course, you don't, you cretin!" spat Saf Tah. "I wouldn't expect you to. It's politics!"

"Saving your life is politics?" questioned Jus Clo.

"In its purest form!" the vice president insisted. "Who do you think benefits from such a blatantly selfless gesture?"

Mol Gat blinked. Twice. "Is that a trick question?"

Saf Tah grabbed a bottle half-filled with black liquor from a side table, ripped out the cork with his teeth, then took a long swig whilst pausing to admire a framed painting of the Malatian's home world.

"Aren't we the ones who benefitted?" asked Jus Clo.

Saf Tah spun to glare at his subordinate. "Of course not!" he snarled. "Are you insane?"

"I didn't *think* I was," admitted Jus Clo. "But since we started this conversation, I'm not so sure..."

"Morons!" bellowed Saf Tah before taking another long drink. He began to pace again, reveling in the painful burning sensation as the fiery liquid made its way down his throat.

"Now that those bastards from the Etheric Empire have so gallantly saved our lives, we're forever in their debt," he growled. "Well, *I* am, at least. I'm not sure keeping you shit-eaters from the next life does anyone any good whatsoever, least of all me!"

"So, would you rather they *hadn't* saved our lives?" questioned Jus Clo.

"Of course!" Saf Tah sneered. "I should have been the one to save *their* pathetic souls! Then they would owe me a debt, and I'd have all my pieces in place for the endgame."

Mol Gat rubbed at his forehead. "I think I need to lie down."

"Don't you get it?" demanded the vice president, taking a final swig of liquor before tossing the empty bottle aside. "Once I realized I was in the debt of those mongrels, I had no option but to suggest I was reconsidering Tor Val's naive plans to join the Etheric Empire."

"So, we're *not* going to do that?" asked Mol Gat.

"Quite the opposite!" replied Saf Tah. "I was always going to agree to align Alma Nine with them."

"You were?"

"Certainly, but under *my* terms."

Jus Clo looked to Mol Gat, but his colleague shrugged. "Your terms, sir?"

Saf Tah smiled, but this was not the pleasant smile he had presented as he was leaving the presidential office suite.

This smile was colder. Darker.

"My terms, gentlemen, and the terms of like-minded individuals across the Ordanian Hub, and beyond."

Finally, the vice president stopped his pacing, and turned to face one of the large bookcases lining the walls of the room. Reaching up, he removed a book with a nondescript cover.

There was a click, and the painting of Malatia rolled up inside its frame to reveal another piece of artwork hidden underneath.

Artwork featuring a symbol painted in black, red and white.

The symbol of an organization some would call freedom fighters, but most would call terrorists.

The symbol of Dark Tomorrow.

Saf Tah's cold smile widened as he saluted the painting with pride.

"Tomorrow, the blood of our enemies shall rain down from the heavens!"

23

Alma Nine, Taron City, Weather Control Center, Temporary Laboratory

Jack peered through the eyepiece of the microscope. "I can see it," he said, "but I'm still not one-hundred-percent certain what it is."

Zeb Lok gestured to the picture on the computer screen linked to the cracked glass case. "It's a nanobot," he explained. "One designed by our chief scientist, Yan Mil."

"And you say it's holding *gravity*?" quizzed Adina.

"Believe it or not, yes," Zeb Lok replied. "We've colored it orange to make it visible to us, but that tiny sphere the nanobot is gripping in its pincers is a graviton; a single particle of gravity."

"You've found those things?" asked Tc'aarlat.

"Yan Mil did, several years before we left Malatia," replied Zeb Lok. "He designed the artificial gravity system for the *Dessia*, the ship we came here aboard. It was, essentially, millions of nanobots embedded into the *Dessia*'s shell, each holding a graviton."

"That still doesn't explain these gravitational waves," Jack pointed out.

"Actually it does," said Zeb Lok with a sigh. "It's the same nanobots. They're snatching gravitons from outside the atmosphere and dragging them down to ground level."

Adina looked back at the screen. "These things have gone rogue?"

"That was what we thought at first," said Zeb Lok. "But, unfortunately not. They've been reprogrammed to do this deliberately."

"What?!" exclaimed Tc'aarlat. "Who would do that? Was the system hacked?"

"That's what we're looking into now."

"And the unpredictable weather?" asked Jack.

"The same nanobots, I'm afraid," said Zeb Lok. "Yan Mil figured out a way to get them to multitask."

"Perfect!" sighed Tc'aarlat. "So, we're at the mercy of millions of tiny robot bastards."

"Try trillions," responded Zeb Lok. "Whoever did this also took control of our back-up swarms, and those dedicated to moderating the weather in other areas of the planet."

"Can't you just catch them all with a big net?" Tc'aarlat asked.

"Unfortunately not," replied Zeb Lok. "We don't have anything with a fine enough mesh. They'd just fly right through."

Tc'aarlat's mandibles tapped together in thought. "What about zapping them with an electro-magnetic pulse?"

"The nanobots have a built-in shield," Zeb Lok explained. "All we'd succeed in doing is trashing every bit of technology we might be able to use to track them and protect the public."

Jack stepped aside so that Adina could take his place at the microscope. "There must be *some* way to get them back under control. What has Yan Mil had to say about the situation? He designed them, after all."

Zeb Lok sighed heavily.

"That's the other thing..."

Alma Nine, Taron City, Weather Control Center, Yan Mil's Apartment

Jack led the group off the elevator and onto the small landing. "This is it?" he asked, gesturing to a closed, white door.

"That's it," Zeb Lok confirmed. "In the early days of the colony, Yan Mil was working so hard on perfecting his weather control system that he often decided to spend the night in the lab, sleeping on the floor. When Tor Val found out, she arranged for the top floor office to be converted into a small apartment for him to use."

Adina pressed her ear to the door. "And he's been in there ever since his wife died?"

Zeb Lok nodded. "No-one's seen, or heard from him."

"Even with all the problems his own invention is causing?"

"We're not sure he knows it's down to his nanobots," said Zeb Lok. "We've called, sent messages, tried everything we can think of. But, we don't know whether he's getting them."

"Well, that ends now," declared Tc'aarlat, taking a few steps back. "You want Yan Mil? I'll get you Yan Mil."

"I'm not sure that's wise," warned Zeb Lok.

But Tc'aarlat ignored him.

He whistled to Mist, who flapped twice to cross the tiny landing area and sit on Adina's shoulder, then he turned side on to the apartment door...

...and charged.

Tc'aarlat slammed into the door with a sickening crunch, bouncing back a short way as everyone else winced.

"Fuck a fucking bistok!" he bellowed, staggering away from the still-closed door. "What the fuck is that thing made of?"

"Yan Mil's apartment was originally a data storage room," said Zeb Lok. "The government installed special security doors as protection against any intruders who might want to access the servers without permission."

Tc'aarlat stared at the scientist. "And you didn't think to tell me that before I tried to break it down?"

"I wasn't aware you were going to hurl yourself directly at it," said Zeb Lok. "Trust me, if there was the slightest chance of getting inside by breaking the door down, we'd have already done it ourselves."

"Well, as amusing as that was to watch, it doesn't get us any closer to speaking to Yan Mil," said Jack. "Can we drill the lock out?"

"Unfortunately not," said Zeb Lok. "The metal the lock is made of is designed to melt if it detects any attempt to tamper with it."

"What about windows?" asked Adina. "Can we get in through one of those?"

Zeb Lok shook his head again. "We thought of that," he said. "But we're seven floors up, and the windows only open enough to allow air to vent in and out." He crossed to the window in the tiny hallway and turned the handle to demonstrate. The mechanism allowed it to open a gap of around eight inches wide.

"Even if we had someone who could get up this high, they'd have to be small enough to fit through that gap. It's pretty much impossible."

Adina smiled, reaching up to scratch the top of Mist's beak. "Nothing's impossible for *The Freedom Squad*!"

Jack stared at her. "The who, now?"

"Freedom Squad," Adina repeated. "I thought that might be a good name for us."

"Only if we were all 12 years old and solved spooky mysteries from a treehouse in Tc'aarlat's back yard," Jack scoffed. "No, I think we can do better than that."

"Whatever," said Adina. "My point is, if there's a window open, Mist could fly to it and squeeze through the gap."

"And then what?" demanded Tc'aarlat. "Unlock the door from the inside? I know she's a smart bird, but there are limits to her abilities."

"SQWARRR!"

"It's not an insult!" Tc'aarlat countered to Mist. "You just don't have the equipment needed to work the lock."

"SCURRR!"

Adina waited patiently until Tc'aarlat had finished making his point. "Zeb Lok said the master key was likely to be in there with Yan Mil," she reminded him.

Zeb Lok nodded. "He keeps his own key on a side table just inside the door. I imagine that's where he's put the master key as well."

"So, we know where it's likely to be," continued Adina. "We can send Mist in to get it."

"She can bring it back to us and we can open the door from the outside," finished Jack. "That's brilliant!"

Tc'aarlat smiled. "I do my best..."

"Not *you*," argued Jack. "It was Adina's idea."

"And Mist is my hawk!"

"It doesn't matter whose idea it was," said Adina. "We just have to hope one of the windows is open."

Zeb Lok pulled a handheld communicator from his pocket and flipped it open. "Jal Fen," he said into the device's microphone. "Can you check if any of the windows in Yan Mil's apartment are open, please?"

A tinny voice responded. "Will do. One moment..."

The group waited anxiously, all hoping they might have finally hit upon a plan to get inside and quiz Yan Mil for a way to regain control of the rogue nanobots.

"Zeb Lok..." hissed the communicator after a short while.

"Well?"

"One of the apartment windows is open to its full extent."

"Yes!" exclaimed Adina. She turned her head towards Mist, sitting patiently on her shoulder. "You know what to do?"

"Hang on," protested Tc'aarlat. "She's my hawk, remember?"

"OK, go on..." sighed Adina with a shake of her head.

Tc'aarlat stepped up to face the Raal hawk. "You know what to do?"

"SKERRR!"

Tc'aarlat nodded earnestly. "She's good."

Adina crossed to the window. Outside, the icy wind was still whipping the snow into freezing white vortices. Mist ruffled her feathers, plumping them out against the cold air blasting in through the gap between the window's glass and frame.

"Will you be OK out there?" Adina questioned.

Mist purred softly in Adina's ear, then leapt through the window and disappeared into the storm beyond.

Alma Nine, Taron City, Weather Control Center, Front Steps

Bundled up against the fierce snowstorm, Jal Fen peered through his binoculars at the lone open window of Yan Mil's top floor apartment.

It was, in fact, the only window currently open in the entire building now that Adina had slammed hers shut again.

He could just about make out Mist's red feathers high in the blizzard above him; the only patch of color in an otherwise world of white. Buffeted by the pounding winds, the Raal hawk fought against the elements to reach the open window.

Once there, Mist paused on the ledge outside, presumably to catch her breath and regain her strength, then she disappeared into the leading scientist's locked and sealed apartment.

Less than a minute later, she was back - and she had something clenched tightly in her beak. Something credit card sized, and a bright, vibrant green in color.

Jal Fen knew exactly what this was from the identical object tucked into one of his own pockets.

It was the key to a door inside the building.

The key to accessing Yan Mil.

Alma Nine, Taron City, Weather Control Center, Yan Mil's Apartment

Mist landed awkwardly on the ledge outside the window the nervous group were waiting at, a gust of wind almost blowing her back in the direction she had appeared from.

"There she is!" proclaimed Tc'aarlat as his precious partner's jet black eyes peered through the toughened glass and met his own.

Adina twisted the handle and swung the window open as far as it would go. Jack reached through the gap, grabbed hold of Mist, and hauled her back inside.

In all the months he'd known and worked with Tc'aarlat, this was the first time he'd ever touched his hawk. She felt much smaller in his hands than he had anticipated, and she was shivering hard.

"That's the key!" cried Zeb Lok, taking the plastic card from Mist's beak. "She did it!"

"She certainly did!" beamed Tc'aarlat, reaching out to take Mist himself, but Jack already had her tucked inside his own coat, holding her against his chest in an effort to

GRAVITY STORM

reward the successful conclusion of her risky assignment with some much needed warmth.

Tc'aarlat's wide eyed and wide mandibiled look of surprise was only outdone by that of Adina. Without the mandibles, of course.

"I never thought I'd see the day," he breathed.

"Nor me," said Adina with a shake of her head. "She's not trying to bite his nipples off, or anything."

Jack frowned at his fellow crew members. "Don't get the wrong idea," he warned. "This isn't the two of us bonding in any way. It's simply the easiest method for providing warmth to a colleague in dire risk of hypothermia."

A muffled caw came from beneath the Captain's coat as if to confirm his words.

"We're in!" exclaimed Zeb Lok as the door to the apartment opened with a satisfying click. "You guys ready?"

Jack, Adina and Tc'aarlat all nodded as Zeb Lok pushed open the apartment door and stepped inside.

Aside from Zeb Lok, none of them knew exactly what to expect the inside of Yan Mil's accommodation to look like, so the choice of decor came as something of a surprise.

The walls were painted a soft mint green, which complemented the thick, grey carpets beautifully. All the furniture was built from dark wood, the delicate grain of which matched the thick frames of the exquisitely chosen pieces of art hanging on the walls.

Many of the paintings had fallen to the floor due to the surges in gravity, their glass fronts now shattered. Yet, under the subtle hidden lighting, even they appeared to

259

have been purposely placed there in an effort to add to the overall design.

"This is amazing!" hissed Adina, her eyes sweeping the sumptuously fitted apartment. "I'd give your left nut to live in a place like this."

"She's right," said Tc'aarlat. "This place doesn't exactly scream 'geeky science nerd', does it?

Despite the urgency of the situation, Zeb Lok chuckled. "It was at first," he told the group. "A fold out cot, a wobbly chair and an old card table covered with ripped and stained fabric."

Tc'aarlat tried to picture the apartment's original style. "So, what happened?"

"His wife happened," Zeb Lok replied. "Once Vix Mil got a look inside the place, she kicked him out for a week and had the place redecorated at her own expense."

"Sounds like a wonderful woman," Jack commented.

The sadness showed in Zeb Lok's eyes. "She was."

A few seconds of silence followed, broken by Tc'aarlat. "So, where is this weather genius of yours?"

"Most likely in his study," replied Zeb Lok, taking a left turn and leading the group along a short corridor.

"Yan Mil," he called out as he reached for the door handle. "It's Zeb Lok, and some friends. Don't be alarmed when we come in."

Twisting the handle, Zeb Lok swung open the doorway to the apartment's study and froze.

Jack, Tc'aarlat and Adina stopped quickly behind him.

"Oh, shit!" croaked Adina.

There, hanging by the neck from a length of computer cable, was the dead body of Yan Mil.

24

Alma Nine, Taron City, Weather Control Center, Yan Mil's Apartment

Jack turned to Zeb Lok. "Are you OK?" he asked softly.

The Malatian didn't reply. Instead he continued gazing up at the face of his deceased superior. The normally teal colored skin now a deep avocado green, the swollen tongue hanging limply from between bloated lips, the eyes - still open - bulging wildly from their sockets.

Adina placed a hand on the scientist's arm. "Come on, I think you should sit down in another room.

But Zeb Lok brushed her hand away. "I knew he was hurting," he said, his throat suddenly dry. "I knew he missed her. I just didn't think it was this bad. I was his friend. If I'd known..."

"You couldn't have done anything," Jack reassured him. "No-one could."

"But, if I'd got him talking..."

"He locked himself away," Jack reminded him. "You

tried everything possible to get through to him and check he was OK. He didn't want help."

"Is there a note?" Zeb Lok asked, still not looking away from Yan Mil. "Did he leave anything?"

Tc'aarlat and Adina exchanged a glance then turned, eyes scouring each and every surface around the room. But, there was nothing to see.

"I'm afraid not," said Adina. "He may not have wanted to-"

"Wait a minute," said Tc'aarlat, interrupting her. "There a red light flashing on his computer. Is that anything?"

Finally, Zeb Lok tore his gaze away from the corpse. He looked over at Yan Mil's personal computer, seemingly struggling to focus for a moment.

"It means there's a live file on the system," he said.

Stepping over to the computer, he reached out and tapped a button on the keyboard. The screen lit up instantly, the Weather Control Center logo vanishing to be replaced with the face of Yan Mil.

"I don't know which of you will be the first to find this," said the man on the screen. "I don't know which of you will find me."

Jack tapped the button again, pausing the footage.

"Why did you stop it?" asked Zeb Lok.

Jack's gaze flicked up to the figure still dangling from the ceiling, then back to Zeb Lok. "I think we should move Yan Mil before we continue."

Nodding silently, Zeb Lok took his communicator from his pocket and called down to the temporary laboratory to explain the situation, and ask for assistance.

Then he, Jack, Adina and Tc'aarlat relocated to the

apartment's dining room to wait while medics arrived to cut down the corpse, zip it into a body bag, and lay it onto a long, thin cart.

Zeb Lok stood in the dining room doorway and watched as Yan Mil left his apartment for the very last time, two medics wheeling the cart onto the landing area, and then into the elevator.

As the elevator doors closed, Adina shut the apartment door gently. "Now, let's see what he has to say."

The group made their way back into the study, Jack and Tc'aarlat each bringing a wooden chair from the dining room. Adina perched on the edge of the large, polished desk while Zeb Lok took the padded chair.

Mist, now properly recovered from being out in the freezing winds of the storm, flapped up to the curtain rail above the window and perched there, preening her dark red feathers.

"Ready?" asked Tc'aarlat, his finger hovering above the 'enter' button on the computer's keyboard.

Zeb Lok nodded. The video began again.

"I don't know which of you will be the first to find this," said the image of Yan Mil on screen. "I don't know which of you will find me.

"But I do know I will no longer be alive when you finally gain access to this apartment."

From the corner of her eye, Adina saw Zeb Lok lower his head, unable to look at the video clip any longer. But he did continue to listen.

"I have lost Vix Mil, the only reason I had for living. She was my all. My reason for breathing. My love.

"But who else knew her? No-one! No-one knew her!"

Zeb Lok looked up again quickly. He frowned at the screen.

Yan Mil's demeanor began to change. He was still grieving, but now there was an anger to his words and body language.

"All we've seen and heard for days is Tor Val this, and Tor Val that. News channels are filled with footage of her opening hospitals, visiting the elderly, reading to children.

"Experts chatter non-stop about how worthy her life has been, how much she did for us, and how she will be missed."

By now, the scientist was shouting at the camera, flecks of spit flying from his mouth.

"Vix Mil died on the same day as the president. But who's talking about her? Who's filming sobbing members of the public laying flowers at the spot where she took her final breath? Where are the newspaper articles about all the good things she did for society, and how she'll be missed?"

Fury flashed in Yan Mil's eyes as he bellowed.

"What about Vix Mil?!"

He rested back in his chair - the chair Zeb Lok was now sitting in - and took a moment to catch his breath.

"So, I have decided that you will *all* remember Vix Mil. In fact, you will never be able to forget her. Hers will be the last name the people of Alma Nine ever hear."

The scientist paused, then stared right down the lens of the camera.

"Vix. Is. Coming."

The screen hissed as the video file ended.

No-one spoke for a full minute.

"That was a bit... full on," Tc'aarlat commented.

Adina scowled. "He was upset," she pointed out.

Tc'aarlat held his palms up. "Hey, I wasn't saying he was wrong. I get it, he missed his wife, couldn't live without her."

"Yes, but what does 'Vix is coming' mean?" queried Jack.

Tc'aarlat shrugged, then he caught his breath as an idea struck him. He turned in his chair to address Zeb Lok. "When you guys die, you don't... you know. Do you?"

"Don't what?"

"You know..."

Tc'aarlat stretched his arms out in front on him, rolled his eyes back in his head and groaned like a zombie from a cheap horror movie.

"BRRRAAAIIINNNS!"

"Don't be ridiculous!" barked Jack.

"Alright, keep your hair on," said Tc'aarlat, turning back. "Someone's got to ask these things, haven't they?"

"No!" Jack retorted. "That's just not the sort of question any sensible, sane person would ever ask!"

"You can't make an omelet without breaking a few legs, Jack!"

"EGGS!" Jack bellowed. "EGGS!"

Tc'aarlat frowned. "You can't make eggs without breaking a few legs? That doesn't make sense."

"There's another light!"

Everyone turned to Adina, and then to where she was pointing on the computer keyboard. "A blue one, this time."

Zeb Lok scooted the desk chair forward on its wheels until he reached the computer desk. "It's another file," he said. "Scheduled to play after that last one."

"Another video?" queried Jack.

"No," Zeb Lok replied. "This is one of our weather program's timelines." He looked up at the others. "Should I play it?"

Jack nodded his head, and he Tc'aarlat and Adina leaned in closer to the screen.

Zeb Lok hit the button.

This time, the screen showed a satellite image of the coast line on which Taron City sat. Layered over the pictures of the land and the sea, were sweeping lines showing areas of air pressure and symbols detailing temperature, wind speed and more.

"Oh, fuck!" croaked Zeb Lok, swallowing hard.

"What is it?" asked Adina.

Zeb Lok pointed to the far right of the screen where a mass of swirling white was gradually approaching Taron City from the east. It grew in size as it traveled, spinning faster as the mass grew darker.

"What is that thing?" said Tc'aarlat.

Zeb Lok typed a series of commands into the computer, giving him a closer look at the raw data behind the graphics. "It's a storm," he said after reading and re-reading the lines of numbers. "A big one. The biggest this planet has ever seen."

He pointed to where three lines of digits were flashing orange. "And that's another group of gravitational waves."

"Headed this way?" asked Jack.

Zeb Lok nodded. "We've got about three hours until it hits land."

"And then?"

"It will destroy the city."

"Wait!" cried Adina, pressing a finger to a side box of text at the top left of the screen. "That says 'Yan Mil'. What does it mean?"

"That box shows the name of the person who programmed the nanobots to create this weather system," Zeb Lok explained.

"Yan Mil did this?" exclaimed 'Tc'aarlat. "On purpose."

"I'm afraid so," said Zeb Lok. "One minute - I'll see if I can access the program and cancel it."

Leaning forward, his fingers danced across the keys, flashing through screen after screen of green computer code on a black background.

Suddenly, he stopped, stared at the naked code, then slumped back in the chair. "I can't get in. He's password protected everything."

Adina looked at him in horror. "You can't stop the storm?"

Zeb Lok shook his head. "I can't stop it, can't divert it, can't even reduce its ferocity. Plus..."

Jack turned to the scientist. "Plus what?"

Zeb Lok swallowed hard as he reached out for the keyboard once more. "He's named the storm after his wife."

"The storm is called 'Vix'?" questioned Jack. "I don't understand."

Zeb Lok hit the 'enter' key, and the screen went blank. Then three words written in bold, red text slowly faded into view...

VIX IS COMING.

Jack turned to face his fellow crew members. "Oh, fuck."

. . .

Alma Nine, Taron City, Saf Tah's Residence

"Are you out of your mind?" exclaimed Saf Tah. "We can't evacuate the entire city in under three hours! Have you *seen* how bad the weather is out there?"

Jack wiped his hand through his dripping wet hair and thrust it in the vice president's direction. "Seen it?" he snapped. We've just been in it! But it's going to get worse. A *lot* worse!"

"So you claim..."

"It's true," Zeb Lok put in. "The storm heading our way - Vix - is the most powerful we've ever seen, both in terms of severity of the weather, and the surge in gravity.

Saf Tah blinked, not understanding. "The storm has a name?"

"All storms are named," Zeb Lok confirmed. "It's how we log them for future reference, rather than refer to them by date or location."

"But why Vix?"

"That's the name of the chief weather control scientist's late wife," Adina explained. "Vix Mil."

Saf Tah held up a hand. "Slow down... You're telling me the guy who invented our weather control system has programmed it to destroy the city with a killer gravity storm, and named it after his *dead wife*?!"

"Pretty much," said Tc'aarlat.

"Then get him to un-program it, on the orders of the president!"

Standing behind Saf Tah, Jus Clo gave out a timid cough. "Er... vice president, sir."

"*Vice* president, then!" spat Saf Tah.

"I don't think he'll listen..." began Jack.

"Then *make* him listen!" Saf Tah roared. "Threaten him with demotion, jail time, deportation back to Malatia, anything!"

Tc'aarlat took a step towards the vice president's desk. "You can't threaten a dead guy."

Saf Tah sat up in his chair. "He's dead?"

"By his own hand," Adina confirmed. "And he locked everyone else out of the system beforehand."

"Which is why you *have* to give the order to evacuate Taron City now!" exclaimed Jack. "Time is running out."

Saf Tah fixed the group before him with a fierce stare. "Do you have any idea how much mayhem and confusion that will cause?" he demanded. "Yes, some people will be able to abandon the city without assistance, but then there's the elderly, the infirm, hospital patients. If we try to move those individuals in these conditions, many of them will perish in the process."

"They'll all die if they stay here," snarled Jack, "and more besides."

"All thanks to a mad scientist, driven to insanity by the death of his wife." Saf Tah's expression remained stern. "If I sound the alert to evacuate Taron City, the resulting deaths will be on *my* hands."

"You pint-sized, piss-faced prick!" thundered Tc'aarlat. "You're condemning people to die so you can keep your reputation?!"

Saf Tah fixed the Yollin with a fierce stare. "If people want to leave the city under their own volition, they can. They don't need me to tell them what they should do."

TOM DUBLIN & MICHAEL ANDERLE

The Yollin took another step towards Saf Tah's desk, but Jack held him back. "We're leaving," he growled.

Jack, Zeb Lok and Adina all made for the door. Tc'aarlat continued to glare at the vice-president for a few seconds longer before following.

As the door began to close behind the group, Mol Gat tossed his clipboard onto Saf Tah's desk, then scurried after them.

Saf Tah frowned. "Where do you think you're going?"

"I don't, um... really know to be honest," Mol Gat admitted. "I just know I'm not staying here to work for a witless pile of cockroach droppings like you, any longer."

Saf Tah's eyes grew wider than the embittered political assistant had ever seen.

Mol Gat paused before leaving, and looked back. "Um... Fuck you, and every odious little spunk bubble like you."

With that he left the office and slammed the door behind him.

Alma Nine, Taron City, Outside Saf Tah's Residence

Mol Gat stomped down the steps outside the house, his feet sinking into the deep snow. Lifting his knees high with each step, he walked past the group that had left just before him without saying a word.

Jack watched him struggle on down the street until he was lost among the swirling torrent of snow.

"So," said Adina. "What now?"

"I should return to the lab," said Zeb Lok. "I don't know how to crack Yan Mil's password to access the system and stop the storm, but I have to at least try."

Tc'aarlat's mandibles tapped together as he thought hard. "Can't you, I dunno... use a computer to hack into Yan Mil's computer." He realized the others were staring at him in surprise, and added: "Hey, I'm not the tech genius scientist here..."

Jack frowned. "You don't say..."

Adina turned to Zeb Lok. "Is that, whatever Tc'aarlat just said, is it possible?"

"It's possible," Zeb Lok replied. "But we don't have a computer anywhere near as powerful as you would need to do that in the time we have remaining. To stand any kind of chance, we'd need a system working almost at artificial intelligence levels."

A smile crept across Jack's face, leaving Zeb Lok confused. Especially when Tc'aarlat and Adina began to smile as well.

"Zeb Lok," beamed Jack. "There's someone we'd like you to meet..."

25

ICS Fortitude, **Bridge**

It took the group 40 minutes to slog their way through the rapidly expanding snow drifts to reach the ship. The snow was now so deep that TV and radio stations were issuing travel warnings due to the safety risk.

And, even if some valiant driver was brave enough to attempt an automobile journey, they wouldn't have been able to get very far at all.

Piles of rubble that had, until recently, been houses, stores and offices now resembled smooth, snow-covered hills, awarding the many scenes of death and destruction a temporary air of serenity.

Except for those areas where body parts still jutted from the icy covering at disturbing angles.

Jack pulled off one of his gloves and tapped his key-code into the panel beside the door.

"Two hours left until the storm hits," announced Zeb Lok, checking the countdown he'd set on his personal communicator.

One by one, the crew and Zeb Lok stepped inside, stomped the snow from their boots and made their way onto the bridge.

"Captain Marber!" exclaimed Solo as she spotted Jack. "I've been so worried about you."

"You have?"

"Of course!" Solo replied. "You didn't call even once to let me know you were safe."

"Oh, er... sorry," said Jack, throwing a concerned look towards Adina. "I didn't realize I was supposed to."

"How else am I supposed to ensure you haven't been hurt, or worse?"

Tc'aarlat held his arms wide towards the face on the view screen. "Adina and I are both here and unharmed as well, Solo."

Solo turned to smile at the pair - a little too condescendingly for Tc'aarlat's taste.

"I can see, that."

Finally, Solo turned her attention to Zeb Lok. "And we have a visitor," she smiled. "Welcome to the *ICS Fortitude*, sir. Would you care for something to drink, or a light snack perhaps?"

"If he does, will you be the one preparing this mini-feast, Solo?" Tc'aarlat inquired.

"As you are aware, I do not have the necessary body parts to undertake such a task," said Solo.

"So, one of us lot would have to do it?"

"I'm merely welcoming our guest," Solo replied. "I would be forced to leave the logistics of the situation to someone more... mortal."

Tc'aarlat turned and whispered to Adina. "I agree with

Jack," he hissed. "Check she was installed properly, first chance you get."

Zeb Lok smiled politely. "Thank you," he said to Solo. "I don't need anything just now."

"As you wish."

"I'm afraid we don't have time for drinks or snacks, Solo," said Jack, pulling off his heavy coat and dumping it over the back of his chair. "There's a gravity storm heading this way, and-"

"Storm Vix," interrupted Solo to everyone's surprise. "I am aware of the impending catastrophe."

"You are?" Adina frowned. "How?"

"While alone, I took the liberty of monitoring local news broadcasts for any mention of Captain Marber," Solo explained. "While none of the major channels saw fit to mention the arrival of the esteemed delegate from the Etheric Empire, they have been reporting about the incoming storm."

The E.I.'s avatar shrunk in size and slid to the top corner of the main screen. In its place, six individual windows appeared, each featuring a live broadcast from one of Alma Nine's television stations.

Tc'aarlat made a mental note to remind Solo later on that they were *all* official delegates and asked. "How did they find out about that?"

Adina turned to Zeb Lok. "Did you tell them?"

"No," he replied. "I gave the order for a news embargo on our way to see Saf Tah."

"Actually," Solo commented, "I believe the originator of the storm, Yan Mil, arranged for copies of his recorded suicide message to be sent to all available news outlets before he took his own life.

"They were delivered electronically approximately 13 minutes ago."

Jack sank into his seat. "There's going to be mass panic."

"That is also my prediction," agreed Solo.

"We need your help, Solo," said Adina. "Can you work with Zeb Lok to hack into Alma Nine's weather control system?"

Solo's avatar shifted to form an expression of concern. "I'm not sure I should get involved in such an activity, Adina. Hacking into computer systems is highly illegal."

"Even if it could save thousands of lives?" questioned Tc'aarlat. "Maybe tens of thousands?"

"The end does not always justify the means," Solo replied. "I, like the rest of the ship's crew, am on this planet as a guest. If I were to break a law, no matter how worthy the cause, the political fallout could be-"

"Forget the legality of the exercise!" Jack commanded. "Can you hack into another computer system or not?"

"Yes, Captain. I believe that would be possible."

Jack stood, grabbed Zeb Lok's arm and steered him towards his captain's chair. "Right, stop talking and get to work, both of you."

Taking a deep breath, the Malatian began to hammer at the ancient, springy keyboard built into the console. Solo responded by flooding each of the bridge's many screens with rapidly scrolling lines of code.

Jack gestured for Tc'aarlat and Adina to join him in the doorway. "We need a back-up plan in case they can't get into the system," he said. "I'm thinking we could-"

"We're in!" announced Zeb Lok, throwing his hands into the air.

Jack's brow knitted. "Already? Are you sure?"

"Absolutely!" said the scientist, spinning to face the trio. "Solo is incredible!"

"Don't say that in front of her!" groaned Tc'aarlat.

Zeb Lok ignored him and continued. "She found a hidden back door into the system in under three seconds, and was inside five seconds later."

"So, you can delete the program running Storm Vix?" asked Adina.

The Malatian nodded. "All we have to do is work out which format Yan Mil used for his password, and we-"

"We can't do it," said Solo, flatly.

Zeb Lok spun back to face the screen. "What? Why not?"

Jack, Adina and Tc'aarlat hurried over, eager to hear Solo's answer.

"The password securing the storm's programming is unhackable."

"Unhackable?" queried Jack. "That's impossible, isn't it? Surely there's no such thing as 100 per cent digital security?"

"Ordinarily, that would be true, Captain," said Solo. "However, it appears that Yan Mil has discovered a way to protect his code with a unique form of password, if it can even be called that."

"I don't get it," admitted Adina. "What do you need to get into the program and cancel the storm."

"DNA," replied Solo. "The 'password' required for access is a sample of an unknown individual's DNA."

"Yan Mil's?" suggested Tc'aarlat.

"I'm afraid we have no way of knowing," said Solo. "Not without a range of samples with which to try."

Zeb Lok slumped back. "Then, it is impossible," he said. "We can't stop the storm, and now we don't have enough time to evacuate even a third of the city."

"Not necessarily," said Jack. "Remember what Yan Mil said in his video message..."

"That he didn't know which of his lab assistants would find his body?" said Tc'aarlat.

"Not that bit," said Jack. "He said-"

"Vix is coming!" Adina finished.

Jack nodded. "He said everyone would remember the name Vix Mil, that hers was the last name the people of Alma Nine would ever hear. He was referring to the storm. That's why he named it after her."

"It's all about Vix Mil," Adina pointed out. "*Everything* is about Vix Mil."

Tc'aarlat's eyes grew wide as he finally caught on. "So, chances are high that the DNA required to access the system will be hers!"

"Exactly!" cried Jack. He turned to Zeb Lok. "Has she had her Journey Back yet?"

"No, all funerals were postponed until after Tor Val's had taken place."

"So where would her body be right now?" asked Adina.

"In the morgue," said Zeb Lok, jumping up. "All bodies are taken there to be prepared for their Journey Back."

Tc'aarlat scowled. "*The* morgue?" he demanded. "A planet this size, and you only have one morgue?"

"The morgue is twice the size of any government building," Zeb Lok explained. "It's always full, but the staff seem to cope."

"So, what are we waiting for?" asked Jack, grabbing his coat and sliding his arms into the sleeves. "We can't be certain Vix Mil's DNA will unlock access to her husband's program, but it's worth the gamble."

"There's just one problem," said Zeb Lok.

"What?"

"The morgue is on the other side of town. At least an hour's walk in this weather, and the roads are still closed off."

Adina sighed. "So, not enough time to get there, find Vix Mil, get a sample of her DNA, and make it back to the lab before the storm hits."

"Unless," said Tc'aarlat, his eyes alive with excitement. "We take The Pegasus."

ICS Fortitude, **Concealed Rear Hanger**

"I don't care if you *are* the captain of the Fortitude," insisted Tc'aarlat. "I've got the rapid reflexes needed to control *The Pegasus* in this vile weather. *I'm* driving!"

"It's got nothing to do with being captain!" Jack retorted. "It's about having the experience required to handle a craft such as this! I was trained to fly ships like this in the *SAM*!"

Adina leaned forward, thrusting her head between the two plush pilot's seats of *The Pegasus*. "Can you two leave your 'manliest among men' contest until *after* we've saved everyone in the city?" she demanded.

Slumping back, she turned to Zeb Lok and added:

"Honestly, take anything black and shiny and fill it with buttons and blue LEDs and men get all googly eyed."

Before either Jack or Tc'aarlat could comment, Solo appeared on the forward screen. "Actually, *I'm* the one who will be piloting *The Pegasus*," she pointed out. "The controls in front of you are for use in emergency situations only."

With that, the sleek spacecraft rose smoothly into the air as the rear cargo doors of the *ICS Fortitude* slid open to reveal the swirling white nightmare outside.

The inside of *The Pegasus* was just as luxurious as the exterior, if not more. Black leather seats sat in rows of two, seating a total of six passengers. The tinted windows doubled as computerized touchscreens, with essential data also projected onto the windshield as a heads up display.

"This is incredible!" breathed Zeb Lok from beside Adina in the second row of seats. "And your A.I. can control this ship as well?"

"Actually, Solo isn't a full Artificial Intelligence," Adina replied. "She's an Entity Intelligence, but I think she has hopes of evolving."

"Don't say things like that!" commented Tc'aarlat over his shoulder. "I don't want to crap myself at the thought of Solo with real power."

Solo reappeared on the view screen, staring at Tc'aarlat. "I shall do my best not to cause you to lose control of your bowels," she said flatly. "Now, does everybody have their safety belt fastened?"

A series of clicks followed, accompanied by a barely audible "For fucks' sake!", and then they were off.

The Pegasus shot out of the rear doors of the cargo

hold and swept effortlessly through the streets of the city approximately six feet off the ground.

To Jack and Tc'aarlat, the gusts of snow whipping past the front windshield resembled a movie special effect of a spacecraft making the jump to warp speed.

However, while the two men shared their barely concealed excitement with their respective inner children, Mist appeared to find the combination of such high speed and poor visibility disconcerting. Tightening her grip on the back of her master's seat, she tucked her head under her wing and stayed there.

Zeb Lok studied the interior of *The Pegasus* in fascination. "What's powering this?" he asked, his eyes wide.

Solo faded into view on the window beside him. "*The Pegasus* contains two unique anti-gravity engines developed by a trio of Etheric Empire engineers known as Team BMW."

"Well, they certainly know their stuff," enthused Zeb Lok. "I don't suppose they have any vacancies, do they?"

"I shall download your resume from the Weather Control Center's database and ensure it is delivered to them at the earliest opportunity," promised Solo with a smile.

Ten minutes later, *The Pegasus* slowed as it arrived at the main entrance of Taron City's only morgue. The side doors hissed open, swinging upwards like the wings of a bird, allowing Jack, Tc'aarlat, Adina and Zeb Lok to climb out.

Jack looked skywards, but the top of the vast building disappeared among the thick clouds and worsening snow fall above.

"You weren't wrong about the size of this place," he said to Zeb Lok.

Tc'aarlat turned back to the car's interior and tapped his leather shoulder pad. But Mist refused to move.

"Come on," the Yollin urged. "We haven't got all day."

Mist turned to face away from Tc'aarlat. It was clear she wasn't going to leave the warmth of *The Pegasus* voluntarily.

"Suit yourself," said Tc'aarlat, "but if I come across anything tasty to eat in there, I'm not bringing a doggy style back for you."

"The phrase is 'doggy bag'," corrected Jack with a small shake of his head. "And what, exactly, do you imagine you'll find that is 'tasty to eat' inside a morgue?"

Tc'aarlat shrugged. "Depends what ends up in the autopsy bowls set aside for stomach contents," he stated.

Feeling her own stomach flip, Adina turned and hurried up the steps towards the main door before she was able to hear any more of the Tc'aarlat's suggestions.

Alma Nine, Taron City, Morgue, 14th Floor, Pathology Lab 9

Finding the room where Vix Mil's body was being kept proved to be easier than expected. The reception desk in the building's lobby had either been abandoned or hadn't been manned at all that day due to the weather.

The computer terminal in the small office behind the desk wasn't password protected, so Zeb Lok didn't require Solo's help this time.

"Got it!" he said, standing up from the chair. He checked the countdown on his communicator. "An hour and five minutes remaining."

Jack nodded. "Let's go."

The music piped into the elevator was far too jolly for such somber surroundings, according to Tc'aarlat, and he was still griping about the chosen playlist when they stepped off on the 14th floor.

A long corridor stretched away in each direction, well-lit but just as deserted as the lobby.

The group hurried in the direction the signs posted outside the elevator had indicated where the lab they needed would be, knowing they were on the clock and didn't have time to spare.

Eventually, they reached a laboratory with a large number '9' painted onto the slate grey door and stepped inside.

A row of five metal benches lined up from one side of the room to the other, four of them occupied by figures lying motionless under soft, white sheets. Behind them, a bank of 12 square steel doors where fitted into the rear wall.

"Not many people about," Tc'aarlat commented.

Adina gestured to the corpses lying covered on the tables. "What, these guys don't count?"

"I meant living people," countered Tc'aarlat. "People you can talk to."

"Nothing to stop you chatting with these people," said Adina with a slight shrug. "Not sure you'd get much of a response, though."

"Can't be any worse than the one-sided conversations I used to have with my parents back home," Tc'aarlat said grimly.

"Got it!" announced Zeb Lok. While Tc'aarlat and Adina had been prowling among the post-autopsied bodies on the tables, he and Jack had been busy searching for Vix Mil's name on one of the pieces of card fixed to the outside of each of the refrigerated storage unit's doors.

Jack snatched up a scalpel from a table of fierce looking instruments. "OK," he said, gripping the handle. "Let's get a sample, and go."

Taking a deep breath, Zeb Lok pulled back on the door handle and slid out the long metal shelf inside.

The drawer was empty.

"I don't get it," exclaimed Zeb Lok. "This is definitely the lab listed on the computer."

"Maybe she's in another one of these storage things," suggested Tc'aarlat. Starting at the top left, he began to open each door and slide out both the tray and occupant inside.

Zeb Lok checked both the face and toe tag of each cadaver, concerned that the slackening of facial muscles after death might make Vix Mil difficult to recognize in her current state.

But she wasn't there.

"What now?" questioned Jack. "Do we check the other labs, other floors?"

"We don't have time," said Zeb Lok, holding up his communicator for the others to see the screen. They were just 42 minutes away from the full force of the storm reaching Taron City.

"I say we get as many of your team out of the lab as we can, and blast off in the *Fortitude*," offered Tc'aarlat. "Get out of the atmosphere completely to avoid those little gravity-hugging nanobot bastards."

"And leave the rest of the city to perish?" demanded Jack.

"We can't help everyone," Tc'aarlat responded. "We never could."

"I... I don't know," said Zeb Lok. "My family is here. I can't just abandon them."

"What do you think, Adina?" Jack asked. He turned

when he didn't get a reply and found her rifling through paperwork in a filing cabinet drawer.

"Adina?"

"I've found Vix Mil's autopsy report," Adina said, slamming the drawer shut with her shoulder.

"So, she *was* here," said Jack.

Adina nodded, her eyes flicking down one page after another as she speed-read the report.

"OK...," she said. "Basic stuff - height, weight, eye color... Evidence of early repetitive strain injury in her wrists, deep cut on the index finger of her right hand, and... Cause of death, knife wound to the heart."

She stopped, sighed, then tossed the paperwork aside. "Yan Mil claimed the body yesterday."

"But, he never left his apartment," exclaimed Zeb Lok.

"He clearly did," countered Tc'aarlat. "He must have slipped past you somehow. No wonder you couldn't get a reply from him."

"He knew someone might work out Vix Mil's DNA was the key to stopping the storm," said Jack. "He's been one step ahead of us all along."

"Or has he?" asked Zeb Lok, reading the autopsy report Adina had cast aside.

Jack's brow furrowed. "What is it?"

Zeb Lok held up a hand while he finished reading the section that had piqued his interest. "Vix Mil came to the laboratory the night she died," he said. "She had made Yan Mil some soup because I'd told her he was so engrossed in his work that he wasn't eating."

Tc'aarlat blinked. "So...?"

"She had a cut on her finger where she had slipped

slicing vegetables for the soup," said Zeb Lok, his finger stabbing at the mention of the deep gash on the report. "She was wearing a band-aid when we saw her."

Adina's eyes widened. "So, that knife might still be sitting in her kitchen," she proffered. "With Vix Mil's blood on the blade."

"Blood containing her DNA," added Tc'aarlat.

"It's possible," nodded Zeb Lok. "She was attacked on her way home from the lab, so she didn't get chance to clean up - unless she did so before bringing Yan Mil his food."

Jack was already running for the door. "It's our only hope!" he cried. "Let's go."

Alma Nine, Taron City, Weather Control Center, Main Entrance

The Pegasus was battered about by gale force winds blasting every corner of the city as it came into land outside Yan Mil's house.

Jack peered out through the front view screen. In the short time he and the others had been inside the morgue, the seemingly endless snowfall had been replaced with torrents of torrential rain.

By the time they had arrived at the house Yan Mil had shared with his wife, the deep snow drifts had already started to melt away.

It had taken Zeb Lok little more than two minutes to bypass the home's fingerprint security system, then he and Adina had dashed inside while Tc'aarlat and Jack stayed with the ship.

A quick search of the kitchen had come up trumps. There, still sitting on one of the work surfaces was a cutting board, discarded pieces of vegetables, and a knife with a smear of blood still on its sharp blade.

"All of the computers at the Weather Control Center have multi-purpose scanners built in," Zeb Lok had explained once he and Adina had returned to The Pegasus. "We can input just about anything we want into the system with them - nanobots, samples taken from crops, even a vial of rainwater to study what, if any, pollutants it contains."

"So, it should be able to break down that spot of blood to retrieve Vix Mil's DNA?" Jack had asked.

"We have to hope so," had been Zeb Lok's reply. "If it doesn't work, Taron City will be hit by the approaching gravity storm, and hit hard."

The group had witnessed hundreds of people urgently trying to escape the path of Storm Vix by fleeing the city however they could. Cars raced by, privately owned space-craft blasted off from rooftops and backyards.

And scores of residents without access to transport were making the desperate journey on foot, heads bowed as they battled on through the fierce, unforgiving downpour.

Men, women and children all pulled their coats and jackets tightly around themselves in an effort to stay warm as they made for the outskirts of Taron City in the hope of avoiding the nightmare heading their way.

"If that bastard Saf Tah had done as we asked and ordered an evacuation, these people could have been loaded onto buses and driven to safety hours ago," Tc'aarlat had snarled.

Families pushed carts piled high with their belongings, individuals ran for their lives, dodging between and around slower groups, elderly couples plodded along, hand in hand, determined not to give in to fatigue or the brutal, unforgiving weather.

Adina saw a group of young men push two girls from their bicycles, then ride off - two pedaling, the other pair balanced on the handlebars - leaving the teenagers hurt and shaken in the gutter. She wanted to stop and help them, but Solo had reminded her that time was short and, if they stood any chance of stopping the worst of the storm from striking the fleeing refugees, they had to continue onwards.

As the strength of the gravity steadily increased, buildings began to crumble. Having already endured two onslaughts, damaged apartment blocks and entire streets of compromised houses finally succumbed to the effects of these repeated gravitational poundings.

Roofs collapsed, walls tumbled and windows exploded as the once strong and sturdy infrastructure lost its battle with the forces of nature. Cries for help rang out from each and every demolished structure, but there were very few people left to assist in the rescue of those unfortunate victims trapped beneath the rubble.

What few first responders remained did their best to offer aid, but the pounding rain and hurricane-like winds made the task difficult to the point of being impossible. On more than one occasion, fire and ambulance crews were forced to make the heart-breaking decision as to which of those suffering could and would be rescued, and which would have to be left to perish in the coming hours.

Finally, they arrived at the entrance of the Weather Control Center. As The *Pegasus* came in to land, Zeb Lok checked his timer.

"Fourteen minutes," he said. "Storm Vix is almost here."

Jack nodded, swinging open his door. "Let's go."

Click!

The barrel of a long, jet-black shotgun rose up, both barrels pointing directly at Jack's face.

"Give us the ship, and no-one gets hurt!" growled the man holding the weapon. The small gathering of three other people - a man and two women - standing behind him stared menacingly in an attempt to reaffirm the gun-wielder's sentiments.

"Actually, that's not strictly true," said Tc'aarlat as he walked round from the other side of The Pegasus, Mist perched on his shoulder. "If we give you the ship, someone *will* get hurt. We will, when the storm arrives in just under fifteen minutes' time."

"That's too bad," snarled the shipjacker. "But, so long as it ain't us, I really don't care. Now, step away or I'll be forced to shoot your friend here right in the head."

Tc'aarlat gave another demonstration of his now perfected human shrug. "Go ahead," he said flatly. "I don't care."

The gunman frowned, clearly not expecting this response.

"You don't care?"

"Not one bit," Tc'aarlat replied. "The guy's a dick, and he

was saying some terrible things about you just as we were landing. Really nasty."

One of the women frowned, appearing confused. "He was?"

"Absolutely," said Tc'aarlat, addressing the gunman directly. "He said you were short, you were fat, that you looked stupid with that bird clinging to your face..."

The man blinked, allowing the shotgun to drop an inch while he processed the supposed insult. "I ain't got no bird clinging to my face!"

Tc'aarlat sighed heavily. "You really walked into that one, didn't you?"

He let loose a sharp whistle and Mist launched herself from his shoulder. Whizzing past Jack's ear, she spread her wings wide, thrust her feet and claws forward, and dug deep into the Malatian's teal cheeks.

Screaming, the shipjacker staggered backwards, inadvertently pulling the trigger of his weapon. Two sizzling projectiles shot past Jack's ear as he dodged to the side.

He straightened and saw the second man running at him, fists raised. Jack shot out his right arm to block the first punch, then ducked to avoid the second.

Bringing his leg back around, he caught his attacker in the ankle and knocked him off-balance. The man crashed to the ground, giving Jack enough time to draw his Jean Dukes Special.

"That's enough, motherfucker!" he spat, glancing at the weapon's settings and seeing it was dialed to eight. "You hear me?"

With Jack distracted, one of the two women took the opportunity to race past him towards *The Pegasus*. She reached for the handle of the front door on the pilot's side but, before she could lift it, she felt something press against her ribs.

"You really don't want to do that," said Adina softly, clicking off the safety on her own gift from Jean Dukes' lab. "Solo, keep our scientist friend safe, please."

There was a solid thunk as every door into *The Pegasus* locked at the same time.

Adina winked to her would-be thief. "Sorry!"

The woman cursed, then flicked her eyes to look over Adina's shoulder.

Realizing there was likely someone approaching from behind, Adina leapt into the air and spun, executing a move John had taught her back on Base Station 11. As she turned, she saw the group's second female dashing towards her, a small but deadly looking knife gripped in her fist.

At the apex of her rotation Adina flicked out her foot, the tip of her boot just catching the sharp point of the blade and kicking it from the woman's grasp.

The knife spun back towards its owner, the handle catching her in the forehead before it clattered to the ground.

Adina was down, securely balanced with one foot on the discarded blade before the Malatian at the business end of her weapon had time to react.

The man on the ground made to push himself up, but stopped when Jack's finger began to tighten around the trigger of his weapon. "This ends now," he declared, "or you will."

The furious assailant slumped back with a growl.

Tc'aarlat calmly strode over to where the shotgun

handler was stumbling around and flapping his arms as he tried to dislodge Mist from his face. The Yollin stooped to pick up the discarded gun and took aim.

"Mist!" he called.

CAAAWWW!

Almost reluctantly, the Raal hawk unhooked her talons from her victim's ragged cheeks, then flapped back to her master. She landed on his leather shoulder pad, shook out her feathers, then calmly lifted one foot to lick the covering of scarlet blood from her claws.

Furious, the man took an angry step forward.

Tc'aarlat pumped the fore-end of the shotgun to reload it. "Don't," he said, matter-of-factly. "Just don't."

Jack straightened up, but kept his gun pointed at his attacker. "We get it," he said, looking at each individual in turn. "You're scared. Everyone is. But, we're trying to stop this storm, and all you're managing to do is hold us up."

The gang's leader said nothing. He stared back at the shotgun pointed in his direction, chest heaving and blood cascading down his ragged cheeks.

"Get out of here!" ordered Tc'aarlat. "Before we change our minds."

The man at Jack's feet scrambled up and joined the two women as they raced off along the street. The ringleader hesitated for a moment.

Tc'aarlat chuckled. "You're not getting this back, cocksplash!"

With a snarl, the man wiped the back of his hand across the tattered flesh of his face, then turned and ran after his friends.

Jack and Tc'aarlat stood together to watch the group depart.

"Fun way to begin the last quarter hour of our lives," commented the Yollin. "Nice bunch of people."

"And we've got more on the way," warned Adina, gesturing to another clutch of citizens hurrying in their direction. "Solo, we need Zeb Lok."

Solo unlocked the rear doors of The *Pegasus*, allowing the scientist to climb out - the blood-stained knife in one hand, and his communicator in the other.

"Less than ten minutes to go," he said, a look of concern on his face.

Jack nodded as he spun the dial up on his Jean Dukes Special. "Then it's time to split up."

Alma Nine, Taron City, Weather Control Center, Main Entrance

Tc'aarlat eased himself into the pilot seat of *The Pegasus* and grinned. "Now, that's what *I'm* talking about!"

Perched on the headrest behind him. Mist let out a squaw of agreement.

"Shut up and fly the bastard thing!" yelled Jack, holding the gun out in front of him as a warning to the angry mob of Malatians keeping a wary - but, in their minds, temporary - distance.

On the opposite side of *The Pegasus*, Adina was doing exactly the same thing. Some members of the gathering were clutching lengths of metal pipe or long pieces of wood scavenged from one of the buildings that had collapsed elsewhere in the city.

And it was clear they weren't afraid to use them.

Zeb Lok watched the agitated crowd nervously from the passenger seat. Every few seconds, one of the mob would take a step towards the ship, only for Jack or Adina to swing their weapon in their direction, causing them to step back into the horde.

Everyone, no matter which side of the stand-off they were on, knew they wouldn't be able to hold back the tense refugees for much longer.

"They all want *The Pegasus*!" cried Adina.

"They can't have it if it's not here!" replied Jack. "Solo - get Tc'aarlat and Zeb Lok up to the apartment now!"

"Certainly, Captain Marber."

With that, *The Pegasus* shot vertically up the side of the building, leaving Adina and Jack alone at the center of a growing circle of terrified refugees, all desperate for a way out of the city and the impending violence of the storm.

The two humans cautiously stepped backwards, the restless circle closing in around them.

"What's the bet that Saf Tah's safely tucked away in a lead-lined bunker somewhere right now?" asked Jack as he felt his back touch Adina's.

Adina laughed. "He's probably got his two flunkies feeding him grapes."

"*One* flunky," Jack reminded her. "One of them walked out on him just after we left, remember?"

"Oh, yeah..." said Adina, swinging her gun to the left to stop a stocky, snarling Malatian with tightly curled silver hair from rushing at her. "I guess he found where he left his balls."

"Remind me to go look for mine after this lot have torn them off," quipped Jack.

Suddenly, one of the men on his side of the circle dashed forward, something resembling a broken table leg clutched in his hands.

"Bring your ship back down!" he roared, running toward Jack.

Thinking quickly, Jack spun the dial of his Jean Dukes Special down to three and fired at the man. The blast hit the aggressor square in the chest, throwing him backwards for a few feet before he crashed to the ground, out cold.

"He's OK!" Jack yelled to the horrified mob. "I only shocked him. He'll be fine in an hour or so."

But his words did little to calm the increasingly jittery gathering. If anything, the sight of the unmoving man only served to focus the feeling of fury among the uneasy throng. Together, they began to advance on Jack and Adina, fists clenched and makeshift weapons raised.

"Shitty luck, huh?" chuckled Jack. "Getting torn apart on our first mission, and we didn't even settle on a team name. Unless, by some small chance, the domain deadfuckers.com is still available for Nathan to purchase after they find the last few pieces of us."

But Adina didn't reply. Instead, she closed her eyes and began to concentrate.

Alma Nine, Taron City, Weather Control Center, The *Pegasus*

The Pegasus came to a sudden stop and hovered outside the windows of Yan Mil's top floor apartment. Tc'aarlat and Zeb Lok stared at the deserted residence through the front view screen in silence for a few seconds.

"OK," said Tc'aarlat, rubbing his palms together in anticipation of some kind of action-packed plan. "What happens now, Solo? Have you got a plan to get us inside?"

"I do indeed, Tc'aarlat?"

The Yollin grinned with excitement. "Let's hear it then..."

"Well-" began Solo, but the sentence was cut short.

"Ooh, I know!" Tc'aarlat proclaimed. "Zeb Lok will climb out onto the front of The *Pegasus* while you get us closer to that open window Mist got through earlier. He'll squeeze inside, then unlock the program controlling the storm with the DNA thingy, cancel it, and we're home and dry."

"Not quite," said Solo.

A frown troubled Tc'aarlat's brow. "But... *I* can't fit through that gap in the window; I'm too big. And I'm not that keen on balancing on the front of the ship either, if I'm perfectly honest."

"That wasn't my plan, either," said Solo.

"Then, what *is* your plan?"

The Pegasus began to fly in reverse, backing away from the building and the apartment's windows.

"Please fasten your safety belts and take hold of something solid," advised Solo.

"Wait, no!" cried Tc'aarlat as Zeb Lok fastened his belt beside him. "You're not about to do what I think you're about to do, are you?"

"That would depend," Solo responded. "As I am not connected to any implant you may currently have embedded inside your skull, I am unable to accurately ascertain exactly what it is you think I'm about to do."

"I think you're about to ram this beautiful, pristine ship directly into the apartment windows as a way to get us inside!"

"Oh, well in that case, you are absolutely correct!" said Solo happily.

"But-"

"Hold on..."

With a blast of energy from the rear boosters, *The Pegasus* shot forward like a bullet from a gun.

Tc'aarlat just had time to click his seatbelt into place, grab Mist and press her to his chest before the front of the ship made contact with the side of the building.

There was an almighty shriek of tearing metal and an explosion of glass as the windows caved inwards. The entire dashboard of the ship lit up with red, flashing lights and alarms blared out from every speaker.

The *Pegasus* slammed into the floor of the apartment's living room, tearing up the carpet and gouging a deep channel into the concrete below as it skidded towards the far wall, gradually turning slightly to the left as it moved.

"Collision detected," announced Solo.

"No shit, Sherlock!" bellowed Tc'aarlat, pulling his legs in to avoid slicing them open on the razor sharp edges of the twisted metal jutting from the front of the cabin.

The momentum of *The Pegasus* carried through the far wall and into the kitchen, where it finally came to a screeching, grinding halt against the refrigerator, the appliance leaning in through the shattered windshield.

As Tc'aarlat and Zeb Lok finally allowed themselves to breathe again, the door to the ice box swung open, allowing a whole, frozen chicken to slowly slide out and land directly in the Yollin's lap.

SSQQAAAWWWW! cried Mist.

"Oh, fuck off!" spat Tc'aarlat. "That is *NOT* your ex!"

Somewhere far beneath the piercing alarms emanating from whichever speakers hadn't been smashed, Zeb Lok became aware of a tinny ringing sound. He thrust a hand into his trouser pocket and pulled out his battered communicator.

"Shit!" he exclaimed. "Two minutes 'til Storm Vix!"

"Then go!" commanded Tc'aarlat. "You snooze, you bruise!"

"The knife!" said Zeb Lok urgently, looking around the battered cabin. "I must have dropped it when we crashed in through the windows."

Both men began to fumble around among the debris at their feet, pushing aside broken pieces of the ship's shattered command console as they frantically searched for the missing blood-stained blade.

"Where the fuck is it!" yelled Tc'aarlat, scrabbling through the sharp-edged fragments of what had once been electronic circuit boards.

"90 seconds!" cried Zeb Lok.

"I've got it!" shouted Tc'aarlat, spotting the handle of the knife jutting out from the leather upholstery of his seat.

The Yollin yanked the blade free, held it up to the light to make sure the bloodstain was still present, then he thrust it into Zeb Lok's hands.

"GO!"

As the communicator beeped to signal the start of the final minute before Taron City fell victim to the deadliest storm the planet had ever known, Zeb Lok grabbed the door handle and pushed.

But, the door was jammed and wouldn't move.

.   .   .

Alma Nine, Taron City, Weather Control Center, Main Entrance

Jack stared in horror as Adina dropped to all fours, her eyes screwed shut and her gun skittering across the sodden road surface.

The wretched mob around them froze, silent, as they too watched her writhe in agony from the spears of pain coursing through her body.

Adina threw her head back and screamed as her spine splintered in pieces, vertebrae snapping apart and reforming in new, more animalistic configurations.

The skin of her arms and legs pulsed and rippled as the flesh beneath twisted and knotted into thick, solid muscle. Blood spurted from her fingertips as razor-sharp, yellow talons burst through tearing off a number of her own fingernails in the process.

Then came the fur. Dense, grey and quickly flattened by the pouring rain. Her shirt ripped at the seams, falling away as her body continued to grow and reshape itself. Her dark blue overalls - arms tied around her waist - soon following.

Her screams of pain dropped several octaves, becoming growls, and eventually a primal roar as her face stretched out to become the snout of a wolf. Adina's teeth were pushed aside in her gums as glistening fangs pushed through the agonized flesh.

Her ears rose up to sit atop her skull, her nose widened, turning black as it sniffed at the air, picking up the scent of the terrified mortals gathered around her.

When her eyes finally opened again, they were yellow. Angry. Hungry.

Suddenly, the gale force winds ceased and the pounding rain stopped as if someone had turned off some giant faucet in the sky.

Far above, the trillions of microscopic nanobots responsible for the downpour hovered motionless as their new programming - the lines of code that would bring Storm Vix into being and slaughter tens of thousands of people in the city below - began to stream into their memory banks.

But the people surrounding the werewolf didn't seem to notice the change in the weather; every ounce of their concentration was fixed solely on the creature in the center of the circle as it scanned from left to right, taking in each and every one of the lesser beings surrounding it.

The wolf tossed back its head and howled, the piercing cry echoing around the now silent streets outside the Weather Control Center.

The sound broke whatever spell was holding the Malatians who had wanted *The Pegasus* as their own and, as one, they turned and ran in fear of their very lives.

Thunder boomed across Taron City as the nanobots' reprogramming was finally completed, and Storm Vix officially began.

Alma Nine, Taron City, Weather Control Center, Yan Mil's Apartment

BEEP! BEEP! BEEP!

"It's started!" croaked Zeb Lok.

Almost instantly, the already dented roof of *The Pegasus* began to buckle under the first surge in gravity, the thick metal and torn silky material of the lining bulging downwards to press into the top of Tc'aarlat's head.

Still wrapped in his arms, Mist gave a shriek and fought to break free. Tc'aarlat resisted for a few seconds, then relented, allowing her to half jump half fly to the floor at the rear of the compartment where she huddled, trembling, behind his seat.

"SOLO!" yelled Tc'aarlat. "Can you get us out of here?!"

The last working speaker inside the ship crackled with static before the E.I.'S voice responded. "I'm s-s-s-s-o-o-o-r-r-r-yyyyyy Tc' Tc' Tc'. Ple-ple-please fas-ten-ten-ten yourrr ssssseeeeaaaaatbel-"

Then, silence.

Raising his hands, the Yollin tried to push back against the sudden pressure pounding The *Pegasus*. Pressing his palms flat against the twisted metal, he locked his elbows and fought to keep the roof from collapsing any further.

But it was of little use. *The Pegasus* may as well have been inside a commercial car crusher at a junk yard. With both Tc'aarlat and Zeb Lok still inside.

Zeb Lok felt himself being shoved lower and lower in his seat, fingers trembling as he tried to keep his grip on the handle of the knife stained with Vix Mil's blood.

Through the shattered window, he could see the Yan Mil's computer and scanner sitting on its desk, just a few yards away.

They'd been so close to saving Taron City.

The surge in gravity was worse this time. Zeb Lok's vision began to fade, diamonds of blackness seeping in from the sides as his consciousness slowly slipped away.

He battled to keep his eyes open with every ounce of

strength he had left in him, knowing that once he finally closed them, they would never open again.

There was a sudden shout of anger as Tc'aarlat lost his fight with the caving roof. Slumping down in his seat to stay lower than the bulging metal, he scrambled for his Jean Dukes Special.

He worked as hard as he could against the steadily increasing force of gravity, he turned the barrel towards the noisily collapsing roof, spun the weapon's dial to 11, and fired.

Alma Nine, Taron City, Weather Control Center, Main Entrance

The first surge in gravity knocked almost every single one of the fleeing Malatians to the ground.

They screamed, yelled and cried as the combined fear of the freshly arrived storm and the furious werewolf finally found a voice.

A building further along the street began to crumble to the ground. The people dragging themselves away from its entrance on their bellies disappearing beneath the mountain of falling brickwork.

The wolf began to prowl first in one direction, then another. Its paws slipped on the wet ground as the gravity pressed down upon the confused animal. Whatever was causing this feeling of weight upon its body, it was only serving to make it angrier by the second.

Finally, the creature's piercing yellow eyes fixed on one of the fleeing figures as it dragged itself away from the snarling beast. It was a man, his long, silver hair lank and wet from the recent rain, his left foot jutting at an awkward angle, his ankle having shattered when the blast of gravity had struck..

He glanced over his shoulder, saw the wolf slowly stalking after him, and redoubled his efforts to drag himself to safety.

Others quickly realized he was the focus of the were-wolf's rage and battled to pull their bodies away from him, leaving the target alone and very, very afraid.

"ADINA!"

Just a few feet from its first victim, the werewolf stopped and turned, something about the name called that seemed to spark a slight flicker of recognition deep within the animal's brain.

Slowly, painfully, the Were turned to see who had shouted the name.

Ahead, Jack lay on the ground, flattened by the surge in gravity like everyone else. His eyes gazed at the wolf, pleadingly.

"ADINA!" he yelled again. "Don't do this! Please!"

Snarling, the wolf began to approach Jack, its muscles burning as they continued to fight the incredible pressure weighing down upon its body.

Something about him seemed to attract the wolf. Something the creature couldn't understand, and had no way at all of explaining.

"That's it, Adina," groaned Jack, his own consciousness beginning to slowly drift away. "Don't be scared. It's only me."

The werewolf sniffed at the air. It could still smell the overwhelming scent of fear flooding the city, but now there was something else. Another scent, more subtle, but much sharper.

A scent that signaled danger.

The werewolf stopped dead as it spotted the barrel of a gun sliding out from beneath Jack's prone figure and taking aim in its direction, a high-pitched whistle rising in tone as the weapon quickly charged.

There was a whumph!

Then everything went black.

_____

ICS Fortitude, **Adina's Cabin**

"I think she's coming round."

"Well, she'd better wake up soon, or I'm going alone. I'm not missing the opportunity to show off this fine, fine cape!"

"You still think that thing suits you?"

"You know what they say, Jack - beauty is in the eye of the bee folder."

"*Beholder* you dipshit!"

"Really?"

"Yes! Who do you think's going round folding bees?!"

"I did wonder about that bit..."

Adina forced her eyes open, gazing up at the two blurry figures dressed in purple standing beside her bunk.

"Can you two take the comedy routine somewhere else?" she grunted.

"You're back!" exclaimed Tc'aarlat.

SKAAARK! cried the purple blob balanced on the

Yollin's shoulder. Adina squinted, bringing Mist and her recolored feathers back into focus.

"How do you feel?" asked Jack.

"Like there's a herd of bistok thundering through my head," replied Adina. She tried to sit up, winced in pain, then slumped back. "What the fuck happened?"

"Jack shot you," said Tc'aarlat flatly.

This time Adina did sit up.

"You did *what*?!"

"It was set on stun," Jack explained, "and I didn't have much of a choice, to be honest. It was either that, or be torn apart by a werewolf."

Adina groaned, resting back against her pillows again.

"When were you going to tell us about that?"

Adina rubbed her hand across her eyes. "Ideally, never," she admitted. "I haven't fully transformed since I was a teenager. I take pills to dampen those strings in my DNA and stop it from happening."

"They don't work," Tc'aarlat pointed out.

"Hang on," said Adina, frowning in the Yollin's direction. "You weren't even there. You and Zeb Lok went up in *The Pegasus*, and..."

She sat up quickly.

"The storm!"

"We stopped it," beamed Tc'aarlat. "Although, it wasn't all good news. I made it out alive, but..." His eyes brimmed with tears. "So twisted and broken, I've never seen so much damage!"

Adina sighed. "Zeb Lok didn't make it?"

"Oh, he's fine," replied Tc'aarlat, blowing his nose with

the corner of his cape. "I was talking about *The Pegasus*. She's utterly destroyed."

"We're hoping Nathan will see fit to provide us with a replacement when we get back," said Jack.

"So, the knife worked?" asked Adina. "Vix Mil's DNA, I mean?"

Tc'aarlat nodded. "I had to blast a hole in the ship's roof and carry Zeb Lok over so he could slide the knife into the scanner, but yeah. It unlocked the program, and he was able to cancel it."

"The Malatian's have spent the last 24 hours clearing up in preparation for Tor Val's funeral," added Nathan.

"24 hours?" cried Adina, swinging her legs off the bed. "How long have I been out?"

"Thirty-five hours and seventeen minutes," announced Solo through the cabin's speaker. "Would you like me to pause the timer now Adina has regained consciousness, Captain Marber?"

Jack smiled. "Yes, thank you, Solo."

"You're welcome, Captain. And I'd like to take this opportunity to remind you that the late president's Journey Back service begins in around ninety minutes' time."

Adina spotted her purple dress hanging on the back of the cabin door. "Then I'd better get changed," she said, standing up and taking a moment to test that she was in full control of her balance.

She was.

"Right you two - out!"

Ushering Tc'aarlat and Jack out of the cramped quarters, Adina closed the door and rested against it, taking a deep breath.

Reaching over to the small drawer beside her wash-basin, she pulled it open and retrieved the washcloth from inside.

Beneath the cloth was the bag of black pills, each with a single yellow dot stamped onto one side.

She reached out tentatively towards the medication...

Alma Nine, Taron City, Central Park

Flags of navy blue and lemon fluttered everywhere.

Tens of thousands of people, all dressed in the official Malatian color of mourning, lined the rapidly cleared streets of the city, hemmed in behind miles of barriers delivered by the *ICS Fortitude*.

They bowed their heads in contemplative silence as Tor Val's coffin was driven along the route of the funeral procession, many tossing flowers behind the hearse as it passed.

Walking behind the hearse were three figures - Bay Don, and the president's two daughters, Mas Val and Ran Val.

Jack, Tc'aarlat, Mist and Adina were among the dignitaries from other worlds gathered in the park, quietly waiting for Tor Val's body to arrive.

As was the tradition, she was encased inside an organic casket which, following the ceremony, would be blasted into space where it would explode, returning Tor Val's constituent elements to the universe among the gas fields of the Ordon Nebula.

Only, in a change to convention, Tor Val would not be alone.

Already arranged in rows upon the grass were over 120 caskets containing the bodies of everyone who had died in the recent gravity storms. Among them, both Vix Mil and her husband, Yan Mil.

Saf Tah, in a rare show of compassion, had pardoned Yan Mil of his actions in creating the storms, declaring him to be not guilty by reason of insanity following his wife's homicide.

Investigations were now ongoing to locate the individual behind Vix Mil's murder, with investigators due to question Hen Wic in his prison cell the next day.

New safeguards had been programmed into the weather control system by the new department head, Zeb Lok. He and his assistants had worked tirelessly to reset the trillions of nanobots required to ensure today's weather resembled a perfect, sunny Fall day; crisp, but not too hot.

That didn't stop Tc'aarlat from clutching his cloak around his body and shivering. "Why the fuck have nanobots that control the weather if you're not going to make the entire planet a tropical paradise every day?" he hissed.

Jack and Adina, both wearing coats over their purple mourning attire, shared a sly grin.

"You could have worn something over - or even, under - your cape," Adina suggested. "You didn't have to turn up as though you were some sort of beach-ready gladiator."

"Currrr!" trilled Mist in agreement.

Tc'aarlat snarled up at her. "Don't *you* start, as well!"

The park fell silent as Tor Val's casket arrived, carried from its hearse by junior members of her government.

They laid it at the end of the final line of caskets, only the dark blue and yellow flag covering it differentiating it from any of the others.

The funeral service itself was short, but heart-rending.

Mas Val stepped up to a podium to give a pre-prepared yet impassioned speech about her mother and everything she had done for the colonists of Alma Nine. Her sister Ran Val stood, quietly sobbing, at her side.

From a specially built gantry, Cal Car and a Channel Three News camera operator listened to the speeches in deferential silence, the newscaster occasionally jotting down a few words of notes in readiness for his next piece to broadcast.

All across the city, people watched the proceedings on huge view screens set up purposefully erected for the day.

Jack kept a close watch on Saf Tah, fidgeting as he eyed the podium eagerly. Beside him, his one remaining aide stood rod straight, clearly moved by the sentiment of Mas Val's words.

When the time for talking was over, each casket in turn had its inbuilt thruster activated, then it was gently lowered into what looked like a large skyward pointing cannon.

The name of the deceased individual was read out, the entire gathering bowed their heads, then the casket was launched into the atmosphere with a thundering BOOM!

Taron City remained under a blanket of silence as the occupant of each of the caskets was shown as much respect as all the others, before being fired into the clear, blue sky.

Finally, only Tor Val's casket remained. Together Bay Don, Mas Val and Ran Mal helped government officers to carry their mother's body to the machine. A uniformed cadet removed the flag, folded it and handed it to Mas Val as the casket was loaded inside.

Then, BOOM!

Everyone watched as the final casket rocketed up into the sky, growing smaller and smaller by the second.

Tor Val had left Alma Nine forever.

A small group of mourners in the street outside the park gates began to applaud. The sound seemed strange and out of place at first but, as the applause spread along the street and out across the city, it took on a sense of warmth and joy.

Soon, everyone in Taron City - and probably those living in the small towns and farms beyond - were clapping together. Showing their love and appreciation for everyone who had lost their lives over the past few days.

One man wasn't clapping, however. Saf Tah straightened up at the sound, believing the applause to be happening to signal his turn to stand at the podium and swear himself in as the new president.

Grabbing Jus Clo by the arm, he marched towards the microphone, surreptitiously flicking a switch on a battery operated gadget in his pocket that changed the string of LED lights threaded through his hair from the respectful purple color of mourning, to his bright political hues of red and green.

He stopped just short of the podium and pushed Jus Clo forward.

"What?" queried the bemused assistant. Everyone in the park turned to study the pair as the sensitive microphone picked up both men's voices.

"I'm the new president, fuck for brains!" Saf Tah spat. "Pull your head out of your ass and go introduce me!"

A mumble of dissatisfaction swept across the gathered crowds.

Jus Clo took a moment to compose himself, then he stepped up to the microphone, and said nothing.

For a full minute.

"What the fuck are you waiting for?!" Saf Tah hissed. "These people are waiting to get to know their new president!"

A flicker of a smile crossed Jus Clo's lips. Nodding, he reached into his pocket and produced his personal communicator, tapping on the screen to locate the file he needed.

Saf Tah took the opportunity to run his fingers through the tips of his hair, pleased that his idiot aide had finally done something right in preparing an introduction to read on this important occasion.

But Jus Clo wasn't looking through his communicator for a speech. Instead, he found a voice recording, hit play and held the gizmo up to the microphone in order to amplify the words coming from the tiny speaker...

"Tomorrow, the blood of our enemies shall rain down from the heavens!"

Jack's head snapped up. He stared over at Jus Clo. "That was Saf Tah's voice!" he growled, setting off at a run. Tc'aarlat and Adina were quickly on his heels.

Saf Tah looked up in terror at the sight of the dignitaries from the Etheric Federation racing across the park towards him.

Meanwhile, at the podium, Jus Clo was playing the

audio clip over and over. Angry voices rose up among the crowds as they recognized the vice-president's words as the motto of the galaxy's worst most hated and feared terrorist organization, Dark Tomorrow.

"Breaking news here at Taron City's central park..." thundered Cal Car down the lens of the Channel Three News camera.

"No! Wait a second!" Saf Tah pleaded, backing away, hands raised as Jack, Tc'aarlat and Adina reached him. "You don't understand..."

"I understand perfectly!" roared Jack, swinging out his fist and punching Saf Tah hard in the face.

The vice president fell backwards, clutching at his blood-soaked nose.

"You're a pissing terrorist sympathizer," Jack continued, drawing his Jean Dukes Special. "And you are SO fucking under arrest!"

Tc'aarlat and Adina joined Jack to stand over the trembling, sobbing politician, also with their weapons trained on the prostrate figure.

"What shall we do with him?" demanded Adina.

"Take him back to Base Station 11 and hand him over to Ricky Smith," said Jack, noticing with some satisfaction that Saf Tah's horrified expression betrayed the fact that the Ranger's reputation had clearly reached this section of the galaxy.

"Come on, you sack of shit," spat Tc'aarlat, reaching down. "Time to get up. We're taking you for a little ride."

"Excuse me," said Jus Clo, stepping down from the podium. "Just before you take him away. May I...?"

Jack stepped back, allowing the political aide access to his former boss. "Be my guest..."

Snarling, Jus Clo took a short run up, then kicked Saf Tah as hard as possible in the groin.

Thanks to the relatively close proximity of the microphone, this time Saf Tah's scream was heard all across Taron City.

ICS Fortitude, Bridge

"Please fasten your safety belts in preparation for take-off."

Flicking a frustrated glance up at Solo's avatar on the front view screen, Jack muttered unhappily under his breath as he clicked his seatbelt in place.

"I promise I'll check her just as soon as I get the chance," Adina whispered once she secured her own safety belt.

"Saf Tah's locked away securely for the trip!" announced Tc'aarlat as he stepped onto the bridge and made for his seat.

Mist, perched on the top right camera, let out a squawww and flapped her now-red-again feathers to fly down and land on his shoulder.

"Where did you put him?" asked Adina.

"In that rear hangar now that it's empty," the Yollin replied.

"Where your precious *Pegasus* usually goes?" question Jack with a smile.

"I don't want to talk about it!" Tc'aarlat declared as he sat down.

Adina also smiled. "But, you *are* going to carry on wearing the cape?"

Jack tried to hold back a snort of laughter, but failed.

"You two just don't understand," said Tc'aarlat, smoothing down the soft, purple cloth as it draped over his shoulders. "It's called style."

Before either Jack or Adina could argue, Solo's face reappeared on screen. "You have an incoming video call from the president of Alma Nine."

Jack looked to his crew mates before replying. "Put it on screen."

Solo faded away to be replaced by Mas Val. She was sitting at the desk in the inner presidential office, dressed in navy blue and lemon. Both Bay Don and her younger sister, Ran Val, were with her.

"Greetings, Madam President," said Jack. "How are you settling in?"

"It's a little overwhelming," Mas Val admitted, "but I grew up with both my mom and dad doing this job, so I know many of my decisions will be guided by how I saw them take on this huge task. Plus, I'll have Bay Don by my side. She's already had Hip Win arrested for his role in the assassination. He'll stand trial very soon."

"Hey, don't forget me!" exclaimed Ran Val. "I can help, too."

"We're sure you'll do an amazing job," said Jack. "And we look forward to paying a return visit under happier circumstances when you're further along with your negotiations to align with the Etheric Empire."

"Yeah," agreed Tc'aarlat. "They're not too bad, as all-powerful, galaxy-wide invaders go!"

"I see you've adopted your mom's political colors," said Adina.

Mas Val glanced down at her dress, then nodded. "They kinda suit me, I guess. Thank you for everything you've done for Alma Nine."

"You're more than welcome," said Jack. "And, if you ever need us again, we'll be waiting in the shadows to hear from you."

The trio fell silent as Solo cut the communication link, then continued her preparations for take-off.

"The Shadows," mused Adina aloud. "I like that."

"Actually, I do, too," said Tc'aarlat. "You know, in a kind of 'always there, yet remaining hidden' kind of way."

"Sounds good to me," said Jack. "OK... Solo, please send word to Nathan Lowell that we are now officially known as The Shadows."

"Certainly, Captain Marber," responded the E.I. "But not until Tc'aarlat listens to my request to fasten his safety belt so we can take off!"

"This again?!" spat Tc'aarlat, pulling the belt across himself and fumbling through his cape to locate the buckle. "You know, Solo... Keep this up and you'll very quickly start to - as you humans like to say - rub me off the wrong way!"

The Yollin scowled as the other two Shadows' laughter filled the air. "What did I say this time?" he demanded.

Jack winked to Adina. "Are you going to tell him, or shall I?"

FINIS

AUTHOR NOTES - TOM DUBLIN

FEBRUARY 2018

Hello! I'm debut author, Tom Dublin.

Actually, that's not true at all. Forget I said it.

I'll start again...

Hello! I'm UK-based author, *Tommy Donbavand*. However, as most of my 100+ published books to date have been for children and young readers, I'm *calling* myself Tom Dublin as a pen name so that kids can't accidentally stumble across these novels and read anything inappropriate.

Such as one character calling another a 'cockwomble' or a 'grade-A ferret fister', or a line of dialogue claiming 'a chubby secretary broke his dick'.

See what I mean?

So, for all of my indie books aimed at adult readers – including the novels I write in the Kurtherian Universe - I'll be *Tom Dublin*. And I don't mind you knowing that one bit.

I'm incredibly grateful to Michael Anderle for the opportunity to write the *Shadow Vanguard* series, and to Craig Martelle for ensuring I didn't stray from the path and write anything that fans of the *Age of Expansion* wouldn't enjoy.

That opportunity came when Michael found out that I was in poor health.

In March 2016, I was diagnosed with inoperable stage four throat cancer, and I quickly underwent intensive courses of both radiotherapy and chemotherapy. Almost immediately afterwards, I contracted double pneumonia and sepsis, and was rushed into Intensive Care where my family was informed that, unless I started to respond to treatment, I had approximately two hours left to live.

I even remember experiencing the whole 'white light' situation. It was that close.

Thankfully, I did respond, spending a week in ICU, and then another month on a cancer ward for further tests and treatment.

When I was finally allowed home, I struggled to both speak and eat. I was very overweight when first diagnosed – tipping the scales at 312 pounds. Over the next year, I would lose 189 of those, ending up at just 123 pounds and resembling a badly wrapped skeleton. As you can imagine, this left me very weak indeed.

I slowly began to recover, gradually putting weight back on, learning to walk again (albeit with the use of a cane), eating small amounts of soft food and undergoing speech therapy until I could make myself understood.

But, there was nothing that could be done to revive my career.

I'd lost almost all of my children's book work, and I could no longer visit schools to teach creative writing and help promote a love of reading for pleasure.

Suddenly, life was even more of a struggle.

Then Michael contacted me, and asked if I'd like to write in the *Kurtherian Universe*, and I jumped at the chance.

It took me a lot longer than I'd hoped to write this first book, *Gravity Storm*, not least because – after being cancer free for over a year – I was told the disease had returned, this time in my lungs.

However, now that I've nailed down my three main characters – *Jack*, *Adina* and *Tc'aarlat* – their ship and E.I. *Solo*, and the way they receive their missions from *Nathan Lowell*, I'll be able to write the next books much faster.

I will be going into treatment for my lung cancer at some stage, but I promise not to make you wait too long for further adventures from *The Shadows*.

You may also be interested to learn that I have previous experience of writing in a successful sci-fi universe. As a lifelong fan of *Doctor Who*, I was thrilled to be commissioned by BBC Books to write a novel to help celebrate the 50th anniversary of the TV show, back in 2013. The result was *Shroud of Sorrow*, featuring the Eleventh Doctor, as portrayed by Matt Smith, and his companion, Clara.

I even wrote a series of my own with both vampires and werewolves among the main characters! *Scream Street* is a collection of 13 books aimed at 7 to 11 year old kids which has now been adapted by the BBC as a stop-motion animated TV show! And it looks great!

Scream Street currently plays in the UK, Australia,

Central America, Germany and many other countries worldwide. The producers are still negotiating with several US broadcasters, and I'll be sure to announce which channel the show will appear on as soon as I know myself.

In addition to writing more *Shadow Vanguard* books, I'll also be launching my own indie published series this year (2018). If you'd like to hear further details as they become available AND receive a free short story giving you a taster of what is to come, please visit my *Tom Dublin* website and sign up for my, er... *his* newsletter here...

www.tomdublin.com/free

Finally, I'd like to thank you for reading this book. I'm incredibly grateful that you chose to spend some of your time in the company of *The Shadows*.

If you have any comments or questions, please feel free to hit me up online. You can find me on Facebook under my real name, on the *Tom Dublin* page, and in the excellent *Kurtherian Gambit Group For Fans And Authors*.

I always do my best to reply.

Tom Dublin (and Tommy Donbavand)
February 2018

PS – BIG shout out to Kurtherian gambit fan, John Reilly, who was the inspiration for the character of Jon Rey in this book. Sorry for the grizzly death, man.

First, THANK YOU for not only reading this book, but these authors notes as well!

I was able to meet Tommy D. last weekend in Runnymede-on-the-Thames just outside of London last weekend.

Two things: the first is Barry Hutchison (Tommy's best man at his wedding and an author himself) is flipping tall, which makes Tommy D. seem short by comparison. (Don't worry, Barry makes me look short as well.) The reason I bring Barry up is because he was instrumental with me reaching out to Tommy.

Tommy Donbavand is a freaking legend in his area of expertise, and had written for Doctor Who. I didn't want my offer to see if he would care to write in the Kurtherian Universe to be understood as anything less than an offer to see if he would like to write in a genre where he wouldn't need to go to schools as part of the sales pitch efforts.

You know, for adults.

And, who the hell was I to ask someone of his stature? So, I chickened out.

I called his best friend and pitched Barry, first.

It went something like this:

Mike (on Facebook): Barry, this is Michael Anderle. I was wondering if I could chat with you for a moment on the phone or Skype regarding Tommy's situation?

Barry (on Facebook): Sure (or something nice like this... the exact words are fuzzy. Barry's Scottish, so who the hell knows...but, I translated it as 'sure.')

We setup a call, and I get Barry on the phone to talk a bit about Tommy, and I pitch Barry with my offer to see if he thought Tommy would be interested. Now, I wanted to help but let's be real, I didn't want to be embarrassed either because...

Once again, *TOMMY DONBAVAND.*

Barry thought Tommy would be receptive and the rest is now history. He accepted my offer and if you have read Tommy's notes, you know what he went through before he was able to write again.

Now, let's fast forward to Craig Martelle, the Age of Expansion manager.

A few weeks ago, he and I had been discussing Tommy's challenges and he told me that he was expecting Tommy's book soon. Both he and I were waiting, *anxiously*, to see what Tommy had written.

The challenge is neither of us knew if Tommy's skills were transferrable, or how much we might have to tweak the story and soon enough, we had our answers.

Craig texts me in Slack, "Got Tommy D's script. It's fabulous!"

And that, was that. There were a few tweaks to change some characters that needed to be switched out, and we are blessed to have a freaking wonderful author here in the Age of Expansion.

Now, for that second thing (that I mentioned above.)

When I met Tommy this past weekend, it was towards the evening and I meet him and Barry in the back of the room (it was full of authors) and Tommy says 'hi' and 'I'll see you later' because he has run out of energy, and has to go to his room. However, he promises to be back the next day, because he is ABSOLUTELY going to heckle Barry during his presentation.

I can't remember any heckling, but I trust that he might have done it.

The thing is, Tommy is shorter than I am. But, his charisma even through the situation with lost weight, lost energy and EVERYTHING... is still jaw-dropping amazing to me.

I parted company with him as he went to his room, and I remember thinking that I really, *really* wished he would be around that evening during the after dinner meetings that would be going on so I could speak with him.

Just from that two minutes of introduction with him and Barry.

It's kinda nuts as I think back to it. This man, whom I don't know well, has me wishing I could just sit and talk with him and wondering just *what* stories he would be able to tell me.

Now, we have one here, and I'm damned proud to know it is in the Kurtherian Universe.

Thank you for reading this story, and I hope you enjoyed this and then the next one, and the next one after that and so on, and so on…

Ad Aeternitatem,
Michael Anderle